Hassood simply **wasn't** *anymore.*
Where he had been there was only
the dark outline of his shape

"What the…?" Grant muttered, staring at the screen as it locked on a fixed image of the wall with the stain that had been Hassood marked on its surface.

Grant turned back to his colleagues, the four of them as transfixed by the screen as he had been.

"What happened?" Domi asked. "It didn't make sense."

Grant was about to answer when, in the moonlight that seeped into the roofed passage, he saw silvery lines cutting the air, winking on and off like Christmas lights. From the screen behind him, Grant heard his own voice, although with a barely restrained urgency he didn't remember: "Hassood? Come in."

He watched as the silvery lines cut through the air, each of them like a knife caught in the moonlight. It was water, pouring from the roof above them, dripping down to the floor where they stood.

"They're made of water," he declared, "and they're here."

As he said it, Rosalia's dog began to bark. Something was taking shape behind its mistress.

Other titles in this series:

James Axler

Outlanders®

DRAGON CITY

A GOLD EAGLE BOOK FROM

WORLDWIDE®

TORONTO • NEW YORK • LONDON
AMSTERDAM • PARIS • SYDNEY • HAMBURG
STOCKHOLM • ATHENS • TOKYO • MILAN
MADRID • WARSAW • BUDAPEST • AUCKLAND

Recycling programs for this product may not exist in your area.

First edition May 2012

ISBN-13: 978-0-373-63874-1

DRAGON CITY

Copyright © 2012 by Worldwide Library

Special thanks to Rik Hoskin for his contribution to this work.

Printed in U.S.A.

"They're dragons now, and that's that. Normality has shifted to accommodate it."
>—Charlie Brooker, *The Guardian*,
>   *2006*

"He alone, who owns the youth, gains the future."
>—*Adolf Hitler,* 1889–1945

The Road to Outlands—
From Secret Government Files to the Future

Almost two hundred years after the global holocaust, Kane, a former Magistrate of Cobaltville, often thought the world had been lucky to survive at all after a nuclear device detonated in the Russian embassy in Washington, D.C. The aftermath—forever known as skydark—reshaped continents and turned civilization into ashes.

Nearly depopulated, America became the Deathlands—poisoned by radiation, home to chaos and mutated life forms. Feudal rule reappeared in the form of baronies, while remote outposts clung to a brutish existence.

What eventually helped shape this wasteland were the redoubts, the secret preholocaust military installations with stores of weapons, and the home of gateways, the locational matter-transfer facilities. Some of the redoubts hid clues that had once fed wild theories of government cover-ups and alien visitations.

Rearmed from redoubt stockpiles, the barons consolidated their power and reclaimed technology for the villes. Their power, supported by some invisible authority, extended beyond their fortified walls to what was now called the Outlands. It was here that the rootstock of humanity survived, living with hellzones and chemical storms, hounded by Magistrates.

In the villes, rigid laws were enforced—to atone for the sins of the past and prepare the way for a better future. That was the barons' public credo and their right-to-rule.

Kane, along with friend and fellow Magistrate Grant, had upheld that claim until a fateful Outlands expedition. A displaced piece of technology…a question to a keeper of the archives…a vague clue about alien masters—and their world shifted radically. Suddenly, Brigid Baptiste, the archivist, faced summary execution, and Grant a quick termination. For Kane there was forgiveness if he pledged his unquestioning allegiance to Baron Cobalt and his unknown masters and abandoned his friends.

But that allegiance would make him support a mysterious and alien power and deny loyalty and friends. Then what else was there?

Kane had been brought up solely to serve the ville. Brigid's only link with her family was her mother's red-gold hair, green eyes and supple form. Grant's clues to his lineage were his ebony skin and powerful physique. But Domi, she of the white hair, was an Outlander pressed into sexual servitude in Cobaltville. She at least knew her roots and was a reminder to the exiles that the outcasts belonged in the human family.

Parents, friends, community—the very rootedness of humanity was denied. With no continuity, there was no forward momentum to the future. And that was the crux— when Kane began to wonder if there was a future.

For Kane, it wouldn't do. So the only way was out—way, way out.

After their escape, they found shelter at the forgotten Cerberus redoubt headed by Lakesh, a scientist, Cobaltville's head archivist, and secret opponent of the barons.

With their past turned into a lie, their future threatened, only one thing was left to give meaning to the outcasts. The hunger for freedom, the will to resist the hostile influ-ences. And perhaps, by opposing, end them.

Prologue

We are water.

The composition of the adult human body is, on average, about sixty percent water. In children the figure is higher, frequently as much as eighty percent. That is to say, up to four-fifths of the human body is water. Which means that every living, breathing person is little more than water sloshing around inside a skin suit like waves against the beach.

Enlil saw this. Enlil, who saw all of eternity laid out in front of him when he closed his eyes. Enlil, overlord of the ancient Annunaki, the superior race who stood as masters of the Earth.

The Annunaki had ruled the planet for millennia and their history had been incorporated into human culture as Sumerian myth. Some would argue that, before the Annunaki, there had been no human culture to speak of, that it was all just cave paintings in blood and clubbing one's fellow apekin with a blunt rock for the duration of each man's very short life. The Annunaki, by contrast, were an incredibly long-lived race, whose lifespans had been extended even more so by two developments. The first was that each Annunaki shared a group memory of the past, so things that had happened a thousand or a hundred thousand years ago were as vivid to each individual Annunaki as things that had happened just minutes ago. The second devel-

opment came in the form of their increased longevity
courtesy of an artificial rebirthing process, a memory
download into their next body shell. In essence, dead
Annunaki were reborn, over and over, in new forms,
to pick up where they had left off when their previous
body had withered and died, their memories infallibly
complete.

In another race, these incredible developments
might have led to some form of enlightenment, a mu-
tually agreed upon concept of a higher purpose, a phi-
lanthropy even, or perhaps a philosophy that was as
far beyond the ability of mortal creatures to comprehend in their own abbreviated lives as the nature of
the combustion engine is beyond the ability of a ter-
mite to understand. This was not the case in the Annunaki, however. Instead, the near-infinite memory
cycles had stultified the whole race, bringing about
only a boredom so pervasive, so bone-deep that the
whole race seemed destined to die from sheer apathy,
the indifference to their own lives consuming them
like a flame. That was until Anu, forefather of those
who would walk the Earth, had ventured beyond the
skies of their home planet of Nibiru, carving a trail
through the cosmos in the sacred starship *Tiamat* and
discovering the primitive planet he had named Ki. The
planet, known today as the Earth, had been bursting
with life, primitive protohumans just dropping out of
the trees to make their homes within the warm, dark,
womblike embrace of the caves. It must have seemed
like a game board to Anu, with pieces beyond number
to be placed and tinkered with based on the whims of
the bored Annunaki.

Shortly thereafter, the bored Annunaki had followed Anu, traveling through the starscape until they

reached this planet, this Earth, to rediscover what it was to be surprised, even if it was just a little, just for one fleeting second of interest in a lifetime that was beyond measure. The Annunaki had landed in the territories known today as Syria and Iraq, where they had settled. Mistaken by the locals for gods, they had built great cities that acted as expressions of themselves, cities that seemed to challenge the very heavens that they had descended from. The first of these cities was called Eridu, and it nuzzled at the banks of the River Euphrates like an embassy, a piece of foreign real estate amid the humans' otherwise unspoiled world. Eridu belonged to Enki, brother to Enlil and a prince of the Annunaki royal family. Soon Enlil had his own city, Nippur, and the other members of the royal family established similar territories: Babylon, Ngirsu, Kish and more. Housed within those cities, as the Annunaki found new creatures to toy with, new places to acquire, they began to squabble. Boredom had given way to greed and greed led to envy, and if hate was the only thing keeping boredom at bay then the Annunaki hated wholeheartedly and fought as if their very immortal lives depended upon it.

But that had all ended approximately four thousand years ago, when the Annunaki seemed to disappear from planet Earth.

They had not died, these so-called gods. They had merely retreated into the shadows, their squabbles become too overblown. And so their charges—the infant race known as humankind—came to be more prolific and more advanced on the surface of their planet as the Annunaki turned their attentions inward. In a final gesture, Enlil had sought to destroy humankind along with his own slave caste, the Igigi, to wipe this blight from the planet with that weapon of such exquisite irony—the weapon called water. The events that Enlil had set in motion came to be known as the Great Flood, but it had been a simple exercise in pest control, an exercise that had failed thanks to his own brother's interference.

And so, from the shadows, Enlil and his brethren watched and waited and secretly guided the events on Earth until they were ready to reveal themselves once more. In the first few years of the twenty-third century, two hundred years after nuclear war had ravaged the planet almost beyond repair, the starship *Tiamat* had reappeared above planet Earth, and the cycle had begun again. The catalyst was set, the Annunaki had been reborn, emerging from the chrysalis shells of the nine hybrid barons who ruled the old territory that had once been known as the United States of America. The Earth, it seemed, was primed and ready for their takeover; humankind would be crushed once and for all beneath their heel. The Annunaki would rule the Earth once again.

Yet within two years, the plot had failed. The Annunaki, an immortal race who had waited almost four thousand years, guiding humankind's development from the shadows, orchestrating a nuclear war to thin the population, to cull the herd, had turned on one another once more, and so their promised reign as kings of the Earth was aborted before it had even begun.

In a final act of despair, *Tiamat* herself, the wombship that had orchestrated their rebirth, had died, sacrificing herself rather than allowing her wilful children to continue taking shots at one another.

Or so it had seemed.

Despite being on board when *Tiamat* had exploded,

Enlil had escaped the fiery destruction via lifeboat, plummeting back to Earth's soil and bringing with him one single seed that formed the essence of *Tiamat* herself. The Annunaki were masters of organic technology and they had developed devices that seemed both sentient and lifeless, crossing the boundaries of what it means to be living. *Tiamat* was one such thing, a dragon-shaped spaceship that was semiliving, that watched and emoted, that felt pain and wished for death. If a spaceship can be said to have a soul, then the seed was that soul.

Enlil had planted the seed beside the banks of the timeless Euphrates, that place where the Annunaki had first established themselves with the city of Eridu many millennia ago. And all those millennia, all those changes and acts and ticking seconds on the clock, had seemed as nothing to Enlil, who viewed time in terms of his own immortality, and so understood how dull time really was.

So now he stood on the banks of the rushing Euphrates once more, as he had thousands of years before, his scales glistening in the sunlight like gold washed with blood. A spiny crest probed the air above his head, plucking at the material of the hooded cloak he wore over his majestic form, the golden armor of his own body. The Euphrates rushed on, timeless and ever-mobile, hurtling to its destination as water will, thriving in the journey, not caring about its end.

Enlil, overlord of the Annunaki, master of the Earth, watched as the water played across the reborn figure of *Tiamat,* lapping at her scaly flanks. Around him, a towering city had grown once more, dominating the lands all around, engulfing them like an infection, for such is what the buildings were.

As he watched the water, Enlil knew what must be done. He would use the water against the humans once again, use it to create his own army with which to enforce his will.

Death by water. The fate of all humans.

Chapter 1

It felt like the head cold from hell.

For the past five months, all Edwards could remember hearing inside his head was that monotonous droning sound, like a choir of tuneless children rehearsing some song they could never get right, never reaching the second note of the refrain. It was a noise, a droning that was so all-pervasive that it had seemed, over time, to obliterate his own considerations, to wipe them from his mind, blocking his ability to form rational thought.

It wasn't as though Edwards was what you would call an ideas man, of course. Over six feet tall with the broad shoulders of his father, a muscular body from hours in the gym and the military bearing of an ex-Magistrate, Edwards was a member of the Cerberus team of rebels who strove to defend mankind against the insidious threat of the Annunaki. Edwards's role had been as muscle, acting as security and bodyguard on field expeditions where the scientists of the organization might run into danger.

He had taken a bullet out in the Pacific, the shell clipping his right ear and leaving it a ravaged lump of flesh. While plastic surgery could have fixed that mangled scar, Edwards had instead chosen to keep that bullet-bitten ear, like some trophy to represent what he was: a man of deeds and not of words.

Right now, Edwards lay in a CAT scanner, eyes

closed as the radiation mapped his brain, layer by layer. In the control room, five people watched as the real-time results flashed across the control terminal. Four of them were Cerberus personnel like Edwards, while the fifth was a man named Kazuko who was the on-site physician for this facility overlooking the Pacific Ocean where the Cerberus team had been forced to make their temporary headquarters.

For years now Cerberus had operated out of an ancient military redoubt in the Bitterroot Mountains of Montana, from which their sixty-strong team had monitored the world and responded to threats at a moment's notice. But just seven weeks ago the once-secure redoubt had been infiltrated and turned against its personnel. Their leader Lakesh and his team found themselves imprisoned within a cavernous prison called Life Camp Zero. The infiltration had been performed by the loyal troops of Ullikummis, an Annunaki prince who had recently returned to Earth to exact revenge on his father Enlil. The incursion had been achieved in a manner that bypassed the redoubt's notorious security—Ullikummis had people on the inside. Ullikummis was a genetic abomination, his body clad in stone, and he had displayed a psionic gift with which he could control the rocks around him. Part of that gift had been to create mind-altering stones, buds from his own body that had planted themselves like seeds within unsuspecting humans. Once planted, these seeds—known as obedience stones—had affected a person's thought process, acting as an entheogen, filling the subject with a sense of euphoria to feel closer to Ullikummis as their god.

When Ullikummis and his army had neared the Cerberus redoubt, utilizing folded space to evade many of the surveillance systems, his presence had triggered the hidden stones that lurked in several of the personnel within, among them Edwards of the bullet-bitten ear, resulting in the whole team's incarceration in Life Camp Zero, a claustrophobic prison carved out of rock. While the Cerberus team had ultimately managed to overpower their jailers, one final revelation remained: the warrenlike Life Camp Zero was in fact the Cerberus redoubt, altered almost beyond recognition by the rock-shaping abilities of Ullikummis. The once-proud military base had been rendered unusable by the manipulations of the stone god, and the remaining Cerberus personnel had been forced to flee, dispersing into small groups and hiding themselves across the country as they struggled to survive in a world turned against them. Beyond the walls of the redoubt, the Cerberus warriors found the cult of Ullikummis had grown at an alarming rate, and though they could not possibly know the exact figures, the loyal subjects who would now lay their lives down for their Annunaki master numbered over one million.

It had only been in the past week that Lakesh had begun to establish this new, temporary headquarters for the Cerberus operation. This facility was in actuality an embassy for the Tigers of Heaven, a warrior class operating out of New Edo in the Pacific. The Tigers' leader, Shizuka, was a longtime ally of the Cerberus team, and she had graciously donated the manse for the duration of the Cerberus team's exile from their own headquarters, providing what additional equipment she could and granting the team the added security of a squadron of her own fearsome warriors, the samurai-like Tigers of Heaven themselves.

Thus it was that the director of Cerberus, Mohandas Lakesh Singh, now found himself standing in the hastily established monitoring suite of the CAT scanner, watching the multicolored brain maps appear as the scan carved its invisible path through Edwards's skull. A cyberneticist and physicist by training, Lakesh appeared to be in his mid-fifties, with dusky skin and a well-built body. His high brow and piercing blue eyes gave clear indication of his vast intelligence, while his aquiline nose and small, refined mouth suggested a man of culture, as well as scientific learning. Lakesh's dark hair was brushed back from his face, streaks of white peppering the wisps that ran at his temples and over his ears. While Lakesh, as he was affectionately known, looked to be about fifty-five, he was in fact closer to five times that age; he had been born in the middle of the twentieth century and had worked as a scientist on various military projects, including the development of the mat-trans system of teleportation. Through cryogenic suspension and a program of organ replacement, Lakesh had survived to his 250th birthday. Most recently, an encounter with a Quad V hybrid called Priscilla had regenerated Lakesh's ailing body, fixing him at the physical age he now appeared.

Lakesh wore a white jumpsuit, the standard uniform of the Cerberus personnel. With all of the disruption that the team had suffered over the past two months, Lakesh felt that appearances were crucial to restore that sense of teamwork once again among his dispirited personnel.

Lakesh was joined in the small surveillance lab by Reba DeFore, longtime Cerberus physician. DeFore had long, ash-blond hair, which she had arranged in an elaborate French braid atop her head. She had endured psychological trauma during the attack on Cerberus, and Lakesh was pleased to finally see her appear to be acting more herself once again. The last time he had seen her, her eyes had been red-ringed from continuous crying, and her hair had been in a state of disarray that was utterly out of character for a woman who so prided herself on her own appearance. Like Lakesh, DeFore wore one of the simple jumpsuits, its white contributing an almost ghostlike pallor to her already pale skin. After the attack on Cerberus, she had gone into hiding in one of the safehouses provided by another Cerberus ally called Ohio Blue, an independent trader who had gray-market connections across the country. DeFore had had the difficult job of monitoring Edwards who, after his traitorous turn against Cerberus, had been kept chained and imprisoned while they were in hiding. Even now, as he lay on the bed of the CAT scanner, Edwards's hands were tied with rope, metal manacles being out of the question while in the presence of the powerful equipment that would magnetize them immediately. Like Kazuko, DeFore was here to bring medical expertise.

Though an expert in her own field, the third Cerberus operative in the darkened booth, however, was not there to provide medical insights. A slim, dark-haired woman in her forties, her name was Mariah Falk and she was a geologist, an expert on rock formations and strata. Though not conventionally pretty, Mariah had an engaging manner and an enthusiastic smile that could win the heart of almost anyone she encountered. Even now, she was smiling as she watched the CAT scanner's report take shape, her narrowed eyes alive with interest. Rocks were at the root of Cerberus's problems just now, which had elevated Mariah to the level of critical advisor for the duration of the Ullikum-mis infiltration.

The slim form of Dr. Kazuko pointed to something on the scan, a dark mass appearing like bubbles to the left-hand side of Edwards's head. "This appears to be a foreign body," he explained, "possibly cancerous—it's hard to tell." Despite this alarming news, Kazuko had a calm, level voice that well suited his low-key manner. He was a short man by Caucasian standards, standing at a little over five feet tall, with the golden skin and almond-shaped eyes of the Orient, and short black hair slicked back from his forehead. Unlike the others, Dr. Kazuko was dressed in layers of leather armor the color of red wine, and he wore a long scabbard—currently empty—at his belt. As well as being a medical doctor Kazuko, like all Tigers of Heaven, was a highly trained warrior. "Whatever it is," Kazuko continued, "the pattern and spread suggest that it is not static—it's growing."

Lakesh nodded, a grave look of concern on his features. "A dreadful thing," he muttered.

"My guess is it's the rock," Mariah confirmed as she watched the scan unfold, "but it's difficult to get a proper idea of what's in there."

The final person within the room spoke up then, his voice deep as faraway thunder. Grant was another Cerberus field operative, and he took particular interest in this case not least because he was also an ex-Magistrate like Edwards. Grant was a huge figure, with dark skin like polished ebony and a body that was all muscle, with not an ounce of fat. Unlike the others, Grant wore a shadow suit, a gossamer-thin armored weave that offered protection from radiation, environmental contamination and extreme climates. He had augmented this with a few simple adornments, dark pants and a pale shirt, which he wore unbuttoned like a jacket. The grimness of his bearing could not be mistaken; his interest in this case was personal.

"I remember Edwards having some trouble with his Commtact a while back," Grant said, referring to the subdermal radio system implanted in the mastoid bone of the user. "Seemed he could hear transmissions but his own reports weren't coming through."

Lakesh nodded wistfully as he remembered. "That's correct, my friend," he said. "Edwards had been out in Hope at the time, providing medical help to the refugee populace. We'd had trouble contacting him while he was out there, but other events had seemed to overshadow that problem."

The "other events" in question had included a visit by an alien called Balam, as well as Edwards himself getting knocked unconscious during a religious rally celebrating the coming of Ullikummis.

DeFore spoke up then, her voice sounding rather loud in the confined area. "We need to operate," she announced. "Whatever this thing in Edwards's head is, we need to see what it's doing and how. That could provide a valuable insight into how Ullikummis is spreading his influence."

Dr. Kazuko nodded in assent. "Loath as I am to open a man up like this, it seems the only option left open to us," he agreed. "And if, as you say, it's some kind of stone that's in there, then not doing anything will be far more dangerous than operating. This man's brain is calcifying as the growth spreads. Left unchecked, he could lose his power of speech, his rational will—he would be left as a vegetable."

Lakesh's brow furrowed as he considered what the

two doctors were proposing. "Do we have the facilities here to operate?" he asked Kazuko.

The Tigers of Heaven doctor nodded. "I can call for everything we require," he said. "We could likely operate as soon as tomorrow, if you're agreeable, Dr. Singh."

With weary reluctance, Lakesh slowly nodded. "Whatever it all means, it's time we got to the root of the problem."

WITH THE ASSISTANCE OF two Tigers of Heaven guards, Grant escorted Edwards back on a gurney to a windowless room that was located just belowground level in the vast complex of Shizuka's winter palace. Edwards was strapped down, hand and foot, to the gurney. However, despite being sedated, he still had some fight in him, and he glared at Grant as the larger man escorted him to his cell.

"I don't like doing this much, either," Grant assured Edwards as he saw the rage burning in the man's eyes.

Under Grant's instruction, the Tigers of Heaven prepared to move Edwards from the gurney to the single futonlike mattress that lay against one wall. The guards untied the straps that held Edwards's feet down, but his ankles remained bound to one another so that he had no hope of escape. Then they moved up to his wrists, untying the tight straps and freeing his hands, a guard standing on either side of the gurney.

Grant watched warily from the end of the cot, his face emotionless as Edwards was untied from the gurney. Like everything in the winter palace, the room was pleasantly decorated, the peach wallpaper featuring a flock of white doves soaring over its sunset colors. Despite the austerity of the single mattress, featuring as it did four horizontal straps that could buckle the occupant in place, it still looked typically artistic, the dark swirl of pattern there mixed with gold thread that caught the soft side lighting of the room. A low occasional table had been placed against one wall, a vase of dried flowers in its center to add color to the room. This hidden room had likely been used as servants' quarters once upon a time, and in other circumstances it could seem quite delightful, Grant was sure. As was, however, it had been pressed into service as a jail cell, its lack of windows ideal to prevent any chance of escape. Edwards was sedated and kept restrained, but even so, he was an ex-Magistrate, one of the class of highly trained enforcers in the towering villes that dotted the country. Any enemy underestimated him at their own folly.

But as the Tigers of Heaven guard unstrapped Edwards's bound right wrist, the ex-Mag moved, lashing out with his fist and knocking the warrior backward. Already unstrapped, Edwards's left hand snatched at the other guard's arm, yanking him with such force that the man flipped over the gurney and crashed headfirst to the floor.

"Dammit," Grant cursed as he came at Edwards from the foot of the gurney.

Although they were still bound together, Edwards kicked out with both feet, striking Grant high in the chest.

Grant staggered backward, his breath bursting out of his mouth with a great "whomph." He had righted himself in an instant, and he turned once more to Edwards, his hands forming into fists.

Behind the gurney, Grant saw the twin Tigers of Heaven recovering. Both men were well trained in the arts of ninjitsu, and while Edwards's attack had come as a surprise it had not been enough to render either man inoperative. They circled the gurney, warily approaching Edwards from above and behind his head.

"Kill you!" Edwards spit, mouth foaming, his hate-filled eyes fixed on Grant.

"Not this time, bucko," Grant assured him as he grabbed Edwards's kicking legs, fixing them a moment later in a two-handed grip.

"Kill you!" Edwards snarled again as he writhed in place, batting at the Tigers of Heaven as they tried to restrain him.

"Let's get more sedation," Grant instructed as he held on to those kicking legs. "Quickly now, I've got him."

One of the warriors reached into the cloth bag he wore at his hip on a crosswise strap, producing a hypodermic syringe. In a half minute he had prepped it with sedative, flicking it to pop any bubbles that remained in the clear mixture. Grant continued to hold Edwards's legs as the man kicked back and forth, his body tossing on the gurney like a struggling fish on a hook. The remaining guard tried to hold Edwards's hands above his head and found himself almost knocked aside by several attempts by the ex-Mag.

Then the other guard approached Edwards with the hypo, and Edwards watched it with angry eyes.

"Just be a moment," the Tigers of Heaven warrior promised, his voice calm despite how fraught the situation was.

"Fuck you," Edwards growled, pulling both arms across his body and tossing the other guard across his chest as he hung on there. The guard tumbled over the gurney and slammed into his companion, head smashing against head with the brutal thump of bone on bone.

Grant watched as the two guards slumped to the floor, both of them dazed by the impact as the syringe rolled out of reach. Faster than thought, Edwards folded his body at the waist, aiming his forehead at Grant's. Grant reared back, releasing his grip on Edwards's legs.

"Utopia is upon you," Edwards hissed, the madness burning behind his eyes as he flipped himself on the gurney.

"Yeah," Grant snarled, taking a step toward the rocking gurney, his fist drawn back. "Well, let's not get too excited about it just yet."

With those words, Grant snapped out a solid punch at Edwards's jaw. Grant's fist connected with a crack, and Edwards shook on the gurney as he struggled to defend himself.

"Hate to do it, man," Grant explained as he pulled his fist back for a second blow. But as he did so, Edwards's own struggles proved the man's downfall. The rocking gurney suddenly upended, and Edwards was thrown to the hard floor in a tumble of limbs. With his ankles still tied, the ex-Mag lay struggling there as the gurney crashed down beside him.

Grant watched as the gurney slammed against Edwards's side, and the already sedated man slapped against the floor.

"You still got any fight left in you?" Grant asked as he stood over Edwards's fallen form.

"Kill..." Edwards muttered, blood on his lips.

"Yeah," Grant said as he picked up the hypodermic syringe, "that's what I thought."

A moment later Grant had pressed the needle into

Edwards's vein as the man struggled woozily from the blow he'd taken. Thirty seconds later, Edwards lay restrained on the futon, happily snoring as he drifted off to sleep.

Grant checked on the two guards who had accompanied him to house Edwards. Apart from a little wounded pride, they both seemed pretty much okay. "You need to watch this guy," Grant reminded them both. "Used to be a Magistrate—he's trained to turn impossible odds against you."

The Tigers of Heaven genuflected appreciatively as Grant left the cell.

Chapter 2

For Grant, Edwards's condition was something personal. He made his way through the Cerberus operations center, a temporary arrangement consisting of four laptop computers attached to a powerful server hub that hummed in one corner of the room. The room itself was originally a simple communal area, a sparsely decorated living room with several low tables and a wide mat covering the floor. The mat had been rolled back to allow for the wiring to trail across the room. Donald Bry, the ginger-haired assistant to Lakesh, was busily linking two of the laptop units together. He lay on his back with a screwdriver in one hand and a pen between his teeth, his mop of copper-colored curls in its usual disarray.

Beside him, Brewster Philboyd, another of the trusted Cerberus team, was running a diagnostics check on the expanding computer system. A tall man with a high forehead, dark hair and black-framed spectacles perched on his nose, Brewster was a trained astrophysicist who could generally turn his hand to most technical problems.

"How's it going?" Grant asked as Philboyd caught his eye.

Philboyd held up his hands in mock despair. "It's getting there," he said begrudgingly. "Satellite feeds are scanning properly, but we're still amassing the data."

For years now Cerberus had relied on the data from two satellites in geosynchronous orbit around the equator, the Vela-class reconnaissance satellite and the Keyhole Comsat. The feeds from the two satellites provided empirical data from across the globe and also allowed for real-time communication via the Commtact units that many of the field operatives had had embedded beneath their skin. The task of monitoring these satellite feeds had been interrupted with the recent attack on Cerberus, and it was only now that Lakesh had begun to reassemble his team and initiate the arduous task of checking the information that had been stored in their absence.

Grant continued across the room, walking through the open doorway at its far end and making his way along a wooden-walled corridor that led the way through the building. He passed several doors, each one leading to private bed quarters that had been procured by Cerberus personnel for the duration of their tenancy. Grant arrowed toward one of these, pushing it gently open with a soft touch despite his imposing size.

Within, the drapes of the bedroom were closed, creating a cozy, dark atmosphere. A beautiful dark-haired woman sat in a chair beside the lone bed, her head lolling backward, a mangy-looking dog lying at her feet. As Grant walked in, the dog raised its head, ears pinned back to its head, and let loose a wary growl.

"It's okay, boy," Grant said, leaning down for a moment and offering the dog his empty hand to sniff. "Just me."

The dog was some kind of mongrel, a scraggly-

looking beast with more than a hint of coyote. It had
the palest eyes that Grant had ever seen in a dog, orbs
a white so pure they seemed faintly blue.

The woman in the chair had awoken, too, and she
watched Grant through narrowed eyes. Her name was
Rosalia, a stunningly attractive woman in her mid-
twenties, with long dark hair that fell halfway down
her back, olive skin and long, supple limbs. Rosalia
wore a long skirt that trailed to her ankles, its flower-
ing pattern scuffed with dirt, her dark top askew on
her shoulders where she had slept in the chair. Working both sides of the law, Rosalia had recently found
herself siding with the Cerberus team as they escaped
the imprisonment of Life Camp Zero.

Grant took no notice of her. His dark eyes were
fixed on the still figure lying alone in the bed. Kane
had come to be Grant's brother-in-arms over the years.
An ex-Magistrate like Grant, Kane was a few years
younger than the other man, and he looked terrible.
His dark hair was ruffled, sticking to his forehead in
sweaty clumps, and he had the dark shadow of a beard
around his jaw now. And there was something else,
too—a spiny protrusion growing on his face, circling
and encrusting his left eye like bone before arcing over
the cheek and pulling the corner of his mouth up into a
sneer. Grant looked at Kane as he slept, eyes running
across that hideous protrusion and feeling the frustration rising in his gut. Whatever it was, the growth
had affected Kane's vision, not simply blinding him
but inexplicably triggering some kind of hallucinatory
episodes. As such, it had left Kane grounded while Dr.
Kazuko and the other medical staff investigated the
nature of the intrusion to his flesh.

When he looked down, Grant saw that he had

clenched his own hands into fists. He eased his hands open again, willing the tension from his body. "How is he?" he asked, not bothering to look at the woman he was addressing.

"He's been asleep mostly," Rosalia said, keeping her voice low so as not to disturb the room's sleeping occupant. "Probably a relief."

"I guess," Grant agreed.

"What about you?" Rosalia asked softly, standing and edging toward Grant. "Any word on Edwards?"

"They're still trying to figure out what the condition is," Grant told her, "but they figure it's stone inside his head. So it's a safe bet they're related. Which means the cure to one might just hold the cure to the other."

Rosalia's lips pulled back from clenched teeth. "Damn this Ullikummis," she cursed. "What did Kane ever do to—?"

"Got in his way," Grant interrupted. "We all did. It's what we do. It's what we've been doing for a half-dozen years. Had to take a casualty sometime."

Grant didn't tell her the other thing he was thinking. The third member of their cozy partnership—a trained archivist called Brigid Baptiste—had disappeared without trace, only to reappear in time to shoot Kane in the chest as he lay already wounded. That had occurred out in a cavern near the newly rebuilt settlement of Snakefishville, a cavern Kane, Grant and Rosalia had investigated as it housed an Annunaki artifact called the Chalice of Rebirth. While Brigid meant little to a newcomer like Rosalia, the woman had been a crucial member of the Cerberus team since its inception, and she shared a special bond with Kane himself—the two were *anam-charas,* so-called soul friends linked through eternity.

Rosalia made her way toward the door, encouraging her pale-eyed companion along beside her. "The dog needs some exercise," she told Grant, knowing the man would want to be left alone with his best friend.

Grant looked at her and nodded sorrowfully.

"You'll be okay here, right?" Rosalia asked. "I can stay, get one of the big tough samurai men to take care of this nuisance."

"I'll be fine," Grant told her, "but thanks." As Rosalia pushed through the door, Grant spoke once more, almost to himself. "You know, it's the strangest feeling—finding out we're not as immortal as we thought."

Rosalia silently closed the door and left the ex-Magistrates alone.

Chapter 3

The silent drums were beating and Farrell looked wasted. He was a young man but he was looking old, his sunken skin drawn and pale where he had rapidly lost weight over the past few weeks. His gold hoop earring hung low on his ear, his goatee beard looked a little more ragged than normal and his usually shaved head was growing out in mismatched tufts of ginger and brown. But when Sela Sinclair looked at him across the dilapidated room they found themselves hiding in, the thing she most felt was not sorrow or worry or even desperation—it was hunger. Seeing a man that drawn, that sallow cheeked, made her stomach growl. She wanted so much to feed him, to just see him eat.

That was stress, Sinclair told herself as she looked at him. That was what it had done to him. Was doing to him.

Farrell had been a technician at the Cerberus redoubt, one of those perennial staff members who could turn his hand to any background task to keep things running smoothly. His favorite post had been running the mat-trans and he could often be found checking the diagnostics on the computer terminal linked to the man-made teleportation unit.

When Cerberus had come under attack, Farrell had been among the staff who had been caught with their

pants down. Quite how Ullikummis's forces had pen-
etrated the redoubt remained a mystery to Farrell—
hadn't they had a security perimeter to stop this very
type of attack? Somehow, whatever it was that they
faced in this Ullikummis creature, it was a threat that
could change the rules. And, like the rest of the complement of personnel at Cerberus, Farrell had been
overpowered and imprisoned by those invading forces,
incarcerated in Life Camp Zero to be indoctrinated into
the ways of this new would-be master of the world, this
new world order.

Farrell had played only a minor role in the subsequent breakout. Having spent days locked in a single
cavernlike room with no amenities and only the most
basic foodstuffs, he had been utterly bewildered when
the door had pulled back and a beautiful woman and
her scruffy mongrel dog had stood framed in the volcanic light, granting his release. Everything since then
had been a blur. Kane and the woman—Rosalia was
her name, Farrell learned later—had overpowered the
troops of Ullikummis but they knew their freedom
would be short-lived should reinforcements arrive. It
seemed that the cult of Ullikummis was growing into
a religious movement that was sweeping the country
at an alarming rate, and the Cerberus people were considered a very trivial but very dangerous threat to that
movement. Thus the decision had been taken to evacu-
ate the redoubt-cum-prison, to split up the targets and
keep the fifty or so Cerberus personnel safe. Farrell
had been partnered with Sela Sinclair. Sinclair was a
lean-muscled black woman, ex-U.S. Air Force, and had
been cryogenically frozen back in the twentieth century to be revived two hundred years later. Thanks to
her military background, Sinclair had acted as secu-

rity detail for Cerberus, and was frequently involved in field missions. If nothing else, Farrell should be safe with her.

Lakesh had made swift contact with a black-market trader called Ohio Blue, an old friend of the Cerberus operation whose underworld contacts gave her ideal access to hiding places for the Cerberus team. Thus, Farrell and Sela Sinclair had engaged in a mat-trans jump that sent them to what had once been the southernmost edge of Arkansas, way out near the border of Louisiana, where Blue's operation was centered. Ohio Blue was a glamorous figure. Farrell guessed she was in her late thirties, with a cascade of long blond hair that reached halfway down her back and was swept in peek-a-boo style to mask her left eye entirely. Like her name, Ohio always wore blue; the first time she and her security crew had greeted Farrell and Sinclair at the entrance to the old military redoubt, she had been dressed in a floor-length sapphire gown that glistened with sequins and had a hip-high split that left her right leg bare when she walked.

Farrell and Sinclair had traveled with six other Cerberus staff, including Brewster Philboyd and a weeping Reba DeFore. All of them were split into pairs at the destination redoubt, where Ohio's people led them to various safehouses dotted across the area.

Ohio's people had escorted Farrell and Sinclair to a dead town that had once been a suburb of Bradley. It looked as if a bomb had hit it, which was very likely what had happened. The asphalt of the streets was churned up into broken chunks, weeds and plants and whole great trees emerging through the wreckage that had sat, unrepaired, for two hundred years. Once upon a time, this had probably been a nice neighborhood, the kind of place where you'd let your kids walk their new puppy, where the evening sun would keep you warm as you sat and read a book on the rocking chair hitched on the wooden veranda, the balmy air granting you that indefinable sense of contentment. Now, it looked like a suburb of hell. One half of the street was just gone; it was simply not there, only the occasional markings where houses or apartment blocks had once stood, old pipes overflowing with swarming plant life and buzzing insects.

The other side of the street still looked somewhat like a street. There were houses there, eight or nine of them, but it was hard to be sure given the state of the last two, which looked more like something that had washed ashore from the ocean depths even out here, two hundred miles away from the nearest shore. The other houses stood on ruined foundations. Three of them had sunk into the ground, crumbling so that they sat like the steepled fingers of a pair of hands, propped against one another for support. A conifer grew out of one and into the roof of another, its cone shape striving up through the eaves of the second house and into the sky where birds flocked all around it, cawing and chirruping. The other houses were dirty, weather-beaten and overgrown with moss and mold, but they at least looked durable. If nothing else, the street seemed about right for the state that Farrell found himself in—a blue funk.

The suburb of Bradley was surrounded on all sides by swamp and jungle and forest, much of it impassable even in these days of so-called civilization after the Program of Unification had brought humanity back from the brink of extinction. There were pathways through those jungles, hidden routes that Ohio

Blue and her men knew, ways to reach all of these forgotten little corners of middle America that had been largely ignored since the nukecaust.

Sinclair and Farrell had holed up in one of the broken buildings, choosing the place with the strongest walls and traipsing back and forth to furnish it as best they could from the bombed-out remains of the other houses in the street. Ohio's people visited every three or four days, bringing with them parcels of food, some of it fresh but much of it tinned or dried goods, cured meats that would keep despite the lack of refrigeration or power in the ruined shack. The place itself smelled like the cloying atmosphere of a hothouse, as if they were living in an arboretum. Mold grew a dark greenish-brown up the walls, and some kind of fungus had taken over the bathroom, pretty violet spores popping and bursting from the walls, ceiling and floor the first time Sinclair had pushed open the door. After that, they had left the room shut, and converted what had once been a downstairs home office into a latrine.

In the forty-two days that they had been here, Farrell and Sinclair had barely spoken. They were both in shock, and both were quite unable to comprehend what was going on around them. Days had passed where not more than two words would be grunted between them. Farrell took to staring through the gap in the boarded window at the front of the house, watching the churned-up street as if waiting for a parade to arrive, some kind of parade that only the Devil himself could bring. Ex-military, Sela Sinclair lost herself in a punishing fitness regime, exercising obsessively, well into the night. At least, she thought, if we do get attacked I'll stand a chance.

She was doing push-ups, listening to the sound of distant drums, when Farrell called her to the window.

"Sela? Come quick, look."

Sinclair expelled a hard breath as she curtailed her routine, wiping sweat from her neck and underarms on a dirt-stained towel as she made her way across the cramped front room, boards creaking as she walked.

"What is it?" she asked.

Farrell sat motionless at the window, and the sunlight painted a single stripe across the bridge of his nose where it cut through the gap in the boards. "Someone's coming, I think," he said, his voice little more than a whisper.

Sinclair looked at him, the way his body had become more like skin wrapping over bones these past few weeks. "Blue's people?" she asked as she stepped closer to the gap in the window and peered outside.

Farrell shook his head briefly. "I don't think so. See there? Look."

Sinclair peered through the gap in the window, feeling the thin draft of air stabbing against her face with the constancy of a knife. It was late morning out there, the bright sun burning against the ruined landscape. Bushes and ferns lined the center strip of the old road, their leaves fluttering in the breeze. One clutch of bushes rustled, and Sinclair watched as a white cat came bounding out of them chasing after some insect or other, its prey's wings glistening with the rainbow sheen of oil on water as it took flight.

It was quiet after that, quiet and still, but Sinclair could still hear the noise of the drums.

"You hear that?" Sinclair asked, tilting her head unconsciously, the way a dog might. "Music."

To her it sounded like the drumbeats of a marching

band on parade, and it sounded real distant. It was like hearing the ocean before you could see it, that constant batting noise as the waves crashed against the shore, the heartbeat of the world.

Farrell looked at her, eyes narrowed. "I don't hear anything," he admitted with confusion. They had been holed up here for more than a month now and he had noticed how sometimes Sinclair would stop and listen to something he couldn't hear; sometimes he would catch her drumming her fingers against the arm of a worn-through chair as she took a break from her exercises. He watched her now as she continued to listen to the noise, watched as her hand reached up to touch her face, the strawberry-shake-pink insides of her dark fingers playing across that lump she had right in the middle of her forehead. It looked like a blind boil to Farrell, but it had been there a long time, never quite emerging or retreating the way a boil usually will. He hadn't thought much about it; for the past forty-two days he hadn't thought about much of anything if he could very much help it, just waited and hoped and prayed for Lakesh or someone else from the Cerberus hierarchy to get back in touch with them and call him and Sinclair home.

"You can't hear that?" Sinclair asked, her eyes still fixed on the slit in the windows. "It's getting closer— it's getting louder."

Farrell peered again out at the street, watching that point where he had seen movement before, where he thought he had seen a figure disappear into one of the tumbledown houses along the street. "Music?" he clarified. "I don't—"

Then a figure appeared, pushing its way through the undergrowth that had taken over the road in the past two hundred years. Farrell had fallen silent automatically, watching as the figure pushed through the plants. The figure wore a fustian robe in a dirt-colored brown, the hood over his head, pulled low to hide his features, but Farrell could see the rough salt-and-pepper beard that daubed his chin. He had wide shoulders and he moved with a certain heaviness—a big man, then, powerfully built. A moment later another figure appeared behind the first, this one slimmer but wearing an identical robe, hood low over the face. The robes were largely shapeless, going down past the knees like a monk's habit, but Farrell could tell that this one was a woman from the way she moved her hips. Something glinted on the breast of the robe, a red shield like the Magistrates used to wear when they had guarded the villes, back before the fall of the baronies.

"They're Ullikummis's people," Farrell identified. "We should probably—"

Before Farrell could finish, Sinclair was on her feet and had scampered over to the door in three quick steps. She moved like a jungle predator, her tread silent and fluid, the movement admirably economical. There was a gun there, a refitted Colt Mark IV. Sinclair checked the little eight-shot pistol swiftly, assuring herself the clip was home, and Farrell watched as she flicked the safety off.

"Sela, I don't think we should do anything that's going to attract their attention," Farrell said, keeping his voice to a low hiss.

Sinclair glanced at him. "Come on."

Then, before Farrell could voice further complaints, Sela Sinclair was out of the door and creeping out past the broken wall of the lobby toward the main door to the house. Getting up, Farrell followed. Unlike Sinclair, he was not particularly adept in combat situations, and would much rather keep well away from the strangers. Still, if he had to face them with anyone at his side, better Sela Sinclair than being teamed with one of the Cerberus cooks or Mariah the geologist, neither of whom was much use in a firefight.

Slowly Sinclair pulled the front door to the house back on its ancient hinges. Beyond, the once-immaculate front lawn looked more like the bottom of an aquarium, fronds and ferns jutting out of the churned-up earth. Bradley had been a casualty of the nuclear war that had ravaged the United States more than two hundred years before, and it had been long since lost, an untouched artifact from another age. For Sela Sinclair, a woman born in the twentieth century and cryogenically frozen for two centuries before being discovered and revived on the Manitius Moon Base, it was like stepping into the past half-remembered. Things out here were familiar, yet they seemed strange and ghostlike, as if a forgotten world had come back to haunt her.

Pistol raised, Sela Sinclair stepped out onto the porch, its wooden boards groaning in complaint at her weight. She turned to Farrell and gave him a silent look of warning, indicating the creaking boards beneath them. Farrell nodded.

Outside, three house lengths away, the two hooded figures moved through the undergrowth. They were not being especially stealthy from what Farrell could tell, but just hacked their way through it, two Stanleys searching for their Livingston.

Sinclair edged forward, hunkering into herself as she stepped off the porch and out onto the overgrown front lawn. She was wearing dark clothes, a sleeveless vest-top in a black that had washed out to a green-gray, combat pants and sturdy boots. Farrell wore his Cerberus operational uniform, a white one piece jumpsuit, but he had augmented this with a dark green windbreaker that blended—passably if not well—with the junglelike flora all around. He followed the sec woman as she made her way to the property boundary, passing a rusted pipe that had once formed the exhaust of an automobile, using the plants for cover, her eyes never leaving the hooded figures that approached.

Sinclair stopped behind a clutch of sprouting reeds that had reached over seven feet in height, nosing at them with the muzzle of her gun to see the street. Farrell joined her a moment later, feeling his heart pounding in his chest, pulsing in his ears. The robed figures were moving efficiently along the street, checking left and right without slowing. Their clothes were just like the jailers who had held them captive in Life Camp Zero; there was no question in Farrell's mind that they worked for the enemy.

"Dammit, Sela," he whispered, "they're Ullikummis's people. We need to get out of here right now."

A thin smile touched Sinclair's lips. "We'll be safe," she assured Farrell, her voice low.

Farrell watched the street from over Sinclair's shoulder, glanced at the gun in her hand, back up the street. What the hell was she thinking? That she could shoot them both right here and now? What if she missed? The two recruits for Ullikummis continued making their way along the street toward them, as if sensing their presence. A shaft of sunlight cut through the plants and, just for a moment, Farrell saw the face of the woman of the group. She looked young and pretty, but her blue eyes seemed vacant, as if she was in a trance. He had overheard the Cerberus field personnel who had come into contact with Ullikummis's troops describe them as "firewalkers," as if their minds were locked in a hypnotic state, their actions not entirely under their own control. The way these two moved without discussion made him think there was something in that, like watching two puppets being moved across some grand stage, their strings hidden from his sight.

Sinclair narrowed her eyes as she watched them, the Colt pistol held steadily out in front of her in a one-handed grip. Farrell watched as her other hand came up to add support to the grip, planting it firmly beneath the ball of her hand. Wait a minute, he thought. Is she nuts?

"What are you doing?" Farrell whispered. "You can't shoot them."

But Sela Sinclair wasn't listening to Farrell. She was listening to the drumbeats as they pounded louder and louder, like a thunderstorm raging in her skull.

The robed figures were just a house away now, standing there and looking it up and down like a parody of a newlywed couple choosing their first home.

"They're getting close. We should get out of here," Farrell insisted, nudging Sinclair gently but urgently on the arm.

Sinclair turned, a sudden movement like a lightning strike, and Farrell found himself falling even before he could acknowledge that she had tripped him.

She jabbed the pistol at his face as he landed.

"He's here," Sinclair said, enunciating the words clearly so that they reverberated down the overgrown street. "The nonbeliever."

Chapter 4

It was like a child's toy, Mahmett thought, this city so empty and so devoid of life. Squawking birds circled overhead and occasionally the bark of a wandering pye-dog or the meow of a cat might be heard. But the animals kept their distance, avoiding the place the way they might avoid fire, some instinct they chose not to challenge.

Mahmett was here for two reasons: a city that was empty inevitably contained untold riches. Even more inevitably, he wanted to impress a woman. But now, walking through the echoing streets with his brother Yasseft and his cousin Panenk at his side, Mahmett wondered just how far he would need to go to find one and hence achieve the indulgence of the other.

"People have died poking around there. There are easier ways to get a woman to notice you," Panenk had berated before they had set off for the strange city.

"But this will prove to her that I am brave," Mahmett insisted.

"And if you die, then what will you have proved?" Panenk asked. "Better just to buy a trinket in the market and then tell Jasmine that you went to the city and got it there."

"But I will know," Mahmett had argued with all the naivety and conviction of youth.

"And so will I, and so will Yasseft," Panenk had said, "but at least we'll be alive."

But Mahmett wouldn't hear of it. So now all three of them wandered through the eerily silent streets that shone a creamy white in the sunlight, feeling cold despite the warmth of the afternoon. The city itself had not been here six months ago. It had appeared, like the ruins of some ancient civilization washed up on the shores of a dream. Mahmett had recalled the stories he had heard of America, where a terrible cataclysm had befallen a great society leaving only the Deathlands, where scattered monuments waited for brave explorers to make their fortunes. That had been more than a century ago, but the myth prevailed, the same myth of lost treasure that had been told over and over since the dawn of language.

The city itself was empty. Everything was made of the same substance, a chalky stonelike stuff that slowly crumbled to dust beneath the sun, the streets and buildings and channeled drains all molded from the same. Bisected by the Euphrates, a confusion of spires and domes climbing toward the sky, interior courtyards and ugly, misshapen towers lunging forth as if vying for space among the narrow, alleylike streets. Those claustrophobic streets wound on themselves like string, doubling back as often as not; narrowing and bloating like a series of valves and pipes. Here and there clear water swished along the sides of the streets in drainage channels, reflecting the sun in bright flashes like lightning under glass.

People had gone missing here, traders and settlers, young and old. No one had explored the place and come back to tell of their findings. Mahmett half expected to find the place full of bones, the remnants of the dead, lost perhaps in the labyrinthine streets and alleyways of the dream. And yet there was nothing, no sign of people, no litter or damage. No footprints or scrapings. No trail of string.

If this was the labyrinth, then no monster came to greet them even as they neared the center; instead it remained obstinately silent, just the cawing of the birds and the raindrop pitter-patter of beating insect wings as they navigated by the sun. The insects didn't stop— why would they? Nothing lived here, nothing rotted or discarded, so nothing remained to make them stay.

The three young men had trekked for hours, and Yasseft regaled them with stories of his own womanizing. Yasseft was older than Mahmett and Panenk, and his exploits seemed a thing of wonder to the younger men. They egged him on, assuring each other of what they would have done in the same situation, of how they would satisfy flocks of maidens. It was nonsense, of course, but it was only natural that the young men would choose to dream when walking within a place that seemed plucked from one.

They turned a corner, and up ahead they saw a great saurian head looming over them like some dinosaur from another era, its reptilian smile indulgently benign. The thing had narrow eyes that shone with a faint trace of fire red in the blazing afternoon sun as it glared at them from its high arching neck. For a moment all three men took it to be alive, and they reared back in fear, as if the thing might snap down on that thick neck, the flat arrowlike head reaching toward them down the length of bone-white street. But it did not. It merely waited there, serene in its majesty, a lizard sovereign waiting for who knew what.

"Is it a statue?" Mahmett asked, not daring to look away.

Yasseft studied the head where it loomed high above them like a cloud, blotting the sun where it waited. He estimated that the head was at least as large as a tool-shed; perhaps even larger, like the house of newlyweds.

"I don't like it," Panenk finally said, breaking the silence that Mahmett's brother had left.

"Who made it?" Yasseft said aloud, knowing neither of his companions could supply the answer.

"Six months ago, this whole region was empty," Panenk reminded them. "This place came to life…" He stopped, embarrassed and scared by his unfortunate choice of words.

"There's no life here," Yasseft stated firmly, as if to reassure himself. "Nothing. Not even death. It's empty."

"But people have searched," Panenk said. "People have looked and they have never come back. There are things, man-made things…"

Yasseft fixed him with his stare. "What things?"

"My grandfather spoke of his time with the army," Panenk said. "He saw things that had been made. Not just to hurt people, but to change landscapes. Perhaps this is one of those things."

He turned to Mahmett, asking the lad's opinion but the boy didn't answer.

Though silent, Mahmett had doubled over, his arms wrapped around his stomach.

"Hey, Mahmett," Panenk urged. "Hey, what's up with you?"

Mahmett looked up when he heard his name, and

Panenk saw the way he ground his teeth, the fearful look in his wide eyes. If he had tried to speak, no words had come out.

"Yasseft," Panenk hissed. "Your brother..."

Hearing the edge to Panenk's tone, Yasseft turned his attention reluctantly from the dragon's head at the end of the street and checked on his younger sibling. Mahmett clutched at his stomach as if trying to hold his intestines in place, and sweat beaded on his forehead like cooking oil. "What is it? Something you ate before?" Yasseft asked.

Mahmett shook his head, the movements jagged and abrupt as if he couldn't stand to do so for long. "S-something inside...me!"

As he spoke this last, his mouth opened and a torrent of water rushed up his throat and past his teeth, splashing on the ground in a rapidly forming puddle.

Yasseft grabbed him by the elbow, pulling him close and looking at his brother as the younger man remained doubled over. "Look at me, let me see," Yasseft urged.

Mahmett looked up, his dark brows arching in whatever pain it was that was driving itself through his body like a knife. Yasseft had been there when his brother had been born fifteen years ago, and he saw something in his brother's eyes that he had not seen for a long time. He saw tears, the type that stream like pouring water with no effort from the one who cries. Water streamed from Mahmett's tear ducts, thick lines running down the dusky skin of his face almost as if they were placed there by a paintbrush.

"What is it?" Mahmett mumbled, seeing the fear in his brother's eyes.

"You're crying," was all Yasseft could think to say.

From deep inside, Mahmett felt the swirl of liquid charging through his guts, racing and churning with the power of nearby thunder, rocking his frame and shaking his very bones. "I f-f-feel…" he began, but a stream of saliva threatened to choke him, blurting from his mouth in a wave.

Yasseft's grip slipped but slightly, and Mahmett tumbled to the chalky cobbles of the street. He hit hard but made no cry of pain. It was almost as if he was anesthetized, or more likely that whatever pain was driving through him required more attention than a simple blow to the knees.

Mahmett lay shuddering on the ground, his mouth widening, tears streaming down his cheeks.

"What is it?" Panenk asked frantically. "What is with him?"

"I don't know," Yasseft admitted. "It's like a fever."

They stood there, aware of how helpless they must appear in the face of this. They were the eldest of their little group, they had played together almost since birth and they had had it drummed into them that they were to keep little Mahmett safe. Suddenly a hundred near-misses were remembered: climbing by the power lines, when Mahmett had fallen from an olive tree, and when they had climbed over the neighbor's wall for a ball, only to come face-to-face with his mean-tempered mastiff. And now Mahmett was collapsed on the ground in a strange city with not a soul in sight.

"Shit." Yasseft spit. "We need to get him back. I don't know what's got into him but we can't stay here."

"I didn't even want to come here in the first place," Panenk reminded him, looking at the younger lad with worry. He wanted someone to blame now, and it wasn't going to be him.

Yasseft crouched and placed his hands beneath Mahmett's shoulders. The glistening, sunlit water at the side of the street sparked and shone like a polished mirror at the edges of Yasseft's vision. "Just grab him," he ordered. "Help me. We'll carry him."

Though dissatisfied with the arrangement, Panenk at least had the good grace to raise his complaints while lifting his cousin's ankles. "It took three hours to get here," he said. "It'll take twice that to get back if we have to carry him, and it'll be nightfall long before that."

Yasseft didn't answer. He stood there, his hands clenched beneath his brother's armpits, wincing as a tremble ran through his own body.

"You okay?" Panenk asked.

Yasseft shook his head wearily. "Just…" He stopped. "Feel like I'm going to…"

He dropped Mahmett, the younger man's arms slipping from his grip as he staggered backward. Yasseft's hands reached for his guts. It felt as if he urgently needed the toilet, as if he had diarrhea. He stumbled for a moment, bashing against a wall in the shadow of the looming saurian head and neck.

"What is it?" Panenk asked again.

"Going to…" Yasseft began and then he belched, a watery spume blasting from his mouth.

Panenk let Mahmett's legs drop to the ground, apologizing automatically as he rushed over to Yasseft's side. "My grandfather told me about this," he said fearfully. "Airborne weapons that get inside you, eat you up from within."

Yasseft was not listening. He stood propped against the bone-white wall of a single-story building, vomiting an odorless mix of saliva and water.

Panenk looked around him, searching for some clue as to where this attack had started. "We'll leave," he shouted to the empty buildings. "We'll go. Just leave us alone, please."

His voice echoed back to him, its fear magnified.

In the road at his feet, Mahmett shuddered where he lay in a puddle of water he himself had created with tears and vomit, and Panenk watched incredulously as the lad vibrated faster and faster before finally shimmying out of existence.

"Please," Panenk cried, stumbling away from the pool of water his cousin had been. There was no sign of Mahmett; he had simply ceased to be.

Behind him, Yasseft was clawing at his clothes, pulling his shirt away from his belt as his guts threatened to burst loose. Panenk looked at him, the fear making him shake like a leaf in the wind. As he watched, the older teen began shuddering in place, water streaming from his eyes, his mouth, his nostrils and ears. Water gushed from his hands, spurting from beneath his fingernails and darkening the white walls of the opposite building.

Panenk walked backward, his eyes fixed on what was happening to Yasseft. Yasseft seemed about to scream, but it came out more like a belch, a hacking blurt of noise as if a wind instrument played through water. Then, incredibly, Yasseft seemed to sink to his knees, but his legs had not bent. Instead, he dropped into the ground, his body sinking into the pool of water that had formed around him, sucking him down like quicksand. If he screamed, the scream was lost in the sound of rushing water that washed over his disappearing form. And then, just like Mahmett, Yasseft was gone, and all that was left was a puddle of cool water reflecting the overhead sun.

"Leave us alone," Panenk cried as he backed away. His voice echoed through the empty white streets. Even as he backed away, he felt the first thrum of water in his stomach like a single drumbeat, and he saw the silvery figures approach.

Chapter 5

Staring into the barrel of the Colt Mark IV in Sela Sinclair's hands, Farrell took a moment to process what she had just said. She had called him "the nonbeliever" and she looked damn serious about it.

From nearby, Farrell could hear the approaching footsteps of those robed figures, the troops for the stone god Ullikummis, the people who had sacked Cerberus and put him and Sinclair in this impossible position in the first place.

"What are you doing?" Farrell asked, mouthing the words more than saying them as he met Sinclair's dark eyes.

She fixed him with her stare, and Farrell couldn't detect so much as a hint of emotion or concern there. If this had been a movie, he knew, she'd smile now or wink or say something coded in such an obvious way that he would know without one iota of doubt that this was a ruse, that any second now she would turn the blaster on their human hunters and they'd get out of here breathless but alive. Come on, Sela, he thought, wishing for that little wink or smile, give me a sign.

Sinclair continued to stare into his eyes, the pistol never wavering as she aimed it at the spot between them.

In a few seconds the twin robed figures had joined

them, their hoods still pulled down low over their features.

"Who is he?" the broad-shouldered one said, a man with a basso voice.

"Cerberus," Sinclair replied, her eyes still watching Farrell like a hawk as he lay sprawled in the grass in front of her.

The hooded figures nodded in unison, and the slender one peered closer at the balding man who lay in the grass. "Is that Kane?" she asked, a Southern drawl to her voice.

"No," Sinclair said simply. "Guy's name is Farrell. He's just a technician."

"Overlord Ullikummis wants Kane," the man explained.

Shit, Farrell thought. This should be the point where Sinclair pulled the switch, turned the gun on their enemies, got them the heck out of there. But she wasn't going to do it, was she? She was following the orders of Ullikummis, whether by choice or design, he couldn't tell.

Sela Sinclair looked at the pitiful figure of Farrell, with his hollow cheeks and the dark rings around his eyes, and she heard the crescendo of the drums as they beat faster and faster in her head, their rhythm driving to a frenzy.

"Should I kill him?" she asked.

"Ullikummis is love," the robed woman said. "His will is not to kill."

As she spoke, the woman pushed down her hood, revealing locks of black hair that reached just past the nape of her neck. Farrell's eyes were drawn to the woman's forehead, however, where a bump showed like a spot or a blind boil.

Beside her, the man had pushed back his hood, revealing the graying remains of his hair and the bearded face of a man in his late fifties. Like the woman, he had a protrusion at the center of his forehead, a little ridge the size of a knuckle, resting between and slightly above his eyebrows.

Farrell had made the connection straight away, but still he checked Sinclair's forehead as he lay in the grass.

"Conversion is preferred," the man explained in a tone so neutral it was as if he were discussing paint.

"To embrace his love is glory," the woman added.

"I've only met him once," Sinclair said dispiritedly.

Fuck! Farrell's heart pounded against his chest, throbbing in his eardrums even as he twisted himself on the scrub and tried to run. Sinclair had it, too, that same telltale lump like a single measle or a boil about to erupt. She had always had it, all the time they had been together. And while he had been worrying himself to an early grave, she had been pumping iron and doing sit-ups, toning her already perfect body into a weapon for her new master. All of this, Farrell thought as he struggled to his feet and began to run back toward the house.

It was a second—less than that—and Farrell was sprinting across the overgrown lawn, Sinclair behind him pulling her gun up to take a shot at him. Farrell ran, the world blurring as the adrenaline blasted through his system like a nuclear explosion. He heard the gunshot, heard the man call out at the same time, ducked his head automatically as he ran.

They had taught lessons in survival technique at Cerberus. Edwards had instructed him in basic hand-to-hand combat on the expanse of dirt outside the rollback door of the redoubt; Sinclair herself had shown him how to load a pistol. A hundred instructions and pieces of advice raced through Farrell's mind at that moment, as the .38 bullet cut through the air past him and embedded itself in the scarred frontage of the ancient house in a blossoming burst of ruined masonry. What was it Edwards had said?

"If someone pulls a gun on you, get the hell out of there and don't look back."

Yeah, something like that, anyway, Farrell thought as he ran in an evasive zigzag pattern toward the house.

Behind him, Sinclair pulled the trigger a second time, aiming her blast at Farrell's rapidly retreating form. The loud report of the gun echoed in the empty street, and Farrell dropped, crumpling to the ground like a felled oak.

"He's still alive," the man in the robes insisted as he scurried toward the fallen figure.

Farrell was more than alive; he wasn't even wounded. Just as Sinclair's shot had blasted from her pistol he had caught his foot on something hidden in the long grass and tumbled to the ground, the bullet shrieking its angry trail over his head. Lying there now, Farrell looked all around him as he tried to scramble away. The grass was so long that it hid his prone form. And there, less than a foot from his right leg, he spotted the thing that had tripped him—it was a rusted old exhaust pipe, caught up in a tangle of grass and sod. The pipe was perhaps eighteen inches in length and about an inch and a half across. His mind racing, Farrell grasped for the pipe and yanked it from the earth as he drove his body forward toward the house once again. Rusty pipe in hand, Farrell powered onward to the house, keeping his head ducked and his body bent.

"He's running," Farrell heard a woman shout, but he couldn't discern if that was Sinclair or the woman in the robe. It didn't matter now, as he was at the door to the house, launching himself at the wooden barricade and powering into the sudden darkness of the hallway beyond.

He had lived in this house for forty-two days, knew every ghastly, rotting inch of it. As footsteps clattered on the porch behind him, Farrell darted left into the living room that ran one half the length of the building.

Something had happened to Sinclair, he realized, something that had maybe been there since before they had gone into hiding. That spot on her head, it was his mark—Ullikummis's. Farrell had heard rumors about other members of Cerberus turning, siding with Ullikummis and his people. It was like a cult, a growing movement that relied on the belief that Ullikummis himself was a god from the stars. Which was ridiculous, of course—Ullikummis was Annunaki, a cruel and heartless race of aliens who had held humankind in subjugation thousands of years ago. But Sela Sinclair knew this. Everyone at Cerberus knew this; Lakesh himself had held an information session in the canteen just a few months before when they had discovered the first evidence that Ullikummis had returned to Earth. And yet Sinclair was under his sway somehow, something physical inside her twisting her will, instructing her like an entheogen.

Behind him, hideously near, Farrell heard Sinclair and the other two pushing through the house, shouting instructions to split up and find him. The blood was pounding in his ears, and his breath felt warm in his throat, pumping past his gritted teeth like sandblasting. The room was full of old furniture. A settee had collapsed in on itself to become a sculpture of rusted springs and wood that showed the familiar signs of woodworm. A table was splintered against one wall, while another sagged to the floor with two legs bent out of shape. Farrell vaulted it as the figure came through the door after him, the man in the robes. The man was pulling something from an innocuous pouch he wore at his waist, loading the slingshot in his hand even as he leaped the broken settee and rushed through the room. The enforcers of Ullikummis didn't use guns as a rule, but relied on a more basic weapon, a slingshot-style catapult that launched vicious stones with the force of bullets.

Up ahead, Farrell saw the second door of the room, the one that broke back into the hall opposite the closet, and he drove himself to it as his pursuer launched the first clutch of stones from his catapult rig.

Farrell reached out with his free hand, striking the far door frame with his forearm as he ducked through it. Behind him, a scattershot of rocks struck the frame where Farrell had been, their pitter-patter like hail on a window.

Out in the hallway once more, Farrell found himself face-to-face with Sela Sinclair, the dark metal of the pistol still clutched in her right hand. Farrell caromed into her, slamming both of them against the far wall in a crash of crumbling plasterboard. Sinclair sank back to the floor, spluttering as the plasterboard disintegrated to powder all around her, Farrell landing astride her in a tangle of limbs. Farrell saw the stubby nose of the Colt Mark IV snap up, and he lashed out with the rusty pipe in his hand, knocking the muzzle aside even as it flashed with another ear-splitting shot.

Then Farrell was on his feet again, driving himself along the corridor as Sela Sinclair brought the pistol around for another shot. Beside her, the man in the hooded robes appeared from the main room, the slingshot in his hand spinning over and over, picking up speed before he launched another clutch of pebbles barely bigger than grains of sand toward the retreating figure.

Farrell sidestepped into another room to his right, a chunk of plasterboard turning to dust just three inches from his face where the stones struck. He was in the dining room now, once able to accommodate a six- or maybe eight-seat table. It now housed a pile of broken furniture amid scarred, moss-covered walls. Worse yet, it stank of rainwater, the kind of rainwater that perhaps had been mixed with urine somewhere along the way. Farrell ran through the room, leaping over the shattered remains of a glass-fronted cabinet that had been used as the set for a family of badgers. The robed man hurried through the open doorway behind him, his slingshot whining in his hand as it spun through the air.

Farrell sprinted onward, aiming himself for the twin doors of the serving hatch that stood closed at the far end of the room. The wood was rotten, light cutting through it in bold strips. Farrell heard the robed man unleash another clutch of stones as he leaped, and he used the pipe like a club to smash his way into the serving hatch doors and powered himself through. A smattering of tiny stone flecks peppered the wall around the hatch as Farrell disappeared through it, and his pursuer stopped in his tracks.

Farrell crashed through the serving hatch into the kitchen, tumbling onto the cracked terra-cotta tiles of the floor and rolling forward, bringing himself back to an upright position. He was breathing heavily now, his heart pounding like a jackhammer against his ribs.

The kitchen was a mess of stained surfaces and mold, the faucets and drains overgrown with plants that had climbed through the pipes once human habitation here had ceased, everything going back to nature in the end. There was another door there that led to the backyard, or whatever had once been the backyard. Now it was just as overgrown as the front, a little jungle in the forgotten strip of land. Scla Sinclair had locked this door when they had arrived here, making sure it was secure to stop anyone sneaking in—or that's what she had said. Now Farrell wasn't so sure. He wondered if she had done it to lock him in for the day when her allies in the New Order arrived. Was she even conscious that she was serving them?

Farrell figured he had maybe five seconds to escape. His only advantage was knowing the layout of the building, knowing about the serving hatch to the kitchen. He took the heavy pipe in his hand and smashed it against the ragged boards that Sinclair had placed over the gap of the window. The boards were tough enough, but the nails were brittle and rusted, and the whole door shuddered on old hinges as the makeshift panel crumpled apart.

Farrell was through the window in an instant, wedging his body into the gap before clambering through it with all the grace of a beached fish. Didn't matter—just had to get out of there, to stay alive.

Outside, the backyard was just as overgrown as the front and the street beyond. Farrell was slowing now, the momentary safety giving him a chance to think. He needed to contact Cerberus, find Ohio Blue or locate the nearest mat-trans.

In a moment he had engaged his Commtact, the subdermal communicator that was located just below his ear. "This is Farrell out in the field. Do you read? Over."

As he spoke, a figure came hurrying around the edge of the house, chasing after him through the long underbrush. It was the woman in the robe, the one who had accompanied the man to the deserted street. She must have doubled back. Her arms were pumping as she chased Farrell, and he drove himself onward, confident he could outrun her by dint of his longer legs. Her teeth were gritted and her eyes looked fierce as they fixed on his back, while Farrell darted across the jungle of the backyard.

A moment later Farrell saw the boundary fence that had once marked this property, a simple chain-link line running just above waist height. He kicked his left leg out, leaping high and vaulting over the fence in a swish of dirty white clothing. Beyond, he guessed he was in an access road—probably the kind that had once been used by garbage trucks—though it, too, had been given over to the wilderness, with fronds and reeds growing as high as his waist, some up to his chest.

"Farrell, this is Donald Bry." The voice from the Commtact device reverberated through Farrell's mastoid bone so that only he could hear it. "What's the situation, over?"

Farrell looked behind him, saw the woman jump the fence in pursuit, the familiar form of a leather slingshot now grasped in her fist.

"Bit busy," Farrell explained over the Commtact.

He didn't wait for Bry's response, just turned and faced the woman bearing down on him. She plucked a palm-load of stones from the leather pouch at her belt, loading the slingshot in a swift, practiced movement. With a sound like an angered beehive, the slingshot began to whir around and around, picking up speed in preparation of launch. Farrell looked all around him, searching for cover, some way to get out of the line of fire. He could still see the back of the house through the raging underground, saw Sela Sinclair and the robed man come out the back door chasing their prey. There was nowhere to run.

"And when there's nowhere to run, you stand and fight."

That's something else Edwards had drummed into him in those training sessions.

Farrell was upon the woman in a flash, driving the heavy exhaust pipe at her chest where the crimson shield glinted in the sunlight. The pipe hit with a hollow thunk, knocking the breath out of Farrell's opponent. Surprised, the woman toppled backward, the stones dropping from her slingshot as it momentarily lost all momentum, like a child's bucket-of-water trick.

Farrell stood over her in the long grass, feeling the ghastly weight of that hunk of metal in his hand. She looked up at him, her dark hair in disarray around her face, blue eyes fixed on his. "I am stone," she uttered, the words like a mantra.

It would be so easy, Farrell thought, to hit her again, to crush her skull in a single, savage blow. But no, that wasn't him. That wasn't how he did things.

So he turned and he ran, the breath heavy against his chest as his booted feet pounded against the compacted earth and leaves.

THE DARK-HAIRED WOMAN, whose name was Tanya Stone, struggled up from the grass, urging her body to follow Farrell as he sprinted away. She plucked the leather loop that formed her slingshot from the ground, wiping the dirt from it as she stood, began moving after Farrell. She had taken two paces when her partner, Jackson Stone, called for her to halt.

Tanya turned, seeing Jack and the ebony-skinned newcomer, and she gave him a quizzical look. "I can catch him."

As she spoke, a chill seemed to cut through the air, and Tanya became aware of another presence. She turned around, searching the brush for a moment before she spotted the other figure, the woman with the red-gold hair and eyes the green of the ocean—Brigid Haight. In her late twenties, Haight was poised in the bole of a tree, prowling from its shadow like a stalking cat, her black leather suit covering her entirely, clinging to her limbs like a second skin. It seemed somehow appropriate that Haight had dressed in the dead flesh of animals, surrounding herself with their ghosts.

Haight was the chosen of Ullikummis, his first priest in the New Order, and while Tanya had not met her before she recognized her instantly. And she shivered in the woman's presence as something seemed to crawl along her spine.

Beside her, Sela Sinclair looked at the slender, red-haired woman stepping from the shadows and she felt a stab of recognition. Inside her head, the drums were beating louder and faster than ever before, louder and faster and far more brutal.

FARRELL SPRINTED DOWN the overgrown access road, glancing back over his shoulder to see if he was still being followed. The woman was on her feet and she had been joined by Sela Sinclair and the man in the fustian robes. They seemed to be talking, watching as Farrell ran from them. Their confidence irritated him, made him angry.

He turned back to face the path he was running along, with its tangles of briars and reeds, the moisture heavy in the air where the plants breathed. There was a wall ahead, reaching up almost to head height but crumbling in places, a sickly green creeper clinging to its surface. He stopped when he reached it, conscious of the ache in the muscles of his arm where he was hefting the heavy length of exhaust pipe. He glanced fearfully behind him once again, back up along what was left of the old road. Another figure had joined his three pursuers. This one was dressed in black, a bloom of red hair haloing its head. From this distance with the sun in his eyes, Farrell couldn't tell if it was a man or a woman. But he knew one thing for certain—it meant they had added another member to their hunting group, another body to chase him and capture him and presumably indoctrinate him into this cult of Ullikummis.

"Ccrb-cr-us," Farrell said, the syllables broken by his heavy breathing now. "I need a way out of here, right now." To his right he saw another low chain-link fence, this one bent out of true and with a gaping hole in its center. Farrell moved toward it, keeping one eye on the gathering group at the far end of the little road.

Donald Bry's voice came back to Farrell over the Commtact link. "What's the problem, Farrell?"

"Hostile types just tried to kill me or indoctrinate me, I'm not sure."

"'Hostile types'?" Bry repeated, and Farrell suspected that, wherever he was, the man had raised an eyebrow at the phrase.

"The stone nuts," Farrell grunted, clambering over

the sagging fence. "Ullikummis's people. They tracked me down—I don't know how."

"Is Sinclair okay?" Bry asked, the consummate bookkeeper even in times of stress.

"She's one of 'em, man," Farrell said. He was running now, arms pumping, the pipe swinging in his hand as he pelted across the overgrown expanse of garden toward another shell of a building.

"What do you—?" Bry asked, mild surprise in his voice.

Farrell sprinted past the side of the house, pushing himself on. "I can't explain how," he interrupted. "I think maybe she's always been one of them, like she was just biding her time waiting for the right moment to strike."

He hurried on, out past the churned-up tarmac of the drive where an ancient automobile waited, its red paint bleached white by the sun across its roof and hood, rust marring its bodywork like ringworm.

"Am triangulating your position now," Bry told Farrell, his tone reassuring.

There was a pause, during which Farrell ran down another forgotten Bradley street that now looked like a strip of jungle had been transplanted into the suburbs. Startled birds took flight from a twisting cypress as he hurried past, squawking in ugly caws, their feathers orange and an almost luminescent green.

In a secret location hundreds of miles away, Farrell knew that Donald Bry was even now using his subdermal transponder to track his position, applying it to a map of the local territory and assessing the best escape route.

"Farrell, I have a mat-trans located in a military redoubt about three miles west of your present position," Bry announced over the Commtact. "Do you think you can make that, or do you want me to scramble a team to come to your aid?"

Farrell glanced self-consciously behind him, searching the wreckage of the nearby houses and the towering ferns for signs of movement. The leaves shimmied in the breeze, making whispering sounds as they swayed. But there was no one around—maybe, just maybe, he had lost them?

"I should be able to make it to the redoubt," Farrell told Bry reluctantly. He knew how tight the personnel situation was just now, knew that Cerberus could ill afford to scramble a CAT team to protect one lowly tech. "If I go careful, I think I can avoid any more trouble. I'll let you know when I'm within sight."

"Excellent," Bry acknowledged over the Commtact. "We should be able to remote program a jump for you from here. We'll get you to safety."

Pipe in hand, Farrell hurried on down the overgrown streets of Bradley, far away from the safehouse he had shared with the traitorous Sela Sinclair.

BACK IN THE OVERGROWN remains of the service road, Tanya and Jackson Stone and Sinclair stood with Brigid Haight as the trim figure of Farrell disappeared from sight.

"Let him go," Brigid instructed, watching the retreating figure as he hurried toward the break between the houses where a wall cut across the roadway's path. "He doesn't matter."

"But we'll lose him," Tanya insisted, clenching and unclenching her fists where she held the leather band of the slingshot.

"The world belongs to Ullikummis now, and all who share in his love," Brigid intoned. "Where is there left for him to run?"

Chapter 6

The wind whipped past the retrofitted cargo as it cut through the skies over Syria toward Iraq. Grant sat on one of two long benches that lined the cargo area, head down, his hands held close together so that their steepled fingers formed a rough triangular shape of empty space. Beside him, Domi watched, a confused crease appearing between her white eyebrows.

"What you doing?" Domi asked.

"Concentrating," Grant replied, his eyes still fixed on the empty space between his touching fingertips.

Domi nodded as if she understood, but she was just as baffled as she had been before. Despite being one of the longest-serving members of the Cerberus organization, Domi was still a child of the Outlands at heart, savage and simpleminded in her comprehension of things. She wasn't unintelligent; she just had a more direct approach to things than those who had been educated in the nine towering baronies that dotted the landscape of North America. A little over five feet in height, Domi was a svelte, pixielike figure who had wrapped her chalk-white skin beneath a series of light layers for the duration of this field mission. Her hair, a creamy white, like milk, was cut short around her head, framing her sharp-planed face in a ruffled pixie cut. While albinism had left Domi almost entirely white, her eyes were a fearsome red, like bloody wounds in her face, and they had a disarming effect when she fixed her gaze on an opponent. Despite her youth, Domi had formed a close relationship with Lakesh, the two of them becoming lovers over the past couple of years. If Lakesh had ever seemed worried about sending his personnel into the danger zone, that worry had quadrupled with Domi once the two of them had fallen in love. But the worry was reciprocated; Domi could be like a terrier when it came to Lakesh's safety.

Across the aisle from Domi, sitting between two Tigers of Heaven warriors dressed in armorlike stealth suits, Rosalia smiled contemptuously. "Leave the Magistrate alone," she said. "He's focusing his mojo."

As she spoke, the nameless dog that sat at her feet whined, its expressive, pale eyes wide with worry. The dog disliked the sound of the heavy rotors, and its ears kept twitching so that Rosalia had to keep one hand in the scuff of its neck to keep it settled, rubbing it there now and again. The dog had come with Rosalia here, as it seemed to follow her everywhere. While it might seem a burden at times, the mutt was a fierce fighter when the time came. In fact, there seemed to be something uncanny in its fighting technique, as if more than one creature somehow existed in the same place. Watching it fight was like hallucinating at times, a double or triple image taking up its position.

Rosalia had changed her clothes before leaving the temporary headquarters in the winter palace. Now she wore a dark one-piece outfit that hugged her curvaceous body, her long shapely legs covered by pant legs that tucked into supple leather boots that reached halfway up her calves. Rosalia had tied her hair back in a simple ponytail, which she tucked beneath the black hood of her top to prevent it from flying in her face.

Domi didn't trust Rosalia. There was something about the mercenary woman and her superior attitude that rubbed Domi the wrong way. Compounding that distrust was the memory that on their first meeting Rosalia had been part of a two-person team that had knocked Domi unconscious from behind. Domi had never forgiven the woman for that, even if Rosalia herself had not struck the actual blow.

"He's called Grant," the albino girl said irritably, her red devil's eyes boring into Rosalia's.

"Like Seth," Rosalia said obtusely before turning back to her whining hound to calm it. Despite her brusqueness, it was evident that the mysterious Rosalia was well educated. Her well of knowledge seemed bottomless, yet she frequently saw no reason to explain her comments to those she considered beneath her. Domi very definitely fell into that category.

Grant ignored the two antagonistic females, relaxing his eyes as he meditated on the nonspace created between his touching fingers. It had been fifteen hours since the incident with Edwards, and he had hoped that he might remain while the operation was performed on the man's brain so that he could witness with the rest of them just what it was that was growing there. However, with the satellite feeds back online, something urgent had come up. Via its network of contacts, Cerberus had amassed several reports of people going missing out near the banks of the river known as the Euphrates. Not just one or two people, but dozens, perhaps more than one hundred. Lakesh had replayed Grant the surveillance footage taken from Iraq, close to the mouth of the Euphrates and Tigris rivers. The overhead footage showed a city structure expanding on the banks of the Euphrates. The settlement that had not been there six months before. Constructed of an off-white stone of unknown origin, the ville was expanding at a rapid rate. That wasn't unusual in this age of displaced persons and in itself it shouldn't be cause for alarm. What was alarming was the shape of the burgeoning ville—it quite clearly took the form of a winged creature, drawn across the fertile soil of the riverbank.

"A dragon," Grant had said as he had stared at the incredible surveillance photos.

"Or perhaps a dragon ship," Lakesh had said, emphasizing the word *ship*. His implication was clear. The Cerberus team had become aware of the Annunaki starship *Tiamat* as it lurked high above the atmosphere, and Grant had been a part of the team on board when the ship had begun its self-destruct sequence, watched from space as its exploding form had filled the heavens with light. To have another of the starships appear like this—on Earth—was without doubt a cause for concern.

Well prepared for the briefing, Lakesh had called up backdated surveillance footage showing the expansion of the settlement from apparent nothingness just six months ago. While it appeared to be a city, there was no mistaking the implication of that swooping, winged shape. Several miles across, it crouched by the banks, head pointing off toward the north while the right-hand flank abutted the river itself, a curving tail winding downward in a southerly direction. The mighty wings were stretched wide in imitation of a crescent, the creature's right wing crossing the width of the river in a curving bridge. It was unclear from the photographs, but it appeared that buildings were constructed on the wing-bridge as elsewhere, adhering to the dragonlike shape of the vast settlement.

"We need to look into this," Grant had agreed. "If only we had the Mantas, then me and Kane could…" He stopped, the words turning to ashes on his tongue. He had partnered with Kane for so long that to take on a mission like this without him, even a simple recce, seemed anathema to the way things worked.

"We're just amassing reports from the local area," Donald Bry had explained from his position at another computer terminal in the makeshift ops center. "It seems it's something of a no-fly zone," he explained. "Reports are hazy but there's suggestions that some low-flying aircraft have failed to return from the area in the last few weeks."

"Sounds serious." Grant nodded. "What about the interphaser—could we access a gateway in there?"

The options that Grant was suggesting covered many of the established forms of long-distance transportation that the Cerberus rebels had come to rely upon. The Mantas were transatmospheric aircraft that were stored at the hangar of the old Cerberus redoubt in Montana. The interphaser, the teleportational device that opened a quantum window through space, relied on established destination markers called parallax points. Unless there was one of these in place, the jump to a specific location could not be completed.

Lakesh had pointed to the surveillance photo on screen, indicating the area where the right shoulder blade of the creature would be. "There's a parallax point here," he confirmed, "but I admit a grave reluctance in using it. This specific area was the exact location of the ancient city of Nippur, where Enlil was said to have made his home. It seems too much of a coincidence for this new settlement to have appeared by chance, especially taking the dragon form of the

Annunaki mother, *Tiamat,* as it has. While the interphaser could send you there instantaneously, I'm inclined to think you'd be walking straight into the belly of the beast."

"Almost literally," Grant muttered as he eyed the dragon form.

"And if there is any Annunaki connection at all," Lakesh continued, "the very first thing they would have established is a security detail or automated expulsion system for the parallax point itself. Which is to say, it could well be like walking into a blender. Not clever."

"Sounds reasonable," Grant accepted. "So what do we do?"

"We have established some local connections in the area," Lakesh explained. "We'll open a gateway into an old military base in Syria, and you'll take a ride from there."

"What kind of ride?" Grant had asked warily.

"Helicopter," Lakesh had explained. "A retrofitted cargo chopper."

Retrofitted was right. Whatever its original configuration, the craft had been gutted and refitted so drastically over the years that it looked like a flying junkyard. Grant looked around him now, saw the rusting patches that lined the wall behind Rosalia and the two guards, the sloppily painted plastic-and-ceramic bowl that formed the uneven ceiling. From the outside, the whole airframe was a patchwork of pieces, different-colored plates worked one over another to complete its shell. It had no doubt been found in some military redoubt somewhere, tucked out of sight for a century or more before finally being called into action, pieced together as best the local mechanics could based

on the design. That the vehicle flew—and flew well—
seemed nothing shy of a miracle to Grant, but he had
traveled in worse.

Dressed in dark, supple armor, two Tigers of Heaven
had agreed to accompany the three Cerberus warriors on this reconnaissance mission to find out what
the deserted dragon city was all about. Their names
were Kishiro and Kudo and they displayed that studied calmness that all of Shizuka's warriors seemed to
have. Grant admired them for it.

With Cerberus in disarray, field missions like this
were proving problematic to staff. Kane and Edwards
were out of commission, Brigid was lost and almost
two-thirds of the personnel were still in hiding, spread
out across North America. If they were going to use
subs like this, Grant would rather they include his lover
Shizuka, whose ability with a samurai sword was nothing short of artistic. But the world was different now;
there were dangers on all sides. This growing cult of
Ullikummis seemed to be expanding at a colossal rate,
and even threatened the shores of New Edo, the territory Shizuka governed.

Thus, Grant found himself leading an untested
pairing of teammates into the unknown. He had come
to trust, even respect, Rosalia after their most recent
escapade, and he knew he could rely upon both Domi
and any member of the Tigers of Heaven. Still, racing
across the skies in a rattletrap cargo chopper accompanied by four teammates he only half knew, Grant felt
a sense of unease. Reluctantly he turned his attention
back to the triangular window created by his touching
fingers, willing his worries to slip away. Whatever else
happened, he couldn't change it now.

"WE ARE ALMOST NEAR," a voice called over the fuzzy speaker system from the cockpit. It was the pilot, a local man called Mahood, whose English was heavily accented with the emphasis on the wrong syllables, making it hard at times to decipher.

Grant nodded, inhaling deeply and projecting a sense of calm. "How long?" he asked, his finger depressing the radio comm button set in the wall.

Mahood muttered something in the local dialect, then repeated it in English for his passengers. "Two minutes is maximum."

"Great," Grant said, wondering if the sarcasm in his tone was lost on the foreigner. He hoped it was; the man was risking his own neck for the Cerberus team, skirting the edges of the dubious no-fly zone.

Swiveling on the bench, Grant turned to look out the window nearest him. It was a horizontal slit of perhaps three inches in height, and Grant had to peer closely to get a decent view of the outside. The others crowded over to their own windows, all except for Rosalia, who stayed with her dog, hushing the animal as it whined in time with the straining engines.

"There it is," Grant muttered, pushing his face closer to the window without thinking about it.

Down below, off to the port side of the renovated helicopter, the dragon seemed to crouch at the banks of the wide strip of river. Wisps of cloud cut the view for a moment, a V-shaped flock of squawking geese swooping by, and then the dragon reappeared, ill lit in the dwindling light of dusk. It was hard to assess the size of it from so far away, but Grant had seen the aerial photographs from the satellite and he already had a rough idea. That idea hadn't prepared him for looking at the structure itself, however.

It was not a dragon, even though its shape suggested one. Close up, it was not even a single structure. Rather, a series of buildings were poised along the banks of the Euphrates, with no apparent uniformity to their designs. Here a minaret poked upward to the clouds; there a low, flat rooftop reflected the dwindling rays of the setting sun as it painted the surrounds in orange and vermilion. Yet despite the differences, each building contributed to the whole, each formed a part of the dragon's body, head and wings. As the satellite image had suggested, one of those wings— the rightmost—sloped out across the river itself, the juddering struts of low buildings ridging across its surface. And everything, *everything* was creamy white.

"It's incredible," Domi whispered, her voice hushed with awe.

"More than that," Grant said, "it's like nothing on Earth."

"Then where did it come from?"

"That's what we're going to find out," Grant assured her. "Which means we have to get lower."

With that, the ex-Magistrate flicked the radio transmission button again to speak with the pilot. "Bring us down, Mahood," he instructed. "Let's see if we can find us a landing area."

With a word of acknowledgment from the cockpit, the sturdy chopper banked left, its body rolling closer toward the dragon-shaped settlement. There was something else about it, Grant realized as they got closer. Despite all those buildings, he could see no people out in the streets, no one wandering amid the lifeless structures.

"My cousin Hassood will meet us by the left wing." Mahood's voice came over the radio speaker again.

"There's a flat space out there just beyond city limits where we can land. There'll be a bit of a walk, I'm afraid."

"Fine by me," Grant began, but before the last word had left his lips, a bright burst of dazzling scarlet light flashed outside like lightning and the Blackbird shook as though it had struck something. "What th—?"

A moment later the chopper shuddered violently, and Grant, Domi and the others found themselves tossed across the metal decking. They were under attack.

GRABBING AT WHATEVER PASSED for handholds in the chopper's interior, Grant hurried forward as the craft continued to shake. Behind him, Rosalia's dog was barking fearfully.

"What the hell's going on?" Grant asked as he saw the startled pilot, Mahood, struggling with the controls.

Grant was surprised to see that the piloting system was not the advanced, sleek dash he'd expected. Rather, old-fashioned dials and plates had been wired together and a bucket seat was positioned in front of two stick-style yokes, something like an ancient whirlybird.

Mahood, an olive-skinned Iranian with glistening sweat in the pebbledash stubble atop his head, looked at Grant with wide eyes, shouting something in his own tongue.

"Again," Grant instructed. "In English."

"A light ray," Mahood translated as he fought with the yoke. "Laser. Laser beam."

Even as he said it, Grant saw another blast zap past the cockpit windows, bloodred and ascending in a thick vertical line that was at least a dozen feet across.

"Shit," Grant growled. One hit from that thing and they'd lose a wing...or worse. "Can you get us down?"

Grant asked urgently, placing a hand on the back of
Mahood's seat to keep himself steady as they rolled
and yawed.

"No, no, no, no, no," Mahood spit as he struggled
with the controls, banking the chopper so that Grant
had to hang on to stop his head from slamming against
the ceiling. Through the cockpit window, Grant could
see the narrow crescent of the moon, a thin sliver of
white hanging in the darkening blue sky.

Grant was an accomplished pilot himself and he
stared at the bucket seat that Mahood sat in, his ample
backside resting atop a fluffy pink cushion at odds
with the worn brown leather of the ancient seat belt.
"Want me to take over?" Grant asked.

Mahood pulled up on the stick as another thick blast
of laser light cut through the air ahead of them, its
edges crackling like lightning. "We need to land right
now," he explained in his fractured English. "I got her
but I don't think we're—"

Another blast lit the cockpit, and something on
the far right of the dash suddenly burst into flames.
Mahood stretched out his sandaled foot and kicked at
the flames, stamping them until they went out.

"Must land here, Mr. Grant," he explained. "But
quickly."

"Yeah," Grant agreed, "I can see that."

Mahood banked in on a tight vector as Grant hurried back to the cargo hold, where his four allies were
anxiously waiting. Swiftly he explained the situation
to them as the ancient chopper rocked in the air, illuminated by another of the all-powerful crimson beams
of laser light.

"Be ready, people," Grant said. "We might have to
ditch."

Rosalia looked up from where she was steadying her dog. "What is that light show, anyway?"

"Looks like a pulse laser," Grant explained. "Single shot but deadly as hell. I don't think it's tracking us. Looks more like it's automated to react to anything in the sky. But it's a wide enough beam to cut us if we get unlucky."

"Local defence, huh?" Rosalia hissed. "Painful."

Touchdown was as rough as it was unexpected. Grant opened the cargo door and urged his companions out.

"Been a pleasure, man," Grant said over the radio communicator as he stepped up to the open door. "Clear skies."

He jumped out into the courtyard where Mahood had landed and sprinted for the cover of the nearby buildings.

As Grant reached the edge of the courtyard the laser blasted again, rushing up into the sky in a column of bloodred lightning. From high above there was an explosion as something went up in flames—the chopper, Grant realized.

He peered up, his eyes aching as they struggled to look into the red beam of the laser. And then it switched off, as suddenly as it had fired, and the sky seemed to be plunged into darkness, the single slit eye of the moon a blurred white streak on his retina.

Grant saw that the chopper had been cut in two by the laser light, an expanding ball of flame bursting from its side as the pieces began to drop. He knew that Mahood was doomed, and threw himself into the mouth of an alley to seek shelter from the flaming wreckage falling from the sky.

Chapter 7

Once he confirmed all his teammates were present, Grant tried to establish their location. He estimated they were no more than three-fourths of a mile from the outer wall. He activated his hidden Commtact link, switching to the frequency they had set aside to speak with their local contact, the man called Hassood.

"This is Grant from Cerberus," Grant said, keeping his voice low as he spoke into his subdermal device. Once the pintels made contact, transmissions were picked up by the wearer's auditory canals, and dermal sensors transmitted the electronic signals directly through the skull casing, vibrating the ear canal. In theory, a completely deaf user would still be able to hear normally, in a fashion, courtesy of the Commtact device.

The units also functioned as real-time translation devices, providing they had enough raw vocabulary from a language programmed into their processor. And because they were directly connected to the body of the user, could amplify speech no matter how quiet. As such, Grant chose not to raise his voice when calling for Hassood, so as not to attract any unwanted attention in the mysterious dragon city. The place appeared deserted, but Grant knew he could not test the veracity of that observation. Best be careful, then.

"Local, are you receiving me?" Grant said.

The Commtact receiver remained silent for an agonizing stretch of seconds before a man's voice, high-pitched and reminding Grant of a woman, came back to him. "Receiving you, Cerberus," the man confirmed. "This is Hassood. I saw an explosion. What happenings?"

Grant winced. "I'm afraid we ran into some trouble," he said delicately. "Your cousin...he didn't make it. I'm sorry."

There was silence again over the Commtact, and Grant could feel the eyes of his team burning on him as they listened to just one side of the conversation.

"Hassood?" Grant prompted.

Hassood's voice came back over the Commtact. "Very sad day. Let us not make it any sadder. Where are you?"

"We landed wide of the field," Grant explained. "About a half mile or so into town along the western edge. How close are you?"

"Head west," Hassood responded after a moment's thought. "You'll see a towering thing, like...um... needle, yes? Knitting needle?"

"Gotcha," Grant confirmed.

"Needle is made of white stone, in center of street," Hassood said. "You will see it. I come, wait for you there."

"Okay," Grant agreed. "We're on our way."

Grant led his field team through the eerie, empty city. The lanes were silent, unlit. There were no streetlamps at all, not even the suggestion of ones that might have once worked. It left the city in darkness, shadows genuflecting to the tidal whims of the moon. The dragon city was made up of buildings of all shapes and sizes, everything constructed of a white stone.

The buildings all appeared to be boarded up, every last one of them, doors and windows barricaded with pale-colored struts as if the inhabitants were preparing for a tornado, battening down the hatches. But if they were, then the locals were waiting now in silence—the whole city seemed to echo only with the footsteps of the Cerberus team, the panting of Rosalia's dog sounding like a steam train as it reverberated off the brickwork.

Beneath the single silvery line of the slimmest crescent moon, the roads were narrow and winding, made of dusty cobbles, sand sprinkled between them that billowed up to dance on the tireless eddies of the wind. There were several abandoned vehicles here, the odd motorized cart parked at the roadside, windows and hubcaps filthy with white sand. Grant urged them to continue, heading in a westerly direction to the arranged meeting place with their guide, Hassood. By keeping to one direction, Grant hoped that also they might find genuine signs of life amid the boarded-up buildings. But they didn't. Instead, it felt like they were walking through a photograph, a picture of one of those great American cities just before the nukes had dropped, when people had boarded up their homes and shops in the hopes of surviving the unimaginable devastation to come.

The five-strong Cerberus team walked loosely abreast, spreading out across the road to make for multiple targets should a sniper appear from the shadows and to bolster their chances of survival against a single tossed grenade. They continued past a stripped-down SandCat sitting on blocks, its chassis holed with multiple bullet scars. There was no sign of its occupants.

Before long, twilight had turned to night, the skyline meeting the sand that surrounded the weird city in the shape of a dragon. Grant checked his wrist chron— it was 9:33 on a balmy July night. He and his companions were becoming increasingly aware that they were walking through a ghost town as they continued to make their way west. Mahood's cousin had promised to wait for them until 10:00 p.m. local time, Grant knew, but since he had witnessed the destruction of the chopper he may very well be having second thoughts. Grant tamped down his irritation, feeling no guilt at the man's death, only sorrow and anger. A Magistrate had no time for guilt, Grant recalled, his training protecting him from such useless and destructive emotions.

They kept moving, hoping to find a place that wasn't boarded up. Rosalia's dog whimpered now and again, and she hushed it; the animal didn't seem to have much interest in exploring the city. Instead it seemed scared.

"Feels strange," Domi murmured as they continued down the empty street.

Grant turned to her, his eyes roving the weird, boarded-up structures behind her. "Yeah," he agreed. He couldn't help wishing they had Kane with them. With his uncanny ability to sniff out trouble, his partner's so-called point-man sense sure could help them out right now.

The street they were walking along narrowed, and abruptly they had reached a cul-de-sac, where the towering buildings on either side leaned inward so as to almost form an arch, their highest points touching. A wall sat across the end of the narrow road, blocking the way and reaching up to Grant's shoulders. Grant stared at it, turned back for a moment to make sure they weren't being watched then brought himself close and peered over the wall. Beyond lay another street, really nothing more than the other half of the one they were on, the wall apparently blocking it for no other reason than to be contrary, or like some kind of valve.

"Back or over?" Grant mouthed, his lips moving in silence.

Grant peered behind him once more, eyeballing the street. Domi waited at his shoulder while Kishiro and Kudo hung back, adopting safe positions in the shadows to either side of the street, unarmed but with their hands resting ready at their sheathed swords.

Rosalia was hanging farther back along with her dog, treading on light feet as she peered closely at the boarded windows and doors around them. She stopped for a moment, peering into the dark gap between two pale boards that seemed to have been painted—was it paint?—a creamy white, her exotic brown eyes searching inside for signs of life. Beside her, the dog whimpered sorrowfully as it peered at the boarded door. Rosalia glared at the dog, hushing it with a single look. Grant watched from the distance as Rosalia pressed her ear against the boards.

Other than Grant's own team, the street itself was ghostly empty. More than just empty—it was silent, eerily so beneath the silver light of the thin moon. Weeds grew between the cracks in the cobblestones, life, as ever, finding a way. The buildings themselves looked aged, ancient, leaning toward one another.

Was this place built by human hands? Grant wondered as a nightmarish feeling began to tickle along his spine.

There was definitely something off about it. It had an indefinably false quality, the age of the buildings somehow premature, the apparent randomness of the structures not random at all, forming that great dragon shape from overhead. The mind that had planned this settlement knew what it was doing. But the question was, what was it doing?

Then Rosalia came trotting up to Grant and Domi on swift, silent feet. "There were people in there once," Rosalia said in an urgent whisper, indicating the house she and the dog had been investigating.

"You sure?" Grant queried.

Rosalia glared at him, thrusting her jaw out, hands on hips. "Why would I say so otherwise?" she snapped contemptuously.

"Yeah, sorry," Grant muttered. He was on edge, something about these ghost streets at moonrise worrying at him. With a determined effort, Grant put his mind back to the problem at hand. The road they were on was quite closed in, which meant that if they turned back they would need to retrace their steps for a couple of minutes. That was time wasted. "Let's keep going west," he decided, and the others agreed.

Grant reached up to the crest of the wall and pulled himself up with both arms, bumping his torso against the wall as he peered more carefully over it, arms poised vertically to hold himself up. As before, this street was empty, and in a moment Grant had pulled himself over the wall and dropped down to the other side.

"Come on," he called, keeping his voice low. "It's all clear."

A moment later Domi came scrabbling over the wall to join Grant, a smile on her lips.

"Nice street you've found," she teased. "Different."

Grant looked up the street, peering into the shadows. It was hard to see now with so little illumination from the moonlight, and he reached for the polymer-lensed glasses he habitually carried in the inside pocket of his coat, propping them on the bridge of his nose. The lenses of the glasses were specially treated with chemical, providing a form of night vision that turned the street in front of Grant's eyes into a sort of greenish-gray conglomeration of light and shadow. It wasn't much different from the one they had just left. The buildings continued to stand at odd angles, closing in on them like falling dominoes, blocking out the moonlight so that what little light it gave became just a spear down the center of the street.

Grant turned back, gazing past Domi at the wall that they had climbed over. "What's keeping the others?" he muttered.

ON THE OTHER SIDE OF the wall, less than ten feet away, the Tigers of Heaven warriors were working together to get Rosalia's dog over the wall with as little fuss as possible. The dog grumbled a little but seemed to assent to the treatment, only to shrug the two men away and unleash a sudden bark, affixing its pale eyes on the far end of the street. Kishiro and Kudo held the dog, and Rosalia leaned down to its face, speaking softly to hush it. The dog looked inquisitively at her, then barked again, pulling past her. Again the Tigers of Heaven grabbed the dog as it glared at the end of the street, fighting their grip.

"Hold him," Rosalia instructed, feeling her hackles rise. She looked behind her, trying to see what had worried the dog, eyes scanning left and right. The street remained ill lit beneath the moonlight, a smattering of stars adding nothing to its illumination.

Kudo took the dog while Kishiro reached for the wall, readying himself to climb over it. Suddenly

Rosalia stopped them, holding up her hand for quiet as she peered intensely back toward the far end of the street. Something had moved back there, she was sure of it. Something swift, a silver flash in the subtle moonlight, like a knife blade.

Without a word, Rosalia took three paces along the street, four, placing her feet silently on the cobblestones as she searched the dimly lit surroundings with her eyes.

There was something there; she was sure of it. It smelled like rain—a nothing smell, but a sense, a feeling.

Rosalia peered down the street for a long moment, calming her breathing as she searched, waiting for whatever it was to show itself. Off in the distance, a fox yipped, sounding like a baby crying, the sound faint but still audible in the silence. Was that what had spooked the dog? Nothing moved. Nothing appeared. No matter how much Rosalia willed it, nothing stepped from the shadows, nothing made a noise. Just that smell, like rainfall.

She peered up, eyeing the narrow shaft of the moon, white on indigo, the stars that crept behind it in their Dalmatian-spot patterns. She had known the constellations once, when she was just a little girl. They looked different here, a half step around the world. If the people of Cerberus were to be believed, it was somewhere up there that the Annunaki had begun, conquering this planet with the effortlessness of a man conquering the lightest dusting of snowfall.

Rosalia turned back, placing silent footstep before silent footstep as she returned to the five-foot-high wall where Kishiro and Kudo waited, holding her dog. She gave them the briefest of nods and they resumed their operation, Kudo hefting the dog up while Kishiro clambered to the top of the wall and readied himself to take the hound as it was passed to him.

Taking a single step backward, Rosalia ran at the wall and leaped, her left hand barely skimming it as she vaulted over and landed beside Grant and Domi on the far side.

Grant looked at her. "What kept you?" he asked.

Following Rosalia, the two Tigers of Heaven lifted her mongrel dog over the wall and placed it—squirming and snarling—on the other side. The dog trotted over to where its mistress stood, peering up at her with plaintive eyes.

"Good boy," Rosalia said to hush it. "S'okay now."

GRANT LED THE WAY THROUGH the warren of moonlit streets, cursing now and again as they seemed to turn on themselves, sending the Cerberus field team back in the direction that they had just come. They walked another eight minutes in silence, just the sounds of their footsteps echoing off the hard walls of the strangely boarded buildings. Now and again they would hear a noise, like a shout or a baby's cry, but it was always in the distance, too far away to discern properly. Nocturnal creatures running wild, most likely.

They had the sense that this was a ghost town now. It felt like a museum exhibit, artificially aged to give an impression of how things might have been a hundred years ago, or a thousand. The buildings, too, seemed slightly off, not wrong as such but somehow not right, like something found only in dreams. The way their rooftops reached for one another, the way the streets twisted and curled back on themselves like a scorpion's tail, it all seemed faintly unreal. Grant didn't like it. He had trained as a hard-contact Magistrate and so was a man used to dealing with absolutes. Here, it seemed, there were no absolutes, just labyrinths within labyrinths, mazes within mazes.

Now and then Rosalia's dog would stop in place and growl deep in its throat, as if seeing something that the others had failed to notice. Rosalia hushed the dog with a stroke and a few measured words, encouraging the willful hound onward as they went to find Hassood.

"How much farther to this guide?" Rosalia asked Grant when the dog stopped for the third time in a street so narrow that it could barely accommodate three people abreast.

Grant shook his head in irritation. "Hard to tell," he said. "We keep getting turned back on ourselves. Should be close, though. Hassood said it was at the edge of the city."

The Tigers of Heaven moved to one of the lower roofs that lined the alleylike avenue, where Kishiro gave Kudo a bunk up so that he could peer over it.

"Gotta be here somewhere," Grant growled irritably. "Like a knitting needle, that's what he said."

Domi was about to add her own observation when her eyes became distracted by something. She twitched, her pale head snapping around as she tried to follow what it was, but the alleylike street was empty. There had been a flash there, a silvery trace of lines like…like what?

As Grant discussed their route with Rosalia and the Tigers of Heaven, Domi skulked away, the rubber soles of her soft shoes treading quietly on the uneven cobblestones. It had been here, near a twisting building that seemed gnarled as a tree root, that she had seen that flash of long silvery fingers. As if reading her thoughts, the line sparkled again, like a string of pearls catching the light before disappearing into the building. She knew what it reminded her of now; it was the effect sunlight created on a mirror, reflecting against the wall in a watery shimmer.

The building sprouted upward in sections, entwined like lovers' arms, bending into one another in embrace. The walls were white like stucco, rough to the touch. Here, too, the doors and windows were boarded over, a pale wood it seemed—ash perhaps—blocking out light and unwelcome visitors.

Did anyone live in this place? Domi wondered. Did anyone live anywhere in this ville?

As she gazed at that twisted plait of tower, Domi saw the thing flash again, or she thought she did, up higher, in one of the upper windows where the boards were wider, leaving enough space to peer within. It was a third-story window, and Domi could not get far enough back to see inside. Turning a corner she spotted an opening at the level of her chest, a dark patch on the white wall roughly twelve inches across.

Domi ducked, peering through the square hole in the building's facade. The hole was probably a ventilation shaft of some sort, Domi couldn't tell for certain. Within the hole it was dark, black as a spider's eyes. Had it gone in here, the silver thing?

Close up, the hole emanated a smell, a stench, in fact—the reek of stagnant water. Domi's nose wrinkled as she caught a whiff of it, rearing away without thinking. But it hadn't looked wet. Warily the albino warrior got nearer once again, carefully touching her fingers to the bottom edge of the square hole. As she suspected, it was dry to the touch. Her fingers came away with nothing but a chalky, hard dirt. She pushed her hand back in, running her pale fingers along the walls and then reaching up and finding that it was a shaft. The shaft went upward into the building, for drainage or ventilation.

Her heart pounding hard in her chest, Domi pressed her ear to the slot, filtering out the sounds around her as she tried to listen for noises within. The hole opened into a pipe, and it had that pipe sound, like the wind whistling through distant trees, the ocean in a shell.

"Domi, what is it?"

It was Grant, standing just behind her shoulder, surprising her at coming so close. She had been distracted.

"Not sure," Domi answered, the words muttered, emotionless, as she pushed her face close to the opening once more. She peered into the blackness, trying to see if there was anything within that shaft. What was it that she had seen, and was it that which was creating the smell?

"Need me to take a look?" Grant asked. He had the night lenses on—of course, they would be ideal.

"Borrow your lenses?" Domi asked, holding her hand out in expectation.

Grant handed them to her, watched as she poked her whole head into the gap in the wall and peered inside, rocking her shoulders to get a better angle. Domi looked up into the darkness, seeing the square shaft drawn in greens and grays on the surface of the night lenses, insects scuttling here and there in the gloom.

Domi heard low voices behind her as the Tigers of Heaven discussed something with the others, grit her teeth in irritation as she filtered them out and tried to listen to the empty shaft.

"We're going to keep moving," Grant told her. "We're about two blocks away from this needle thing our man Hassood told us about. Kudo spotted it from one of the rooftops."

Suddenly, Rosalia's dog let out a deep growl, the sound coming from deep in the beast's throat. Domi turned, shocked by the noise, her concentration broken.

"Dammit," Domi muttered as she stepped away from the dark square in the wall. Had she seen something, high up in the pipe? Something shimmering like moonbeams? She couldn't tell now, couldn't be sure if she had seen it or imagined it.

"Domi?" Grant prodded, keeping his voice low.

"This place is giving me the creeps," Domi growled in response. "Does anyone actually live here, do you think?"

"No intel," Grant replied as he led the group down the alley, searching for an alternate route to the nearby stone needle. "People have been seen coming into the city, nomadic farmers mostly, hiding away from the cold nights. But fuck knows if they're still here. I'm guessing not."

"Well, someone's here," Domi said.

"The dog feels it, too," Rosalia agreed. "He's skittish, dumb animal. Not like him."

Domi glared at the dark-haired woman. "Are you ever going to give that dog a name?" she asked, sounding peeved.

Rosalia arched an eyebrow as she replied. "I call him lots of names," she said. "Maybe when he learns to speak we'll settle on one."

Grant hushed them then, raising his hand as he listened intently to the Commtact link. "Hassood? That you?"

There was a pause during which the Cerberus team continued hurrying through the twisting-turning streets, and then Hassood's voice came back over the communicator, urgent and breathless.

"Mr. Grant, they're coming. They're coming now."

Chapter 8

"Back up there, man," Grant instructed over the Commtact as he hurried along the empty street, his footsteps sounding loud as they echoed from the hard stone. "What's coming? What are you talking—?"

A scream came over the Commtact link, the shriek oddly doubled by Grant's proximity to its origin.

"What was that?" Domi asked, searching for the source. The clawing towers of the buildings seemed to close in overhead now, blocking the moonlight and trapping them on the road like bars on a cell.

Rosalia's dog bolted then, scampering ahead of them all.

"Come back!" Rosalia yelled, sprinting after the dog. "Stupid mutt."

The scampering dog turned, its lithe body twisting into a side alley that was almost entirely hidden in the darkness, and abruptly disappeared from view. The alley was less than fifteen inches wide, just a narrow gap between the rough-walled buildings. Rosalia stopped in front of it, peering into the darkness, her nose wrinkling.

"The scream came from this way," she announced. "The dog's right."

"Wait just a—" Grant began, but already Rosalia had ducked into the alley after her dog. "Shit!"

"Might be the quickest way to our contact," Domi

suggested to Grant as they stood at the entryway to the alley.

Grant eyed the narrow gap for a moment, estimating its width. He could tell it would be a tight squeeze for him, and in the darkness it was hard to see if it narrowed any further. "You follow her. The rest of us will go around," he decided.

Domi didn't stop to acknowledge Grant's instruction but just started running, sprinting down the oppressive strip of alleyway, her lean shoulders snugly fitting between the walls. Up ahead she could see Rosalia turning sideways, skipping along crab-fashion to chase after her willful canine, calling for it in an annoyed hiss.

Behind her, Domi could hear Grant speaking urgently to Hassood via the Commtact, then trying to raise Cerberus.

BACK AT THE MAKESHIFT Cerberus headquarters, dour-faced Brewster Philboyd acknowledged Grant's hail from the field.

"My contact's in trouble," Grant explained. "Can you locate him? We're caught in a damn maze here—there's no logic to this place whatsoever."

"I can bring the satellite cam around," Philboyd explained, his fingers already racing across his computer keyboard to do that very thing, "but it will take time."

"Time is something we don't have, Brewster," Grant reasoned. "Any other ideas?"

Brewster Philboyd looked at the countdown clock on his laptop screen and made a quick calculation. "We don't have anything on file," he explained. "It will take...forty minutes to get a street view."

"Damn," Grant growled to himself, the word automatically relayed via the Commtact link.

Philboyd tapped at his keyboard again, hurrying past protocols to try to locate an older record of the dragon-shaped settlement. As he did so, something popped up on screen, a red flashing icon of a dog. Philboyd stopped in his tracks, doing a double take as he took the icon in. "That's…Cerberus," he said slowly.

"Repeat, Brewster," Grant said. "I don't understand."

Philboyd spoke quietly, incredulity in his voice. "I'm getting hailed by Cerberus," he said, almost unaware of the mike pickup he wore for the linked Commtacts. "But that's impossible."

Grant's voice had a hint of irritation to it as it came to Philboyd's ear. "Brewster, you ain't making a lick of sense. What's happening?"

Standing in his seat, Philboyd checked the small ops room that had been set up temporarily on the California site. Donald Bry was running a diagnostics check on two linked terminals, while Lakesh was flipping through the reams of printout that had been produced since Cerberus ops went back online, tracing his missing personnel. Philboyd called them both over, trying to keep the anxiety out of his voice.

"Brew?" Grant's voice was in his ear.

"I'm cutting the call, Grant," Philboyd said briefly. "There's something happening here, and I don't think it's wise to stay online just now."

GRANT MUTTERED SOMETHING to himself as Philboyd cut the radio link. It wasn't in Philboyd's nature to overreact, he knew, so something serious had to be going down at the Cerberus base. Cerberus had been infiltrated just weeks ago and the internal security remained heightened, frustrating though that could be. In the meantime, however, that left Grant and his field team out on their own.

ROSALIA RAN AHEAD, RUSHING after the scraggly-looking mutt who seemed to have adopted her months ago, whether she had wanted it or not. The dog had emerged from out of the Californian desert, a stray found in a destroyed settlement whose inhabitants had been mind-wiped and destroyed by an alien race called the Igigi, whose spirits were searching for new host bodies. The Igigi had once been the slave caste of the Annunaki, dispossessed by their master Enlil.

The narrow passageway ran between buildings in a tightening curve, the stony walls echoing weirdly, the rooftops touching here and there above her. Up ahead, Rosalia could see a hint of moonlight tapering into the far end of the alleyway, and the dog's familiar form was a low blot, tail wagging furiously left and right like a psychotic metronome, its breathing sounding like a steam train as it bolted out of the enclosed space.

The passage itself was getting narrower still. With a grunt, Rosalia shifted herself again, swiveling her body so she could lead with her right shoulder, blowing hair out of her face as she hurried on. She heard foot-steps clattering against the cobbles behind her; Domi was chasing after her, in second place as ever. Rosalia ducked her head into her body, driving herself on down the echoing passage before she lost sight of the dog.

There came voices then, from the far end of the passage. No, not voices, she realized—*a voice*. A man's voice, the words unclear. And then the agonized scream again, the one she had heard before only louder now, closer.

Rosalia saw that the dog had sprung from the far end of the passageway and was running out into whatever lay beyond. "Wait, stupid mutt," she ordered. "Stay."

The dog ignored her, running off into whatever lay beyond the passage. Rosalia willed herself to go faster, her feet skittering across the cobbles as she lunged down the passageway, the walls scraping her, front and back. The voice was getting louder, authoritative. And the screaming had abated, an ugly, strained whimpering taking its place.

The next instant Rosalia burst out of the narrow confines of the passage and found herself in a hexagonal courtyard between buildings. The courtyard seemed vast after the tightness and darkness of the passage, despite being surrounded on all sides, the jagged struts of buildings clawing toward the moonlight above like a crone's twisted hands. A towering spire rested in its center like an upended needle, a prodding lance made of white stone, and beyond that a wider gateway, an arch of stone across its top. Here was the location Hassood had described in his discussions with Grant. So where was he?

Rosalia halted, getting her bearings, looking all around for her dog. The man's voice was echoing around the courtyard along with whimpering and foreign words, both coming from somewhere to her right. Warily, Rosalia made her way toward it, spying the shelter there between a balustrade of curving archways that shone like ice in the moonlight. Something was moving there, but as Rosalia approached the dog came hurrying back out, barking a warning.

The man's words echoed from the covered passage, the words unfamiliar but the tone clear. "Help me," he was saying. "Help me." Rosalia felt sure of it.

Rosalia leaned down, touching her hand to the dog's neck as it looked plaintively up at her. "What is it, boy?" she muttered, keeping her voice low.

At that instant Domi came running from the narrow passage entrance behind her, legs pumping as she rushed to join Rosalia and the mongrel. "Don't...just... run off," she stormed breathlessly. She was covered in dirt from the walls, her pale face powdered with white dust, her hair in disarray.

Rosalia glared at her, left hand raised for silence. Then she indicated the space between the archways. As she did so, a gurgling scream rent the air, echoing around the courtyard like tumbling waves crashing against the shore.

Rosalia hurried forward, drawing a hidden knife from her sleeve as she leaped through the closest archway. The man's voice was loud in here, squawking off the walls like a parrot's caw. There was a figure there in the darkness, a tall man, thin with narrow shoulders, a shimmer of silver glistening beside him like a full-length mirror.

It took a second for Rosalia's eyes to adjust as the dog scurried over to her side, barking again. In that instant, the shadow she had taken to be a man became just another shadow against the wall, and the glistering mirror light winked out as if a cloud had smothered the moon.

Rosalia searched the walled area, hearing the man's voice again, realizing it had an artificial quality to it. It was Grant, his words tinny over the transistor radio pickup—a compact unit no larger than a football crashed on its side against the wall, the microphone hanging loosely on a coiling wire beside it.

"Hassood?" Grant's voice chirruped with urgency. "Hassood? Come in." Water sloshed around the radio, disappearing down a drain.

Domi had entered the covered area now, engaging her hidden Commtact as she recognized Grant's voice. "He's not here." She continued speaking, explaining about the discarded radio receiver, that no one was around.

Rosalia ignored the exchange. Her eyes had been drawn to the dark shadow on the wall, a shadow in the shape of a man, tall and thin with narrow shoulders. Pacing forward, Rosalia touched her hand to the dark stain, pressing her palm gently against it after just a moment's consideration, her eyes narrowing. It was damp; warm and damp.

Chapter 9

"Didn't you get the memo, Kane?" the red-haired woman had said, her emerald eyes narrowed into wicked slits. "All the heroes are dead."

A whisper of gun smoke trailed from the muzzle of the TP-9 semiautomatic in her hand. The handgun was the final piece of evidence—as if he had needed it—that she had been the one who had shot Kane, emptying a clip into his chest as he reached for her in the cavern beneath Snakefishville. Kane had stumbled backward under the impact of those 9 mm slugs, their force dissipated by his shadow suit but still powerful enough to knock his exhausted body back into the Chalice of Rebirth. Its amber mists had wafted in front of his eyes as his vision dimmed and he lost consciousness, and the very last thing he had seen was the redhead—Brigid Baptiste—and the girl called Quav disappear into the hazy glow of the interphaser's quantum window, stepping into nonspace and on to their next destination, leaving Kane struggling for his life in the Chalice of Rebirth.

But it hadn't really been Brigid Baptiste, had it?

Kane lay in the bed, alone in the private room that had been set aside within Shizuka's winter lodge for his recuperation. Sunlight lashed across the bedsheets that arched over his firm chest, bright shards of yellow-white drilling into the room through a tiny break in the drapes. Kane looked at those dazzling yellow strips for a long moment, thinking about Brigid Baptiste and all that had happened in that hidden cavern.

She had shot him. Brigid Baptiste, his *anam-chara,* his "soul friend" through eternity, had shot him full in the chest, emptying a whole clip as if there could be any doubt about her intention. But had she really been Brigid Baptiste? That was the real question tugging at the forefront of Kane's mind.

An operative for Cerberus, Brigid Baptiste had been Kane's and Grant's field partner for as long as they had been a part of the organization. And more than that, they were friends and she and Kane were eternally linked by their *anam-chara* bond. But seven weeks ago, during the attack on Cerberus, Brigid had disappeared; her biolink transponder somehow shut down, rendering her untraceable. For six weeks Kane had waited for a sign, a hint that she was still alive as he knew she must be, as that thing deep inside him, that bond they shared, insisted she must be. But that woman in the cave, with her fiery red hair and emerald eyes, that woman who had emptied the entire contents of her blaster into his chest, that had not been Brigid. It had been something wearing her like a suit, mimicking her actions. She had stood differently, spoken differently, acted differently. Not a clone, but a suit of flesh.

Kane stared at the shaft of sunlight, listening to the growing commotion outside his room. That was what had awoken him, he realized. Something was going on out there, raised voices and clattering feet, people talking over one another in the way of frantic decision makers. Slowly, begrudgingly, Kane pushed the covers from his weary body and hefted himself from the bed on unsteady feet.

He was a muscular man, well built with a powerful torso and arms, the legs of a sprinter. His dark hair was messy now, brushing past his collar, and stubble darkened his jaw, the start of a beard. He moved slowly, as if weary, heavy.

How long have I been asleep? he wondered. It felt bad, cloudy, as if he'd been drugged. Maybe he had— he had taken a chest full of bullets and even the armored weave of the shadow suit could only do so much to cut down that physical trauma, even if it had saved his life.

His eyes ached, and he turned away from the brightness that lanced through the drapes like a blade, rubbing at his face. It felt hard, his face, like bone. There was a ridge there, across his left cheek where the scar had been, a ragged hunk of something reaching out above his brow. His vision wasn't good, either, he realized, testing himself for a moment by running his pointed index finger in front of his nose. He could see, to a reasonable degree at least, out of his right eye, but his left was just a blank, the waggling finger disappearing behind a screen as it passed his nose.

"Shit."

Beneath the ridge, his jaw remained the same, bristly now with days-old beard, sore and itchy and dry, as if the remnants of paste had been stuck there. What's more, he was thirsty, his mouth tasting bad like dead things rotting.

The noises outside the door were getting louder, or maybe he was just becoming more aware of them. Men were talking in raised voices, then a woman's voice, the pitch higher and calmer at the same time. Kane felt like death warmed over as he reached for the robe lying on the chair beside the bed and made his way to the door.

He stepped through the door on unsteady feet, clinging tightly to the handle while he waited for the feeling of nausea to pass. Beyond that, a corridor lined with wood paneling, neatly tooled with a simple but graceful design of lines and curves. The corridor seemed lit by the evening sun, the illumination turning it all orange and tan, the colors of autumn.

Kane hurled himself along the corridor, throwing his body forward and willing himself to—dammit all—stay on his feet. He was fine; he just needed air or food or both.

There was a guard at the end of the corridor, a stern Asiatic face peering querulously at Kane as he stumbled toward him. "Do you require help, Kane-san?" the man asked.

Kane tried to speak, swallowed, tried again. "I'll be okay," he said, each word feeling like concrete being poured down his throat. He brushed past the guard, recognized him as one of Shizuka's warriors. Then he pushed through the twin doors that waited at the end of the corridor, finally locating the source of the kerfuffle.

"BUT IT'S LUDICROUS," Donald Bry insisted. "No, more than that—it's impossible."

Lakesh fixed his usually dour assistant with the cold stare of reason. "Impossible or not, it behooves us to investigate it."

"Investigate what?" Kane asked from the door, grogginess in his voice.

Everyone in the temporary ops center looked around, surprised to see Kane standing there, surprised to see Kane standing at all. Reba DeFore was the first to speak, hurrying over to Kane at a swift trot, her braided hair swinging to and fro as she did so.

"Kane, what are you doing here?" she began. "You shouldn't be on your feet." There was clear concern in her voice, not just the clinical concern of a physician but that of a friend.

"I can stand," Kane said, brushing her away, "so I'm on my feet. My legs aren't broken unless you want to tell me different, Doc."

"But, Kane…"

He held up his hand, halting her midflow. "Investigate what?" he repeated, fixing the others in the room with his steel-cold stare.

After a few seconds' pause, Lakesh finally spoke up, making his way toward Kane to greet him. "It is good to see you up and about, Kane," he said. "You had us all quite worried."

"You're still worried," Kane assessed. "Cut the fat and give me the meat."

"We have had an emergency beacon from a rather unexpected source," Lakesh explained.

"The source being Cerberus," Brewster Philboyd added from his position at one of the three laptop terminals in the room. Something blinked on his screen.

"Cerberus," Kane repeated.

"It's impossible," Donald Bry insisted, pushing a hand absentmindedly through his ruffled copper curls. "Cerberus was evacuated after the attack. It's empty and most of the equipment is offline, unusable."

Kane thought about it for a few seconds. He had been based at the redoubt set in the Montana mountains for so long that it was still difficult getting his head around the change of location. "Was the emergency alarm unusable, Donald?" he asked.

Bry shrugged. "Hard to say. I do have an inventory sitting around here somewhere showing what worked and what—"

"Well, it works now and someone pressed it," Kane reasoned, cutting him off. "Which means someone needs to take a look, right?"

Lakesh agreed and, after a moment, both Philboyd and Donald nodded, too.

"In which case," Kane said, "suit me up and let's get the interphaser fired up."

"Kane, you cannot be serious," Lakesh scoffed, and Reba DeFore added her own concern, too.

Kane ignored them. "I may have been out of it for a little while, but unless something major has changed you don't have a whole lot of field operatives to send," he said. "Check on an alarm—that's a one-man op. I could do it in my sleep. You want me to take Grant with me, that's fine…"

"Grant's out in the field," Lakesh explained, "along with Domi, Rosalia and several Tigers of Heaven. But I could easily request one of the Tigers go look into…"

"I know the redoubt," Kane said. "I'll go."

"I thought you were…blind," Bry noted, feeling terribly self-conscious as soon as he'd made the point.

Kane held his hand up, rocking it through the air just a little like a teeter-totter. "Comes and goes," he said. "But right now, I figure you don't have many other people to send, though. From what I've heard, it's not like Edwards is going anywhere."

Lakesh placed a gentle hand on Kane's arm, the ex-Mag's muscles bulging against the material of his robe. "Kane, you do not need to prove anything to anyone in this room," he said. "While your gesture is appreciated, no one here expects you to investigate this personally.

I shall arrange for one of Shizuka's people to step in while we are undermanned. Their report will be more than sufficient."

Kane stood in front of the older man, his expression hard, the bumping protrusion by his eye looking like a smear. "I'm going," he said. "I woke up for a reason. That call you got, that's Baptiste."

Reba DeFore took a loud breath as if to speak, but Lakesh turned to her and, with an infinitesimal movement of his head, warned her not to.

"I hope you are right," Lakesh said instead.

With that, Kane turned to get ready for a field mission, while the Cerberus ops team prepared everything for him as best they could. Kane was among the best field operatives Cerberus had ever had, probably the best. Even functioning at less than one hundred percent, he was still nothing less than formidable. If anyone still felt that this mission was foolhardy, none of them said a word.

Chapter 10

Grant arrived in the white-walled courtyard like a monsoon, bringing with him an air of tension and barely suppressed rage. He was accompanied by the two Tigers of Heaven, Kudo and Kishiro, who in contrast displayed no trace of emotion. While the Tigers of Heaven checked the area surrounding the hexagonal courtyard, Grant joined Domi and Rosalia where they waited beneath the covered passageway at the side of one of the crookedly towering buildings. Like the others here, this one had no door, just windows that had been boarded up with thick sheets of plasterboard. The whole passageway smelled of wet dog.

"What the heck happened here?" Grant muttered as he looked around the covered passageway, examining the man-shaped stain on the wall and the discarded radio equipment. Domi was just righting the radio unit, propping it back up and turning a handle to power up its internal dynamo-driven generator. "Where's Hassood?"

Standing beside him, Rosalia fixed Grant with her exotic eyes. "You're staring at him, I think."

Grant looked the man-shaped stain up and down more carefully, as if trying to fix a missing piece of a jigsaw puzzle in his mind. Behind him, something started dripping, water plink-plinking down from the low ceiling. "What happened to him?"

"We heard screaming," Rosalia said, "sounds of a struggle. When I looked…" She stopped, finishing the sentence with a befuddled shrug.

Behind her, Rosalia's dog whined, trotting a pace forward and sniffing at the air. Grant wondered if the dog was distracted by the musty smell of tobacco in the area. He looked around and saw a little clutch of cigarette butts in the corner, three crumpled white tabs like teeth made of paper.

Kneeling by the radio unit, Domi flicked several of the knobs and spoke quietly into the microphone, checking its functionality. "Radio's still working," she told Grant. "Whatever came for Hassood did so real quick and they didn't care about nixing his communications. That suggests they moved fast, even though we didn't hear any shots."

"No shots," Grant mused. "Then what…?"

"Wait," Domi added as she tinkered with the radio unit, "there's something. Give me a minute here."

"Wall's still wet," Rosalia told Grant, pressing her hand against it before showing him her palm. The wall appeared sodden to her touch, and her hand came away covered in a watery sheen like dew.

Grant pressed his own fingers against the wall and sniffed them. It smelled of water, which is to say it didn't really smell of anything. There was certainly no scent within it to distinguish it as anything else. He looked back at Rosalia's scruffy mutt where the cur was sniffing at the air, and he wondered if perhaps the dog might be able to smell something that they could not. "What do you think spooked the dog?" Grant asked after a moment's thought.

Rosalia shrugged. "He does as he pleases," she explained. "Who knows why he came down here."

As if on cue, the dog whimpered, tilting its head sideways and staring up at the ceiling with its wickedly pale eyes. As he did so, another droplet of water dripped down from the ceiling, landing between his forepaws with a splash. There was a small puddle forming between its feet, Grant saw, swelling like an inky gloss of black beneath the darkened portico.

"Grant?" Domi said, drawing his attention. When he looked he saw that she had activated a tiny screen light on the top of the radio unit. "Camera."

"Still working, too," Rosalia acknowledged as she joined Grant and Domi.

"Hassood was recording things," Grant realized, gently nudging Domi aside. While Domi was good in the field, her ability with technology could be a little primitive. Grant balanced the radio unit on its back edge, examining it in the moonlight. After a moment his thick fingers reached for a recessed panel in the top and a viewscreen flipped up into position, roughly three inches by two. Pictured in real time on the viewscreen, Grant saw his own face, with the ghostly image of Domi's visage peering over his shoulder.

"Let's see what we have here," Grant muttered as his fingers played across the controls at the side of the communications unit. After a moment the image on the screen blurred slightly as a pop-up menu appeared over it. Grant selected Playback and the trio waited as the internal recording device backtracked through its footage, running backward ten minutes under Grant's instruction.

Ducking a drip of water from the ceiling, Kudo stepped back under the portico while the three companions crouched around the tiny flip-up screen, informing Grant that the area appeared clear. Grant acknowledged that, then turned back to the screen and pressed Play.

On screen, a man's face appeared, bulging out where he was too close to the tiny camera. The man had dusky skin and a dark beard laced with silver where he was going prematurely gray. He spoke with a thick accent, not bothering to look into the camera, and after a moment Grant recognized the conversation—he had been on the other end of it last time, as the man instructed Grant's team to meet him at the stone needle. Automatically, Grant glanced back over his shoulder for a couple of seconds, admiring said needle in the moonlight. Another drip of water cut through his vision as it fell from the ceiling above, missing Grant's nose by just a couple of inches. Rosalia's pale-eyed dog was standing just a step behind her, back arched, its muscles held taut; the mongrel obviously sensed something and was worried.

Grant turned back to the screen, watching the tiny time display in the corner as it marched onward, seventeen minutes behind current time. Grant and the others watched the screen, transfixed. Hassood's hand passed close to the camera lens clutching something metallic.

"Microphone," Domi observed.

Once he had placed the microphone back on its hook, Hassood got up and for a moment the recording showed the familiar image of the covered passageway, the tight arches running along the right of the picture, moonlight through the far end making the automated white balance flicker as it tried to accommodate its inconsistencies. There was a lot of "dirt" to the image, a hazy blue mist across the shadows where the camera could not pick up enough light. Occasionally a scarlet glow would run over the image and it would break up where the laser blast lit the skies above, bathing the covered area in its blood light. For almost three minutes Grant and his allies watched as Hassood paced back and forth, his torso passing the camera from left to right and back again.

Another minute passed, then another. Kishiro joined the group as they watched, transfixed by the image on the screen. Something fizzed to the side of the screen, and again the white balance winked, trying to accommodate the sudden change. Illogically, Grant found himself leaning just a little closer to try to see what was happening, and he realized that the others had done the same, all but Rosalia, whose attention was being diverted by the restless dog at her side. Then Grant saw Hassood's flank at the right side of the image, a puff of smoke wafting across the camera, and he realized the shock of brilliance had been the man lighting a match for his cigarette.

For another minute there was nothing, just the dark shape of Hassood as he smoked his cigarette, rocking impatiently as he waited for the Cerberus team to arrive.

Suddenly, with no warning, the dusky-skinned man came rushing back to the camera, his hand blurring across the image as he grabbed the microphone, frantically peering over his shoulder. Then he was looking at the camera and the whites of his eyes were visible all around the dark pupils. They watched as Hassood spoke into the microphone, his voice fearful, breathless, the words rushing out like water over a burst dam.

"Mr. Grant, they're coming," he said. "They're coming now."

Grant's voice emanated from somewhere off camera, tinny with static at its peaks. "Back up there, man," they heard Grant say. "What's coming? What are you talking—?"

But before Grant's words had finished, Hassood moved speedily away from the camera—whether he had jumped or been pulled was unclear from the angle—and they heard him scream. It was a hideous sound, hearing a grown man scream like that. It triggered something primal in Grant, something he found he was very uncomfortable with. But there was another sound, too, something like a hard rainfall sloshing in the background. The noise hadn't been there a moment before, or if it had it had been too quiet for the camera microphone to detect. It hadn't rained, Grant knew. His team had been maybe 150 yards from this when it had happened; no microclimate was that precise.

The once-static camera angle suddenly whirled on screen as the radio was knocked from its perch, and for a moment the image flickered and cut, shadow and light blurring into a mist of electronic squall.

For a moment there was nothing. Just the camera lens trying to refocus, to make sense of the darkness.

The image reverted but it was sideways now, the familiar arches that lined the wall now running across the bottom of the screen as if that wall was the ground. Sounds of a scuffle, a scream nearby and incessant, cut off as abruptly as it had begun. Stillness on screen, just a flicker of shadow where the tiny lens tried to give definition to the dark walls.

And then they saw it, and Grant heard Domi gasp behind his ear. It was a shard of silver, like a beam of moonlight snapped off, passing across the screen in a blur. It looked like a mirror in the dark, and for a moment Grant took it to be a blade, either sword or knife passing the lens.

Then Hassood's familiar form came hurtling across
from the right, which is to say from above them, and
he slammed down, face-first into the ground that ran
on the screen's left. His skin glistened with a sheen,
silver droplets reflecting the moonlight.

Hassood turned to face his attacker, looking across
to the top of the screen—to his right where the arches
were. The silvery line appeared again, stepping in from
the top, a white streak across the camera image. The
picture blurred as the camera refocused, and then the
silvery line shimmered, moving away from the lens. It
was a man, or at least it was man-shaped. The figure
walked away from the camera, its back to the screen,
its movements flowing like liquid. And it glistened as
the moonlight played across it, the silver now a series
of insubstantial streaks like brushstrokes in the air, ill
defined, darkness between them.

Hassood screamed again, staring up into the thing's
face where its eyes must be. Grant's team watched as
the silvery figure reached for Hassood, grabbing him
by the throat even as he scrambled to his feet. It stood
between Hassood and the camera, yet they could still
see Hassood, not simply over the stranger's shoulder
but through his body, too, shimmering and bulbous as
if the man's image were recast in a fun-house mirror.

Water, Grant realized. They were looking through
a curtain of water.

On screen, Hassood slammed back into the wall as
the mysterious figure gripped him by the throat. Grant
winced as he heard that bone-cracking shunt, and Hassood gurgled, his eyelids flickering as he struggled to
retain consciousness. It was the same wall where the
man-shaped stain was, Grant realized, the exact same

spot. Hassood was saying something over and over, the words foreign to Grant's ears.

Behind him, Grant heard Rosalia mutter a curse, and he turned and saw her shake her head, wiping something from her face.

On screen, the silvery shimmer held Hassood in place, a spasm running through the man's body. It was difficult to see what happened next, the image was so small and dark, and it took Grant a few seconds to notice the change. In front of his eyes, Hassood seemed to be merging with the wall, sinking into it, a shimmer glistening over his face like sweat. Grant heard his own voice come from the speaker of the playback system, calling to Hassood to "respond, please respond." It was eerie hearing his own voice at that moment, a fragment of time echoing over again.

Beneath the sound of his voice, Grant heard a dog bark—Rosalia's pet, urgency and fear in its gruff voice. Hassood was calling again as he sunk into the wall, repeating a phrase over and over as he struggled in the grasp of the shimmering human form standing in front of him.

Then Hassood simply wasn't anymore. Where he had been against the wall there was only the dark outline of his shape, the shimmering thing standing in front of him like a mirror.

"This is where I came in," Rosalia muttered, recognizing the scene.

As if to confirm her point, a dark blur passed over the camera lens from above and Grant recognized it as the wagging tail of her dog. And the shimmering, glistering mirror man dropped, his form seeming to lose its integrity as he sunk into the floor.

"What the...?" Grant muttered, staring at the screen

as it locked on a fixed image of the wall with the stain that had been Hassood marked out upon its surface.

Then Grant turned back to his colleagues, the four of them as transfixed by the screen as he had been.

"What happened?" Domi asked. "It didn't make sense."

Grant was about to answer when, in the moonlight that seeped into the roofed passage, he saw silvery lines cutting the air, winking on and off like Christmas lights.

From the screen behind him, Grant heard his own voice echoing back with barely restrained urgency. "Hassood?" it said. "Hassood? Come in."

He watched as another of those silvery lines cut through the air around them, like a knife caught in the moonlight. It was water, pouring from the roof above them, dripping down to the floor where they stood.

"They're made of water," Grant declared, "and they're here."

As he said it, Rosalia's dog began to bark. Something was taking shape behind its mistress.

Chapter 11

Twenty-five minutes later, Kane led a party made up of Lakesh, Donald Bry and Reba DeFore toward the south end of the lodge's vast grounds. The lodge itself overlooked the sea, a sheer cliff dropping down to the crashing waves of the Pacific, which hurried up a tiny sliver of beach seventy feet below. A weedy-looking fence ran along the edge of the cliff, just two horizontal wooden bars linked by a series of posts, reaching no higher than a man's hip. The fence was a safety measure and nothing more—no one was sneaking up on the lodge via that harsh cliff face.

Kane had washed and dressed, though his hair looked untidy where it fell to past his collar and his jaw was dark with stubble that was almost a beard now. He was a tall man, imposing and well-built, his shoulders wide to accommodate his broad chest. He was built like a wolf, a muscular torso and upper body coupled with rangy limbs that could eat up distance with little effort. There was something of the wolf in his manner, too, the way he automatically slipped into the role of pack leader but seemed a loner all the same. He was dressed in black, wearing the shadow suit beneath a dark shirt and denim jacket, the latter frayed at the cuffs and hem. The shadow suit was the same one he had worn when Brigid had shot him less than a week before, and while it still retained its incredible properties to deflect both blades and light gunfire, the scars of that attack remained across its chest. Dark combat pants and scarred leather boots finished Kane's ensemble, the latter an echo of his days as a Magistrate in Cobaltville, their familiar grooves a comfort in this time of upheaval. Kane's dark hair was longer than he was used to, brushing at the nape of his neck and whipping around his face in the sea breeze.

Kane had secreted several familiar armaments among his clothing, including his faithful Sin Eater handblaster surreptitiously held in a hidden holster at his wrist and primed for swift access. Like his boots, the Sin Eater was a legacy from his days Cobaltville, something both he and Grant had kept after their sudden exile from the Magistrate division. Kane had brought one more thing, securely packed in a scuffed backpack hanging between his shoulders. It was this item that brought him and his companions out here on the beautifully kept lawn.

The foursome hurried briskly across the trimmed grass, making their way to what appeared to be a wholly unremarkable point a few hundred feet from the line of conifers that marked the property's boundary. Kane slowed as he reached this spot close to the farthest reach of Shizuka's territory, sweeping the area with a glance until he spied what he was looking for. There, incongruous amid the neatly trimmed lawn, a patch of burned grass perhaps twelve inches square waited, straw-yellow against the lush green.

Shirking out of his rucksack, Kane stepped across to the patch of faded grass and placed the scuffed bag down beside it. Then, with a swiftness that belied the care he was taking, Kane reached into the rucksack and brought out a metal pyramid roughly twelve inches square and the same measurement to its apex. With practiced efficiency, Kane tapped in the code at the control panel on its base and the pyramid seemed to vibrate, a movement so slight as to exist only on a subconscious level.

Still kneeling on the grass, Kane looked up at his three companions. "We're ready to go," he informed them.

Reba DeFore protested, telling Kane she still felt that this was a bad idea. "If your eyesight should get worse again…" she complained, but Lakesh stopped her.

"Kane is right," he said. "This mayday signal is something that we cannot ignore. And he is the only one of us with sufficient combat training to handle the situation should it prove to take a turn for the worse. Even with his abilities compromised, I suspect friend Kane is still far more capable than you or I or Donald here."

Bry laughed uncomfortably, nodding in agreement. "This jump will take you right into the heart of the Cerberus redoubt," he advised Kane, all business once more. "You'll arrive in the mat-trans chamber as normal, but the chamber itself and the ops room that it leads into have changed beyond comprehension."

"I saw it all—I remember," Kane growled. "Lot of stone work."

Bry nodded somberly. "Just keep in mind that, for all intents and purposes, you are leaping into the unknown here, enemy territory. We believe that the redoubt was evacuated when we left, but it's not beyond the realms of credibility that Ullikummis or his troops have reacquired it for their own usage. Alternatively, with the security compromised as it is, there's a chance

that someone else may have taken up residence there.
They may even be the ones who activated the beacon."

Kane nodded. "Got it."

For a few moments Kane worked at the base of the
interphaser, tapping out a sequence of numbers so that
the device could locate the destination point at the Cerberus redoubt. The interphaser worked by accessing
specific locations called parallax points, which could
be found right across the globe and beyond. While
eminently adaptable, the interphaser still required a
specific departure and destination points, opening a
quantum window between the two points and allowing its user to step through that gateway to a place that
may be a thousand miles or more away. Just now, Kane
was setting the incredible device to send him to the
parallax point located in the mat-trans chamber of the
Cerberus redoubt in Montana, roughly seven hundred
miles away. Once the interphaser was activated, the
journey itself would take just a fraction of a second.

Kane moved back and watched as the interphaser
came to life, an expanding lotus blossom of color
emerging, top and bottom, from its silvery frame. The
twin cones of light were like oil on water, dark with
rainbow swirls glinting in their impossible depths,
hooked fingers of lightning firing through the light like
witch fire. The gateway was opening, carving a path
through the quantum ether to the Montana redoubt.

Kane stood then, and as he did so Reba DeFore trotted over to his side and produced her ophthalmoscope
from her pocket, holding it up to his eyes like a cop's
torch. "Keep still," the ash-blond-haired physician told
him.

Kane looked at her, staring into the bluish-white
light of the ophthalmoscope. "All clear?" he asked.

"Your left pupil is entirely unresponsive," DeFore replied matter-of-factly, "while the right eye is reacting slower than normal. How does it look from the inside?"

"It's okay," Kane said noncommittally. "I've been worse."

Lakesh held his palm out, grasping Kane's hand in a firm grip. "You be careful, my friend," he said. "Brewster will be monitoring your Commtact feed and the transponder you carry beneath the skin. If anything happens, you are to return immediately, do you hear me? Immediately."

Kane nodded. "I'll be fine."

"If things get hot, don't go playing hero," Lakesh warned. "You're in no condition to do that."

Kane looked at him, the steely gray of his eyes cold and full of a repressed fury. "Didn't you hear? I have it on good authority that all the heroes are dead."

Before Lakesh could think to respond, Kane had stepped into those twin cones of light and, in less time than it takes to tell, both he and the interphaser unit disappeared, winking out of existence in front of his very eyes.

"Godspeed, my friend," Lakesh muttered under his breath. "Godspeed."

WHILE TRAVELING BY interphaser was instantaneous, it conversely seemed to exist in a kind of nontime. It was this nontime that had affected Kane on the past few occasions he had accessed it. Now, yet again, he found his brain burning, a searing knife of heat penetrating his frontal lobe.

Within his eye, within his mind's eye, something was stirring, history replaying itself like ancient video footage, the images flickering over and over.

He watched now, a spectator to his own thoughts, as his hand—which is to say, the other's hand—reached for something lying in the sand. It was a blade, short and curved like a scimitar, finished in glorious gold that shimmered in the bright sunlight pelting toward it from above. The hand grabbed it, and Kane saw that the hand—his hand?—was ridged with rock, like an armored glove cinched over his fingers.

There was sound now, too—music. It hurried to Kane's ears, a series of notes played without breaks, like one note, rising and falling, the sounds like rushing water.

Kane—or whoever's vision Kane was witnessing— lifted the knife, judging its weight, turning it over in one hand. Then he looked up from the ground, and Kane saw the arena around him like a gymnasium, targets and weights and beds of spears arranged along its walls, its sandy floor open to the elements. Off to the left, at the edge of a roughly marked circle, sat a creature dressed in simple robes, its skin coarse and scary and ridged. The creature sat in front of some kind of harp, propped upright in the sandy dust of the ground, its frame lined in pearlescent seashell, its taut strings the red of blood. The creature, an Igigi slave, plucked at the strings of the harp with its fine hands, claws running along the side in a swishing motion, creating not a tune really, but just a pleasing sound, running along the octaves with the fluidity of liquid, no rhythm other than the harpist's own. Beneath the harp, where the dust had sprinkled against its underside, Kane saw the tassels at the bottom where the strings were tied through the frame, bloodred twists like scabs hanging in the air.

He turned, and Kane felt a sense of disorientation,

even motion sickness, as the vision swirled around. There, pinned to a large target shaped like a hexagon, rested a woman, held upright, arms and legs splayed. She was naked, tears running down her cheeks as she watched the proceedings, but she made no noise. Her long dark hair fell to almost her waist, clinging to her neck and shoulders with sweat, strands brushing her olive breasts as she breathed hurriedly in and out, in and out. Her dark eyes glistened with tears as she watched the figure with the sword—Kane? Was it Kane?—take a step back, holding his empty left hand up to judge the distance more clearly. It was forty feet if it was an inch, maybe fifty feet; Kane couldn't get his bearings. It was like a magic act, the magician's beautiful assistant waiting on the target as certain death approached.

Then Kane felt his balance shift, felt the long knife hanging behind his head, held low in his hand for a moment as he readied to throw it. The girl whimpered, the noise distant and quiet like a creaking floorboard expanding in the heat. And with the swiftest of movement, the right arm came forward and the blade cut through the air like golden death, spinning over itself in a long, beautiful arc as it raced unerringly toward the human target.

There was a shock of blood then, and Kane wanted to turn away. The girl didn't even cry out; she was dead as soon as the blade struck, her heart cut in two, an eruption of blood spurting from her chest, bones visible like teeth amid the redness.

Kane's viewpoint—forced as it was, unable to turn away—stayed on the girl as she sagged against the target, the deep crimson of her life's blood running down her torso and between her legs, vomiting over the sand at her feet. The golden scimitar remained in her chest, sticking out like some perverted crank handle that might grant her life if only she could wind it.

The eyes Kane looked with went closer, examining the butcher's work on the young woman's body. There were cuts on her body, Kane saw now, and bloody marks on the target here and there where others had presumably died. Kane wanted her to say something, to beg forgiveness, even though he hadn't thrown the knife, only been a party to its deadly toss, mute witness in the body of the thrower.

"Good work, my son." The voice came from Kane's right.

Kane turned, or the figure he was now turned, and saw the speaker, recognizing him immediately. It was Enlil, his burnished red-gold scales rippling with the breeze as he watched from the side of the training area, a red cloak wrapped across his shoulders. He reached out then, holding his lizardlike hand in a gesture that Kane—or the thing Kane now was—recognized as a salute. "Well done, Ullikummis. The speed of your improvement staggers even me."

Ullikummis. Visions of Ullikummis.

THE MOMENT PASSED. The swirling pattern of the interphaser dissipated around Kane and he found himself looking around the mat-trans chamber, its familiar walls of brown-tinted armaglass shimmering into view.

Kane placed a hand to his head, rubbed at his eyes with the heel of his hand for a moment, feeling the pressure there. "What hit me?" he muttered.

Taking a deep breath, he looked around the mat-trans chamber. He had used this mat-trans unit numerous times in his role as a Cerberus field agent; at one point it had formed the main route in and out of the hidden mountain redoubt. The mat-trans was a system of teleportation developed by the U.S. military in the twentieth century, and a number of similar units were located across the country. The interphaser had been rigged to access this same point, allowing the Cerberus operatives to utilize the same location despite the differences in the technologies.

The chamber looked much as it always had, tiled walls and ceiling with its pocks and vents for expunging the gas created by matter transfer. The armaglass looked subtly different, Kane noticed, seeing the vine-like creepers that clung to the exterior like grasping fingers, each one made of rock. There was rock, too, along the edges of the chamber, running where the walls met the floor, piling high in the corners like sand in a beach house left open to the elements. Kane ignored it, reaching for the exit door, automatically powering the Sin Eater pistol into his hand from its hidden holster beneath his sleeve.

The official sidearm of the Magistrate Division, the Sin Eater was an automatic handblaster that folded in on itself to be stored in a bulky holster strapped just above the user's wrist. Unfolded to its full extension, the automatic pistol measured less than fourteen inches in length and fired 9 mm rounds. Kane's holster reacted to a specific flinch movement of his wrist tendons, powering the pistol automatically into his hand. The trigger had no guard. The necessity had never been foreseen that any kind of safety features for the weapon would ever be required since the Magistrates were considered infallible. Thus, if the user's index finger was crooked at the time it reached his hand, the pistol would begin firing automatically. Though no longer a Magistrate himself, Kane had retained his weapon from his days as one in Cobaltville, and he still felt at his most comfortable with the weapon in his hand. It was an extension to his body that seemed second nature now, like the comforting weight of a wristwatch.

Clutching his Sin Eater in his right hand, Kane used his left to tap in the mat-trans door code. He waited, listening to the door's faint hiss as the seal unlocked. Warily, he stepped out into the antechamber room beyond, Sin Eater poised in front of him.

Kane relied on something that had been referred to as a point-man sense, an inherent ability to detect danger before it became readily apparent. It was this sense that had made him so crucial on field missions back when he was a hard-contact Magistrate, and it had ensured his survival countless times. However, while it may have appeared supernatural, Kane's point-man sense was actually a shrewd combination of the traditional five senses, promoting an almost Zen-like oneness with his surroundings and allowing him to pick up on anything that didn't belong.

Right now, however, it seemed almost that the whole room didn't belong. This was the operations center of the Cerberus redoubt, or at least it had been. The room should have been familiar to Kane; he had walked this vast chamber numerous times over the past few years. Once dominated by twin rows of computer terminals, the sleek lines of technology had been replaced with the roughness of stone, its patterns not carved but eroded, a harsh product of nature.

The vast chamber was faintly lit, traceries of volcanic magma glowing in the walls like veins, bringing a dull orange light into the area. Rock covered every surface, the twin aisles of computers buried beneath its suffocating grasp. Even the floor had been replaced, its smooth surface overwhelmed by the jagged roughness of a layer of rock, all of it colored a dull brown like mud.

For a moment Kane was overwhelmed, too, his senses reeling from the familiar made sick, twisted upon itself and turned into nightmare. The security, the sanctity of his base—*his home*—had been breached, changed, besmirched and left in ruins. Kane had seen it before, almost two months ago when he had explored this place under its other name, when it had been Life Camp Zero, prison for the New Order of Ullikummis. Even so, it still shook him to see it like this. It was like revisiting a childhood nightmare, its potency still vibrant years after the dreamer believed it conquered.

Kane's eyes twitched left and right as he searched the ruined room for company. There had been guards here once, troops loyal to Ullikummis, but they had been ejected along with the Cerberus rebels when the place had been evacuated. Deserted, it appeared as if it had simply been left to rot.

But there was someone there now, waiting in the chair that had once belonged to Lakesh Singh, its lines obese where the stone had lashed to its sides like runnels of rainwater. Humanoid, the thing's bulbous head lolled at an angle, the grayness of its skin darker than the last time Kane had seen him, wide, upslanting eyes narrowed as if half asleep, their glossy black wells bottomless as ever. When standing, the pale-skinned creature was about five feet in height, and he wore an indigo smock, a simple item of sheer fabric that reached down his short legs to his feet. There was a two-inch hole in the center of the smock, the material clinging there to the creature's chest, congealed blood sticking to the ruined tunic, plastering it to the creature's chest. Despite his wound, the figure had a stillness about him, but that had ever been so from the first time Kane had met him.

"Balam," Kane said, speaking the creature's name like a curse.

"Kane," Balam replied weakly. "I didn't think you'd come."

Chapter 12

Rosalia's dog was barking frantically, and it sounded loud in the enclosed space of the covered passageway. Grant ignored it.

"Everyone back," he ordered. "Right now."

The dog continued to bark, peppering its noise with plaintive whines as the watery thing began to form three feet in front of it. The dripping water was coming faster now, pooling on the floor in swirling circles dark as an undertaker's diary. There were pools all around them now, Grant saw, subtle drips from the ceiling creating a patchwork of tiny puddles across the hard white cobbles of the ground. Grant could see the first figure emerging from the pool in front of Rosalia and her dog, the water rising impossibly from the puddles and creating limbs and a torso, the whole swaying thing wending in place as it rose and took solid shape.

"Get back," Grant ordered again, recalling the Sin Eater to hand from its hiding place in his wrist holster. The fourteen-inch-long muzzle appeared in his hand instantaneously, its parts clicking into place as the mechanism shot it from its hidden guard.

The water figure shimmered, the moonlight playing off its lines and contortions as it grew taller, its body filling it with a roar like pouring rain. Wide shoulders appeared, curving downward like waterfalls, its limbs long and malformed, the hands shaped like the paddles of a rowboat. It was headless still, twisting in place as its legs expanded out of the pooling water beneath it.

Domi and the twin Tigers of Heaven had shuffled backward, easing themselves swiftly through the rounded archways along the left side of the covered passage and out into the hexagonal courtyard. The light was brighter out here, where all around them the fractured buildings pushed against one another as they grasped for the narrowed eye of the moon.

Under the portico, Rosalia's dog barked, lips pulling back to show its teeth as the water thing grew in stature, swirling in place. The figure was six feet tall now, more than that as its calves and ankles took shape, its feet sucked out of the pooling water like a man dragging himself from quicksand. A sluicing of water broke at its neck—or where its neck should be—the frothing waves twinkling with spindrift as the moonbeams played across them. Grant took a shot at it then, his Sin Eater spitting a single 9 mm bullet at its still-forming head from just seven feet away. The bullet cut the air, the sound of the blaster loud in the enclosed space, and drilled into the wall behind the forming man shape.

"That's the only warning you get," Grant called, apprehensively recalling the terrible demise of Hassood on the video record.

The mongrel growled and barked, showing its teeth to the forming figure of water. Rosalia grabbed the hound by its scruff, pulling it back.

Grant sighted the figure as Rosalia pulled her dog back, trying to make it out. It appeared silver in the moonlight, strips of nothingness, an ever-changing dimension to its body. It was water, clear through, rushing water whose ebbs and flows twinkled like witchfire.

Rosalia was at the line formed by the archways, pulling at her dog's neck, holding it back as best she could. She watched in dismay as the figure made of water stepped forward. No, *stepped* was the wrong word—it flowed, moving with all the grace and temerity and persistence of a raging river bursting its banks.

"We saw you hurt our friend," Grant called. "I'm not going to hold off shooting you if I have to."

The water thing ignored Grant's warning, rushing toward him with the force of a downpour. Grant snapped off a swift burst of fire as it approached, watching as the bullets passed harmlessly into its body, only to emerge on the other side, wet but otherwise unmarked.

The transparent figure glided across the paving stones toward Grant as he backed away, upon him in a second. Grant snapped off another burst of bullets, cacophonous in the tight-walled space, as one of the thing's watery arms cleaved the air toward him. The paddle-like hand struck Grant hard across the chest, lashing against his breastbone and knocking him backward so that he went stumbling into the far wall. Grant lost his footing, kicking out and back as he crashed into the wall, knocking the radio unit flying as he fell to the ground. His chest was soaked, his shirt wringing wet and the shadow suit he wore beneath it clinging to his skin.

He looked up, bringing his Sin Eater out in front of him as the shimmering water man washed through the space between them like rain, sluicing toward him in an unstoppable torrent. Grant's Sin Eater spit again, unleashing another clutch of bullets as the figure hurtled toward him.

Rosalia's dog was barking angrily now, the hair on its back standing up, its tail pointed and stiff as an arrow, and she had to pull it back by the scruff of its neck, keeping it from being hit by Grant's gunfire. The bullets whizzed past both of them, cutting through the first of the water creatures in splashing streaks, cutting lines from its liquid body as they zipped through it and into the crumbling wall behind.

Incredibly, the liquid monster gave no reaction to the bullets cutting through it. Instead it just hurtled on toward Grant where he lay by the radio, its body instantaneously re-forming where the bullets had tried to wound it, leaving no more trace than a stone dropped into the ocean.

Grant rattled off another blast, unable to fully appreciate the strange creature in the insubstantial lighting beneath the portico. In the instant before the thing reached him, Grant saw it as a man drawn in twinkling silvery lines, incomplete thanks to the darkness of the shadows, a blur in the air. And behind that figure, Grant saw something else moving, another of the watery figures emerging from the pools that littered the floor beyond the covered passage.

LESS THAN TEN FEET FROM Grant's position, Domi, Kishiro and Kudo found themselves facing their own menaces. Unnoticed, pools of water had formed in the hexagonal courtyard that led into the covered passageway. They lay there, shimmering darkly in the moonlight as if from a heavy rain. When Domi and the twin Tigers of Heaven had backed out into the courtyard, those pools had suddenly begun to stream upward, forming more of the waterlike men with whom Grant was struggling.

Alerted by some uncanny sense, Domi spun in time to see the first of them wind out of the ground, swirling into shape the way water streams down a drain when one removes the plug. Each of the creatures formed like that, five of them shimmering into ghostly shape as they clambered from the pools in a wash.

"Look sharp, people," Domi instructed. "We've got trouble."

As she spoke, the first of the weird creatures reached the completion stage of its formation, and immediately it was running at her, attracted by her scent or noise or…*something*. Quite why these water creatures had been attracted to the Cerberus warriors—and to Hassood before them—was a mystery right now, but immediately Domi realized it may go some way to explaining why the city seemed deserted, its populace hidden within their locked homes as though in a state of siege.

Like Grant, Domi's instinctive reaction was to pull her gun—in her case, a Detonics .45 Combat Master. The Combat Master was a compact revolver finished in metallic silver, its sleek lines flashing in the moonlight as she pulled it from the holster at the small of her back. Domi reeled off her first shot even before she had her target, bringing her weapon around as she ducked and spun away from the onrushing figure of the human carved from flowing water. With a flash of ignition powder, Domi's bullet shot across the courtyard, snagging the otherworldly figure through the top of its left shoulder in a splash of spilling water. The creature didn't slow for a second; it just kept charging at Domi as she flung herself out of its way like some demented jack-in-the-box.

Behind Domi, the twin Tigers of Heaven warriors

had set themselves in fighting stances at her warning, taking up defensive positions as the strange water creatures grew in stature all around them, their bodies wending into shape from the spilled pools of water. Both Tigers had drawn their *katana* swords, each blade over twenty-five inches in length and stored in a decorative sheath slung low at their hips. The blades sang as they exited their sheaths, the metal vibrating infinitesimally to create an eerie note that ran around the courtyard in a mournful echo like a tolling bell. Every member of the Tigers of Heaven was a highly trained warrior, intimately versed in the traditional fighting techniques of the samurai. However, while the warriors could appear traditionalist in their ways, they were also exceptionally competent in the more modern arts of combat, able to employ handguns and automatic rifles with breathtaking grace.

Standing shoulder to shoulder, both fearsome warriors readied their blades as the first wave of the water creatures rushed them.

Kudo took a pace forward, stepping into his attack as he swung the two-foot-long blade through the air, cutting into the nearest water warrior roughly where its third and forth rib would be. The sword slashed into the water form, its keen edge cutting effortlessly across the figure and slicing a line straight through it. However, even as the sword was passing through the thing's body, the water was reknitting behind it, sealing its path over with the speed of thought.

Surprised, Kudo stumbled slightly as he found his blade cutting through the creature with no more effort than plunging it into the contents of a filled bath. As he did so, the water creature reached out, its shimmering arm glistening as moonlight played across its seemingly solid surface. Kudo ducked, throwing himself out of the path of the creature's thrusting attack even as he regained his balance.

Beside him, Kishiro had favored a two-handed grip on his own *katana,* and he plunged it at his own foe from above his head, the blade cutting downward from an almost horizontal position of rest. The *katana* drove into the humanoid figure's head, driving a line through the center of its forehead and drilling through the water in a rush of foam and splatter. Drops of water spilled from the thing's half-formed face, the moon's silvery rays painting in the suggestion of eyes, mouth and nose where the water rippled across its surface.

The sword remained in the thing's head for a moment, cutting deeper with a minimal effort on the part of its wielder. Then the shimmering figure shoved out with both arms, its curving, malformed hands driving outward until they slapped against Kishiro's chest with the force of a waterfall. Kishiro tumbled backward in a wash of water, losing his footing and slamming into the cobbled road with a fierce exhalation of lost breath. The front of his shirt was soaked through and he splashed against the ground where, all around him, a puddle had formed.

Then, Kishiro began to struggle as he found the water pulling him down, dragging him against the cobbles in a magnetic grip, down into the solid mass of the road itself. His grip slipped on the *katana,* and he felt it leave his grasp, skittering away from his hand.

Kishiro was a brave warrior, trained and disciplined in the art of fighting honorably. He did not scream as the water sucked him down with the power of quicksand; he barely even called for help as he felt his body drawn impossibly down through the solid mass of the street itself.

"Help me, I require assistance," he said, conscious that his companions were already engaged. "Please, someone…"

Kudo turned at his colleague's eerie disappearance, dropping as his own foe swung one of its heavy arms at him. The arm made a sloshing sound as it swept through the air, dappling Kudo's black hair with a sheen of dewy water.

Without turning, Kudo slashed out with his *katana* blade once again, cutting low, slicing through the strange creature's ankles. The thing's left ankle split, the water parting as the blade hacked through it, and it lurched to one side.

Kudo paid it no mind, driving himself onward to where his fellow Tiger of Heaven was disappearing beneath the surface of the dark pool of water in the street. "I'm coming," he assured him as his feet slapped against the cobblestones.

MEANWHILE, JUST A DOZEN feet away beneath the portico, Grant lay on his back, squeezing his Sin Eater's trigger as that furious deluge that was shaped like a man came hurtling across the ground toward him, a dark trail of damp in its wake. Rosalia was watching in trepidation as Grant's shots cut through the watery creature lunging at him, her hand deep in the fur at the scruff of her dog's neck as it strained to get closer.

"Bullets aren't having any effect, Magistrate," Rosalia shouted as Grant blasted another shot into the place where the creature's gut should be.

"Tell me somethin' I don't know," Grant snapped as he rolled across the floor, diving out of the way of one of the water beast's pounding fists. The fist slapped against the ground with the power of a water cannon blast.

The thing was fast, its movements like a raging river about to burst its banks. Despite his large size, Grant could move just as swiftly, and he vaulted aside as the creature spun toward him, each movement accompanied by the sound of gallons of water swirling through the air.

Grant got back to his feet as the fearsome creature passed him in its fury, the nearness of its watery skin leaving Grant covered in a dewlike sheen. Grant turned, bringing his Sin Eater to bear once more and unleashing a triple burst of 9 mm bullets at the thing's head as it glided across the cobblestones to meet him. The bullets zipped across the gulf between Grant and his weird attacker, cutting through the thing's body with blushes of spit water where they hit, only to continue on through the transparent torso and exit. The water man continued to move, unfazed by the impact of the bullets, rocketing at Grant with the ferocity of a monsoon.

Then it hit him like a breaker, a great wave in human form striking Grant head-on, lashing across his body and face in a fearsome torrent. Grant opened his mouth to call out in surprise, only to find the water carom past his teeth and down his throat, causing him to choke as he lost his footing and fell back.

Standing between the arches that lined the open passage, Rosalia saw Grant fall beneath the man-wave, her left hand reaching across her body for the Ruger pistol holstered at her right hip, her right hand still struggling with the dog. Grant smashed into the hard cobblestones with a bone-jarring crunch, the swell of water washing over him in a slick sheen, drowning him where he lay. His attacker no longer looked like a man but seemed to have flattened, swelling over Grant's form as it smoth ered him. Grant's eyes met with Rosalia's, eyes wide in fear as the water poured down his throat in a foamy gush. Rosalia watched as, desperately, Grant's right hand punched upward and the nose of the Sin Eater burst out of the sheet of water that covered him, unleashing another burst of bullets that drilled into the portico ceiling.

Though she favored her right hand, Rosalia was schooled enough in the use of firearms to be effectively ambidextrous. Now holding the Ruger P-85 in her left, she brought the weapon around, searching for a target, some hint of the thing that drove this weird water creature on, some kind of heart or brain. The water shimmered as the moonlight played across it, looking like a hideous clear mask over Grant's taut-mouthed face. A blurting burst of bubbles frothed from Grant's mouth as he struggled beneath the shallow layer of water.

"Come on, Magistrate," Rosalia muttered to herself. "Show me what to shoot."

AT THAT SAME MOMENT, Domi found herself leaping to avoid the swinging punch of another of the water creatures, its clear liquid lines twinkling in the moonlight. Domi had grown up in the Outlands and she was used to relying on her wits. Despite her petite form, Domi was a supreme athlete. Right now, she applied all her instincts in a graceful synergy with her firm muscles, ducking and weaving out of the way as her watery foe approached.

But as Domi ducked another brutal punch, snapping her blaster up and drilling a slug through her foe's liquid body, she realized there was another of the watery figures at her back, just emerging from a dark pool of water there, tar-black under the moonlight. Domi turned, running headlong at the nearest wall, its rough surface looking ghostly under the moon's glow, and the two water creatures flowed across the cobbled stones to follow.

Then Domi was kicking out, twisting her body as her feet hit the wall at roughly the height of her waist. As the twin creatures grasped for her, Domi leaped gracefully over their heads, her Detonics pistol blasting shot after shot through their bodies from above as she swooped through the air in a flip.

The albino warrior landed a moment later, taking her weight on bended knees as she brought her gun to bear on another of the watery creatures.

Beside her, Kudo was running across the cobbles to help Kishiro as he was drowned in the strange pooling water that dominated one side of the courtyard. The pool was ten feet across at its widest point, and Kishiro seemed to be sinking into it. It was impossible, Kudo felt sure—he had checked this courtyard not ten minutes ago, had seen that the area was flat and dry. Even if a pool of water had appeared here in that time, there was no way it could be deep enough to absorb a man.

Yet Kishiro seemed to be drowning, his arms flailing as he sank deeper into the impossible pool, his breath escaping from his lungs in a series of hurried, angry bubbles.

Domi whipped around, ducking the grasping arm as one of the liquid humanoids reached for her, spinning and diving at the same time. She saw Kudo reach for Kishiro as he disappeared beneath the dark water, a final rush of bubbles galloping from his mouth and nostrils to burst at the surface, frothy where his struggles had churned those waters over and over.

In that moment Kishiro was gone, his form sucked beneath the water. All that remained of him was a puddle that bulged for just a moment in the faint shape of a man's body, beside which his discarded *katana* lay still, its burnished silver length shining with the moon's rays.

"Stay back," Domi commanded. "Keep away from the water."

Kudo stopped in his tracks, his sword held ready at his side. They were one man down and there were water creatures on all sides of them now.

BENEATH THE MOONLIT portico, her dog still held firm by its neck, Rosalia felt a growing sense of helplessness as she watched Grant drown in only inches of water. The water clung to his face in a shiny gloss, painting him silver as the moonlight struck it. The corpuscles in his eyes were growing red, turning the whites pink as he struggled to free himself from the impossible trap. His legs were kicking urgently and he reached for her with his free hand, the Sin Eater still clutched in the right where it was doing no good.

If Rosalia touched him, she suspected she would be dragged into the watery prison, too. Whatever it was, however it worked, touching it was almost certainly a bad idea. She glanced over her shoulder for a moment, semiaware of the stuttering gunshots and sounds of movement behind her where Domi and the Tigers of Heaven battled more of these strange liquid combatants. Domi was back-to-back with Kudo, a handgun's familiar length glinting in her hand while the samurai-like warrior held his *katana* out ready. On all sides of them, four more of the water beings ebbed and flowed, swaying in place like leaves on the breeze. Rosalia heard Domi scream a savage battle cry as she hurled herself at the nearest of the water warriors, her pistol blazing as it struck the creature's wet skin.

"Dammit, there has to be some way to..." Rosalia muttered, searching her mind for an answer as she turned back to witness Grant's horrifying predicament.

Suddenly, Rosalia's dog pulled free of her grip, powering itself forward and throwing her back against the upright of the nearest arch. With a snarl, the dog leaped for Grant and the glistening liquid sheen that covered him, jaws widening as its face hit the water.

"No!" Rosalia called, but it was too late.

There was a splash, a splatter as the dog's muzzle broke the surface of the water. The clear liquid burst all around its jaw, lashing against its fur like a living thing—which, perhaps, it was. For a moment, seen only in the tricky half light of the moon, the dog seemed to expand, to become two beings or three as its head shook beneath the water.

Rosalia's heart stopped for a moment in fear, watching but utterly helpless as the pale-eyed mongrel dunked its head in the water, shaking itself as the water hit it. Then, astonishingly, Grant gasped, the sound loud in the covered area, and he rolled onto his side, coughing and spluttering as he finally took breath once more.

"What th—?" Rosalia muttered, observing in incredulity as her dog shook its head and body, the water streaming from it in droplets that painted the walls and floor.

For a moment it appeared that the dog had somehow defeated the liquid thing, causing it to dissipate in some inexplicable manner. But even as Rosalia watched, Grant lying a few feet from her and clutching his chest as he struggled to clear his lungs of water, the droplets that had splattered against the walls began to hurry downward, re-forming into a dozen pools that knitted together in a matter of seconds.

The dog barked loudly as it returned to its mistress's side, and they both watched as the pool—against all sense of logic—poured upward, rushing toward the portico's ceiling and taking shape once more. In less than five seconds, the man-shape stood in front of the Cerberus exiles once more, its body dripping out of the pool around its feet, the tiny green light of the radio's camera unit coruscating and refracting as it flickered behind the creature's transparent body.

In that instant Rosalia knew what she had to do. With a decisive shriek, she pointed the Ruger at the floor behind the liquid creature and pulled the trigger, directing three slugs into the creature's shins. The bullets cut through the water and out, burying themselves in the front of the radio unit where that green signal light glinted. In a fraction of a second, the front of the unit sparked into flame as the innards were pierced by the bullets, an arc of electricity flickering across its surface and zapping the pooling water on the floor in a lightninglike explosion.

Rosalia leaped back, her dog scampering out of the covered area and running off in a flurry of whirring legs. Across the portico area, Grant rolled as best he could away from the sparking figure of the water man as it shuddered in place, the electricity racing up and down its eerie, see-through body.

Then there came a colossal burst of light within the covered passage like a lightning strike, and Rosalia found herself thrown ten feet backward and down to the ground, the metal of the Ruger pistol glowing hotly in her hand so that she had to release it. As suddenly as it had begun, it was over. The light faded and, in its wake, the portico seemed draped in black.

Rosalia lay on the ground, breathing heavily, her left hand pulsing where it had tried to hold the burning-hot Ruger as the electricity fired across it. After a moment she turned, saw something glinting in the moonlight just two inches from her face—it was a *katana* blade, its point aimed straight for her left eye.

"Shit," Rosalia yelped as she forced herself to sit up. A moment more and she realized that the lethal blade just lay there, tossed aside on the cobbled stones of the courtyard.

"You okay, miss?" Kudo asked from behind her. "You took quite a flight."

Rosalia pushed herself up from the cold ground into a crouch, indulging the Tiger of Heaven with a look as she scanned the area. "I'm fine," she said. The water people were gone and the ground around the courtyard was bone-dry.

Ahead of her, she and Kudo could see a figure moving in the arched area beneath the portico. Rosalia reached automatically for the nearest weapon, the discarded *katana,* as that figure stumbled around in the darkness.

As Rosalia stood, her scruffy-looking dog came skittering over, barking happily, tail wagging. "Good boy," Rosalia encouraged quietly. "Good dog."

Then the figure stepped from the shadows, revealing itself to be Grant, rolling his shoulders and wincing in pain as he struggled out of the covered alley on unsteady legs. "What the hell did you do?" he asked as he caught Rosalia's dark eyes.

The long-haired mercenary smiled. "I gave your dancing partner a little jolt," she said. "Surely even a Magistrate knows that water and electricity don't mix."

"All of them disappeared at the same instant," Kudo added appreciatively. "Just winked out like they…evaporated or something. But by then we'd lost Kishiro. He was sucked into one of those pools that—" he looked around embarrassedly "—well, they were here a moment before."

"Sure, they were," Grant agreed, nodding slowly, a blurted cough coming past his lips as he stepped unsteadily forward. His chest ached where the lungs had filled with water, and he felt light-headed, as if his head was spinning on his neck. Without conscious thought, he commanded his Sin Eater back to its hidden holster.

Grant peered around the courtyard, looking at the chalklike facades of the buildings as the moon played across their rough surfaces. "I just got one question," he said after a moment. "Where the heck is Domi?"

Chapter 13

"Son of a bitch, what happened to you?" Kane asked as he examined the wound in Balam's chest.

"I was shot," Balam said simply, his soft voice sounding too loud in the absolute stillness of the abandoned redoubt.

The two of them had moved to the Cerberus infirmary under Kane's instruction, where the ex-Mag might be able to examine Balam's wounds better. Like the rest of the Cerberus base, the infirmary had been overrun with stone growths, spiraling across the surfaces like creeping vines. Balam seemed able to walk at least, although he was slower than Kane recalled from the last time they had met.

Balam was one of the Archons, a race that had confirmed the pact between the Annunaki and the Tuatha de Danaan millennia ago. Balam and his fellow Archons had lived in the shadows for their whole lives, observing and guiding humankind as it battled Annunaki interference. The last of his kind, Balam dwelled in the underground city of Agartha with his charge, the human-hybrid girl called Quav. His contacts with Cerberus had been infrequent but pivotal, each time auguring an end-of-the-world scenario involving the Annunaki. The last time that Kane had seen Balam, it had been four months ago when he had come to warn Kane and his Cerberus teammates of the destruction of the Ontic Library, an undersea storehouse holding the rules of reality. The library had been breached by Ullikummis, the rogue prince of the Annunaki. While there was little love between the two of them, Kane had never wished harm on Balam, and seeing him wounded like this disturbed him.

Balam sat across several chairs within the infirmary. He had slumped as soon as he sat, adopting a pose very unlike his usual erect manner. Kane stood, pacing across to one of the stone-daubed cupboards, trying to recall where Reba DeFore had stored her medications.

Kane snapped several finger-thin tendrils away from one of the cupboard doors and peered inside, checking three of the wall-mounted units until he found what he was looking for. Then, he turned back, producing a bottle of antiseptic, its clear liquid swilling behind a glass bottle that also had a dusting of stone growths obscuring its surface.

"I'll clean and dress your wound," Kane told Balam, trying to sound reassuring, "while you tell me all about it, okay?"

Balam nodded, a slow, deliberate movement of his bulbous head. "Six days ago, an intruder came to Agartha," he explained as Kane tipped the open bottle of antiseptic onto a folded strip of gauze. "I knew the intruder, recognized her immediately, yet I also knew she was there to do harm.

"I sensed that much," he went on. Balam was referring to his telepathic abilities, his natural facility to read and interact with another's mind. While Balam generally refrained from delving into a human's thoughts, he was frequently well aware of the swirling emotions that bubbled at the top of a person's mind, though he usually deemed it politic to keep that information to himself. "The intruder was your colleague Brigid Baptiste, Kane."

Kneeling beside Balam as he applied the antiseptic to the gross wound, Kane took a long breath.

"You're not surprised?" Balam probed.

Kane showed no emotion as he spoke, his eyes not meeting with Balam's. "Tell the story," he said.

"Brigid came for Quavell's daughter," Balam said, "my charge—the girl you know as Little Quav. She kidnapped her, escaping Agartha via the interphase transmitter in the old storehouse.

"I endeavored to stop her, and I received this wound for my efforts," Balam said, indicating the bloody rent in his tunic where Kane was daubing antiseptic. "I used an ASP Emitter," he said, showing Kane the burned-out ruins of the snake-shaped weapon that had been strapped to his right wrist. "Brigid opened a quantum gateway and disappeared before I could reach her, taking Little Quav with her. But I thought myself clever, in this instance, and so I followed, presuming—though it transpired, foolishly—that Brigid would have returned to your Cerberus base here. Obviously, I am out of touch, as I did not realize the base had been evacuated."

"We had a little trouble of our own," Kane explained vaguely as he finished cleaning Balam's wound. Despite himself, Kane was impressed that the shorter creature showed no hint of pain as the burning liquid played across his raw cuts.

"Naturally, I was reluctant to let Little Quav out of my sight for too long," Balam continued, "but by the time I realized my mistake I had lost too much blood. It took all my effort just to bring myself back to consciousness and activate the beacon."

Kane inclined his head, showing Balam a self-conscious, lopsided grin. "Well, we heard it," he said. "Cavalry's here."

Balam held Kane's gaze with his plaintive dark eyes until the ex-Mag turned back to his work of cleaning and dressing his wound. Kane felt Balam's eyes upon him as he worked, the silence between them like a wall.

Finally, Kane lifted Balam's tunic a little higher and wrapped a strip of gauze across his freshly cleaned wound. It had finished weeping at least, though some of the congealed blood was still tacky. "I don't know how long that's going to hold you together, Balam," Kane said. "If you're up to a jump we could phase back to where we're holed up and get Reba to give you the once-over."

Balam continued to look at Kane, waiting for the man to meet his eyes once more.

Kane stepped away, admiring his work. "Field dressing ain't my speciality, but it'll hold for now." Then he looked Balam in the eye. "How's it feel?" he asked.

"We have something to talk about, friend Kane," Balam said. "I have told you my story, but that is only half of the tale, is it not? You of all people would know what Brigid Baptiste was doing, would you not?"

Reluctantly, Kane nodded. "You can see that things have got kind of messed up around here," he said with typical understatement. "Baptiste, too. She's not with Cerberus right now, and I really don't know if what you saw—the person who shot you—was her."

"She was different but she was still Brigid," Balam said with arch simplicity.

"Yeah," Kane agreed, tugging at his shirt and revealing the shadow suit he wore beneath. Its black skin was torn and frayed in places and the area that should cover his heart was missing, the dark hairs of his chest visible through the two-inch-wide tear that lay there. "Baptiste shooting you only makes you a part of an exclusive club," he said.

Balam could barely believe what he was hearing. "S-s-she shot you, too?" he spluttered.

Kane nodded. "Something shot me," he said. "Something with Brigid's face."

Kane paused, and Balam waited as the man struggled with what he had to say.

"She had Quav with her at the time," Kane stated. "I couldn't do anything. It was so fast. It was all so—" he stopped, trying to find the right word but failing "—so fast."

"You and Brigid were friends, close friends," Balam said.

"More than that," Kane acknowledged, recalling their *anam-chara* bond, which linked them through eternity. "But something's gone wrong with her, something inside. And it's Ullikummis's fault, just like this whole base is Ullikummis's fault, this whole damn world and the mess it's now in."

"Kane," Balam said slowly, his voice firm, "I am sorry. I know how much Brigid means to you. I see how you look at each other."

Kane shrugged with impatience. "Well…"

The strange infirmary with its dark tendrils of stone across once immaculate surfaces, grasping like the tentacles of an octopus, was silent for almost a minute as the two figures remained in silence, each pondering his own concerns, his own losses.

"And what of you?" Balam asked finally. "The wound on your chest isn't the only one, I can see."

Delicately, Balam brought his six-fingered hand up to his own face, brushing his long fingers along his cheek by his left eye in indication. "You have taken…a blow of some sort?"

In unconscious imitation, Kane touched at the callused area beside his blind eye. "Something hit me," he explained. "Something alive, I think. My vision comes and goes."

"You're blind?" Balam asked for clarification.

"No," Kane said. "It's hard to see, and sometimes I don't. But I'm seeing something else. *His* memories, those of Ullikummis. I can't explain."

"Kane, you are going into battle with your vision seriously impaired," Balam stated, clearly horrified. "A human would need to harbor a death wish to do that. I understand that you have lost Brigid—"

"No, I haven't," Kane interrupted, anger firing his voice. "She's out there and I'll bring her back."

Balam looked at the muscular figure of the ex-Mag for a long moment, studying for the first time how much Kane had changed physically. He held himself slightly stooped now, as if weary with fatigue, and his hair was ragged, unwashed and caught in tangles that reached past his collar. His chin was dark with a semi-grown beard, tufts of ginger in its muddy brown.

"You are facing an enemy who has destroyed your base," Balam realized, "and taken your friend, perverting her into something that neither of us truly recognize. But, take solace in this fact—you are not alone in your struggle." As he spoke Balam reached up, his long arms shifting across the gulf between himself and Kane, his snakelike fingers grasping Kane's. "I am pledged with the guardianship of Little Quav, a pledge I take seriously. We stand now together."

Kane held Balam's hands in his, feeling how cold the creature of the First Folk's skin seemed compared to his own. "Two wounded soldiers, huh?" he muttered.

"I believe, as you might say, that we still have some tricks left in us," Balam said, smiling in that slight, knowing way that only he could manage.

USING HIS COMMTACT, Kane reported to Lakesh and the others at Cerberus's temporary base, briefly reciting how Balam was present and had set off the redoubt's distress alarm upon finding the base abandoned.

"Do you require any assistance?" Lakesh asked, surprise mixing with concern in his agitated voice.

"Not just yet," Kane reasoned. "Balam might need a medical consort later, but the tough little bastard says he's fine right now. Best not to press it."

After he had reported in, Kane led Balam up to the cafeteria area of the redoubt via elevator. The elevators still worked, despite being recast in ugly stone cladding, their interior lights replaced with a dull orange glow from wall-mounted magma pods, the same magma pods that were used in so much of the refashioned redoubt.

The canteen, too, was a mess of jutting stone and wreckage, one whole section covered over with a wave of rough-hewn stonework, the walls and floor scored with more of the haphazard rock. Blisters ran along the walls as if the room was alive.

"See if you can find us a seat," Kane said, "and I'll grab us a bite to eat."

With that, Kane disappeared into the familiar kitchen area, its doors heavy with dark stone plating, its once-tiled walls lumpy as a rock face. Balam watched him depart, making his slow way over to one of the rock benches that rested in front of a flat stone table where once metal and Formica had ruled.

Despite the changes, much of the canteen remained pretty well intact and Kane soon located the larder area of the kitchen, its cool walls rough now with jagged spikes of gray-black stone like a porcupine's back. Shortly, he returned to the seating area carrying two plastic trays featuring molded compartments in which he'd placed a few items from the canned supplies: cold beans and some brittle flatbreads.

"I couldn't get the stoves working," Kane explained briefly as he took a seat opposite Balam, laying the trays out between them. "But the way you look just now, I figure you won't mind so much."

Balam nodded gratefully, plucking at the beans with a metal spoon. Tiny veins of stone arced across the spoon's handle and bowl, making it rough on the tongue as Balam scooped up the cold beans and ate them.

"When was the last time you ate?" Kane asked as he worked his spoon into his own plate of beans.

"Six days," Balam said through a mouthful of food, tearing at the flatbread with his incisors. Kane had never seen Balam like this; there was something almost undignified in his manner, no longer the archly refined figure he had always seemed before. Balam saw Kane watching him and he smiled. "I can manage without sustenance for a while, but not indefinitely. Your food, however, is good."

"Thanks." Kane nodded, tearing off a piece of his own flatbread. There was a dusting of mold on the flatbread, and Kane tore around it, casting that part aside.

Balam looked around the cafeteria area, transformed as it was, the magma pods glowing redly along the walls to cast a gloomy light on the proceedings. "Something bad happened here," he stated. "Death."

"A lot of things went down when Ullikummis attacked," Kane agreed. "I wasn't here for most of it, had to play catch-up when me and Grant and...well, when we came off mission. We literally walked into all this."

"A lot of things have changed," Balam said with deliberation. "Perhaps if you had warned me, I could have been better prepared to protect Quav."

Kane shook his head. "We didn't realize anyone would come for her. Or for you. How could we guess that?"

"Little Quav is the genetic template of an Annunaki goddess called Ninlil," Balam mused, "as you well know. The reason she was placed in my safekeeping was to shield her from the Annunaki's machinations."

"Enlil's machinations," Kane corrected. "This wasn't Enlil."

Balam looked at the nightmarish devastation that had consumed the cafeteria, feeling the emanations of death all around him. "Things changed when the Ontic Library was breached. Perhaps we have both been naive," he concluded.

"So, you think Baptiste's planning to employ Quav in her aspect as the goddess Ninlil?" Kane proposed.

Balam nodded. "That is distinctly possible. You said that Brigid disappeared during the attack on Cerberus, that she cannot be tracked in your usual manner."

"That's right," Kane acknowledged. "Her transponder isn't broadcasting. It's like she's disappeared off the face of the Earth."

"The transponder could be blocked, of course," Balam suggested through a mouthful of flatbread and beans.

"Theoretically," Kane agreed.

"But Ninlil would be of no concern to Brigid Baptiste," Balam resumed. "She was sent to take the child while my guard was down. Specifically, someone sent Brigid because I would trust her, even though I saw through the ruse swiftly. Another person—Enlil, say, or one of his Nephilim warriors—would be unable to perform the same feat, for I would have removed Little Quav to safety at the first sign of them. As was, Quav recognized Brigid and placed herself in jeopardy almost immediately on your colleague's arrival."

"So, she's working with Ullikummis? How would that make sense?"

"Many are the ways of the Annunaki," Balam told Kane. "Surely I don't need to remind you of that."

Using the flatbread to mop up the last of the bean juice, Kane reached unconsciously for his face, probing at his left cheek with his fingertips.

"How is your vision now?" Balam asked.

"The light in here isn't good," Kane replied sourly.

Balam watched as Kane chewed on the last of the flatbread, leaving nothing but an oily residue on his plastic tray where the beans had once sat, a torn hunk of the flatbread with mold patterning its edge. "Kane, there is a way around all of this," he said slowly. "Little Quav is still a child, not yet three years old. She is not a goddess yet—to achieve that will require a full body download from the genetic hub of Tiamat."

"Which we destroyed," Kane growled.

"Without those codes, without that genetic key to trigger her metamorphosis, Quav will stay Quav," Balam explained. "If we track her down, we would likely track Brigid down, and also Ullikummis."

Kane looked impatient. "And how do you propose

we do that? We've already established that Baptiste's transponder is nixed."

Balam smiled enigmatically. "You have your ways of tracing people, friend Kane, and I have mine."

Kane shoved the tray away with irritation, causing it to clatter across the table. "You are not a soldier, Balam. You wouldn't stand a chance against Ullikummis. And you know it."

"Yes, I do," Balam agreed. "But perhaps together...?"

"No." Kane shook his head. "I faced this monster three times, and two of those times I got my ass handed to me. Look around you—all this destruction, that's Ullikummis, that's his legacy."

Balam waited as Kane seethed with annoyance and frustration, watching the broad-shouldered man tensing with the menace of a caged tiger.

"What if I told you I could restore your sight?" Balam said.

"Cerberus is working on that," Kane responded dourly.

With an abruptness that surprised Kane, Balam reached across the table and grasped Kane's hand, placing his long fingers over Kane's own. Before the startled Kane could respond, he saw something change in his vision, as though a light had been switched on in the room, the dimensions and depths once hidden by shadows clear once more, colors flooding and overwhelming his senses in a blur.

"Balam, what did you do?" Kane said, the words coming as a frantic shout. "What did you do to me?"

"Stay calm, friend Kane," Balam replied. "You have nothing to fear here."

Chapter 14

She had stepped into the water and she had died. Or at least, that's how Domi thought of it as she fought to open her eyes.

While Rosalia and her dog were trying desperately to save Grant from an unimaginable fate at the hands of the sentient water pool, Domi had found herself partnered with Kudo out in the moonlit courtyard. Standing back to back with the modern-day samurai, Domi had walked around, footstep over footstep, as four of the watery beings washed toward them on all sides, like menacing, roiling waves crashing toward some eerie moonlit beach. Behind her, having already seen his partner disappear beneath the dark surface of one of the impossible pools, Kudo readied his *katana* sword, grim determination showing in every muscle of his tautened body.

Domi took another pace to her right, the weight of the Detonics Combat Master glinting as it caught the silvery moonlight. The transparent human forms cut from water flowed closer, ebbed back, flowed closer still. Then, suddenly, Domi moved, kicking off the cobblestone roadway and blasting a shot from the pistol as she hurled herself at the nearest of the sinister forms.

Whatever it was she had shouted, it was unintelligible, just a frustrated shrill of anger as the first of her bullets cut through the surface of the creature and continued on, through its body and out the other side without having an effect.

The thing swung one of its arms at Domi, like a whirlpool spinning through empty space at her head, and she ducked it, feeling the coolness of the water as it speckled her chalk-white skin and dampened her bone-white hair. Domi's pistol blasted again, kicking in her hand as she drilled another bullet into the creature's flank. It had no internal organs—heck, its whole substance seemed malleable, so what was she hoping to hit?

Fuck it!

With another savage scream, Domi kicked forward and drove herself at the swirling pillar of water shaped like a man. Head down, shoulders driving onward, she splashed into the creature as, somewhere behind her, Kudo tried to cut the arm of another of the creatures with his sword. Then, with a splash that seemed to echo through every bone of her body, Domi hit her foe.

It felt like hitting the surface of a freezing cold lake, cracking through a layer of ice so thin it barely registered. The water seemed to swirl around her, clinging to her as she drove through the creature's liquid body, clasping her flesh. Domi felt her feet go out from under her, felt herself trip and drop, the water still holding her, clinging to her face like some terrible mask. She could feel it filling her mouth, nostrils and ears, pressing against her wide-open eyes with the pressure and coldness of the deep. She should have walked through it, shattered it, ruined it, but instead she was still inside the thing, trapped as she toppled toward the hard cobblestones of the path. Sound was different here, too; she felt her finger pull at the trigger of her gun but the spitting bullet sounded deeper and louder, as if the sound had been artificially slowed down.

Then Domi slammed against the cobbles, knees first, connecting with a brutal impact. And still the water swished around her face and body, clinging to her with the consistency of tar. She couldn't breathe. It had been just two seconds, but she was desperately conscious of the fact that she could no longer breathe.

The world swam around Domi's eyes as she rolled against the ground, feeling the coldness and the wetness of the slick cobblestones. Behind her, seen as if through a stained-glass window, Kudo was using his two-foot-long sword to keep the other water beings at bay, hacking left and right, carving splattering lines through transparent limbs that reconstituted in the blink of an eye.

Bubbles rushed past Domi's eyes, her own breath passing her, hurtling for freedom from this terrible prison. Mindlessly, pointlessly, Domi squeezed the Combat Master's trigger again, feeling the mighty handblaster buck in her hand.

Then her head struck against the cobblestones, cushioned by the water that had enveloped her, the impact still hard enough to shake thoughts from her skull. There was redness in the water now. Blood. Her own?

Redness and encroaching blackness, swirling in from the edges of her vision.

Red and black—cards on a table.

PAINTED SILVER IN THE moonlight, the courtyard was eerily quiet now, just the faint sounds of dripping from somewhere off in the distance. Three figures stood in the empty courtyard—Grant, Kudo and Rosalia with her dog—the hound's breathing and the occasional sound of their shoes scuffing against the cobblestones made artificially loud by the silence.

Grant looked all around him as he stood in the courtyard's center, pacing a few steps back and forth in irritation. "Where is she? Where did Domi go?" he snapped.

"I didn't see," Kudo admitted, his head bowed in supplication. "After we lost Kishiro, things started to move awfully fast."

"Lost Kishiro?" Grant mused. "Let's start with what happened to him."

"He was drowned in a pool of water, pulled under," Kudo explained. "I saw him struggling, heard him screaming, but I couldn't reach him in time."

Grant took in the empty courtyard in a glance, searching the gaps between the cobblestones for signs of water. There was nothing; it was dry as a bone now. The color of bone, too, as it happened. "Where did the water go?"

Rosalia was crouching, running her fingers along the cobbles, the dog sniffing at the air over her shoulder. "There's no drainage system," Rosalia said. "Not even any gaps within the grouting that I can see. This may look like stone, Grant, but I don't think it is. It's something more than that."

"Ullikummis?" Grant asked, the name a question. Ullikummis had demonstrated that he could control stone, and he had been the major thorn in Cerberus's side these past few months. While it was dangerous to assume he was behind everything the warriors faced, it was also a reasonable proposition to consider.

Still running her index finger between the cobblestones, Rosalia looked perplexed. "Rocks, yes—but water? That doesn't seem to be his style, Magistrate."

Kudo led Grant over to the part of the open court-yard where Kishiro had been dragged under water. "My brother disappeared here," he explained, toeing it with his boot in a wide circle.

Grant looked at the area, noticing straight away that it was flat, other than the natural protrusions that the cobbles created. Were they really cobbles? There was definitely no space for a pool deep enough to drag a man under. "It makes no sense," he said softly, speaking his thoughts aloud.

Still tracing her fingers along the grouting between the cobbles, Rosalia spoke up once more. "There's a slope," she said. "It's subtle but it's there. Water can move fast, Grant—with another power behind it, it could run away from an area like this in the space of a few seconds, maybe less."

"Doesn't explain the pool," Grant grumbled.

"They all disappeared together," Rosalia reminded him. "There were five of these water creatures but when I hit your one with electricity they all went poof."

"So they're connected," Grant agreed. "It's not five creatures we're facing, it's one."

"Like fingers on a hand," Rosalia proposed.

"Or puppets," Grant mused. "Mannequins. A skilled puppeteer can operate more than one puppet at the same time, bringing to it the illusion of life."

"What, you think someone's controlling these things? Giving them instructions?" Rosalia asked.

Grant nodded in reply. "They weren't predators," he said. "They came for us the way the old sec men would come in the villes, either driving strangers away or killing them."

"Or a kidnapping," Rosalia suggested.

Rosalia's dog whined as she stood, and she tickled

it behind the ears affectionately for a moment. "It's okay," she said to console it. "Danger's passed for now."

Grant looked around the courtyard again, peering up at the moon overhead and pondering just what to do next. "If they are guards," he suggested, "then there's a chance they took Domi and Kishiro in for questioning or whatever."

Belying his usual air of tranquility, Kudo appeared to jump just slightly. "Do you really think so?"

Grant brought his hand up to hush the conversation as he engaged his Commtact. "Domi?" he called. "Come in, Domi. Do you read?"

Grant waited for Domi to respond. Their Commtacts were linked, making this the simplest manner in which to check on her. He waited briefly before trying her again, but the result was the same both times—no reply.

Across the courtyard, Rosalia plucked Kishiro's discarded *katana* from the ground, taking care not to touch its razor-keen edge as she pushed it through her belt. While her competence with firearms was remarkable, Rosalia was far more at home with an edged weapon, knives and swords her specialities. Though she had several knives secreted throughout her clothing, she hadn't brought a sword on this mission herself. Right now, however, this one would do just fine.

Grant spoke into his Commtact, keeping his voice low. The unit itself would boost his words, so there was no need to raise his voice and attract any unnecessary attention. "Cerberus, this is Grant. Do you read? Over."

After a momentary pause Donald Bry's familiar voice reported back over Grant's Commtact, asking for an update.

"We had a little excitement," Grant said with deliberate vagueness, "and I lost track of Domi in the process. Can you locate her from your end?"

"This sounds serious, Grant," Bry replied thoughtfully. "What happened?"

"We're not sure yet," Grant explained. "Let's not worry Lakesh unduly. He has more than enough on his plate there already right now."

AT THE TEMPORARY CERBERUS facility on the Pacific shore, Donald Bry peered up guiltily from his computer terminal to where Lakesh was talking with Mariah Falk and Reba DeFore about the medical implications of Edwards's condition. He was speaking into a headset, so Lakesh couldn't hear both sides of the discussion.

"Is that Grant?" Lakesh asked, noticing Bry speaking into the Commtact's headset.

"Yes, sir, I'm just bringing up some data for him now," Bry confirmed.

Lakesh held his hand up, keeping his voice low. "For now, Donald, let's not tell Grant that Kane is out in the field. The two have been through a lot together, but I wouldn't want to worry Grant unduly."

Bry nodded, barely concealing the smile that threatened to burst to life on his features. It seemed that right now everyone wanted to protect everyone else from something.

After a moment Bry tracked down Domi's transponder signal on his telemetry readout.

"GRANT?" BRY'S VOICE came over the Commtact. "I've found her. She's about four miles from your current location. You need to head into the city itself, toward the river. By my estimate, she seems to be close to the eastern side, near the center. I'll patch through a beacon signal for you, which will register...like this."

Standing in the courtyard, Grant heard a very low pulse in his ear, a single bleep so low as to be almost unconscious.

"When you get nearer, the clicks will become more frequent," Bry explained. "Let me know if it becomes a distraction."

"Thanks, Donald," Grant acknowledged. "Will do."

With that, Grant closed down the communication and began striding from the courtyard, his mismatched partners in tow. "Domi's alive," he told them shortly, "which bodes well for Kishiro. Even money they're being held together, at least for now. The sooner we trace them, the less chance there is they'll have been split up."

Hurrying along at Grant's heels, Kudo nodded once in gratitude. "Thank you, friend Grant," he said. "We must hope that fate is with us."

"Hoping sounds about right," Grant grumbled. "We have a long march ahead of us—four miles across town—and I don't want to get sloshed, so let's avoid bumping into any more of the water babies if we can help it."

Together, Grant, Kudo and Rosalia hurried urgently through the streets of the dragon city, with Rosalia's dog scampering along behind her at a fast trot.

BLACK AND RED—playing cards on a table.

The two colors whirled in front of Domi's eyes, but no matter how hard she tried she couldn't seem to make sense of them, couldn't remember how the game was played.

As swiftly as it had started, the whirling stopped and in its place was nothingness, a soft blackness that might have come from the two colors as they coalesced. Domi peered into that inky nothingness for a long while, trying to recall what had gone before.

She had been attacked, along with her teammates in the courtyard. Finally, she had turned on her attacker, its liquid form like a fractured mirror glistening in the silvery moonlight. And then…

Domi felt the bile surge up her esophagus in a violent rush, the aching clench in her belly, and suddenly her eyes were open and she was vomiting, a tasteless, watery gush blurting from her open mouth before she even had time to think. All she could see were the dark tiles, her face just inches from them as her watery expulsion surged out in front of her, pooling on the tiles, colorless but with a faint smell like brine. Domi shuddered and heaved again, another mouthful of the salty vomit bursting from her mouth, her belly clenched like a fist, forcing her to remain doubled over, lying on that cold floor. The watery vomit washed across the slick, black tiles, and Domi tasted the bitter tang of stomach acid as the last of the vomit drooled out of her, leaving her ribs aching, her stomach shaking, her throat burning.

All around her, the dark tiles stretched off away from her face. They were cold to the touch, and the room—for it was a room, she could tell that immediately from the lack of motion in the wind currents—stretched off, layered with them, the lighting reflecting from their surface in thin white strips. She was cold, too, cold and damp, her scalp wet, her hair heavy with water. She could hear the sounds of dripping coming from nearby, a constant *plop-plop-plop* rattling from several directions at once.

She pushed herself up, every part of her aching, her hands stinging with pins and needles when she pushed them against the hard floor. Her circulation felt poor, her extremities numb—either from the vomit or from the coldness of the room, she couldn't tell which. Perhaps something else, too, the way she had come here, the journey.

It had been like a rollercoaster ride, she remembered then, a rollercoaster ride through a swimming pool. The water had pressed all around her, swirling in a freezing hug, like being held in an icy fist. She remembered its sound against her ears, and when she listened now she could still hear the faint sound of the waves, as if their echo had become trapped in the seashell swirls of her chalk-white ears.

It felt a little as if she had traveled through a broken mat-trans, the journey of discorporality resulting in body sickness when she had been reconstructed. It wasn't the first time Domi had experienced that with a mat-trans; and while she couldn't be sure, this felt similar enough for her to suspect that's what the water thing had been.

But where was she?

There came a groan behind her, and Domi instinctively reached for the holstered gun at the small of her back even as she turned to face the noise. Her gun was missing. She ran her fingers along the waistband of her pants, but it wasn't there. She couldn't feel its familiar weight, either, now that she thought about it.

The light came from above in thin strips, bright as lightning but only a quarter-inch wide and six inches long. Peering up at the ceiling was like looking through a venetian blind.

The room, like the lighting, was narrow with slanting edges where the walls met the floor and ceiling. The walls and ceiling seemed to be made of a glossy, ash-dark substance, like plastic or coral, and there was an unpleasant dampness to the air, making it feel heavy. The room's proportions reminded Domi of a pressure chamber used by divers. That, too, may have been an effect of the method with which she had been transported here, the racing water still primary on her mind.

Automatically, Domi's hand was at her leg, clawing aside the damp material of her pants where it stuck to her, pulling the combat knife she kept stored in a sheath at her ankle.

Lying across the room, slumped against one of the shimmering wet walls, was Kishiro. He lay at an awkward angle, Domi saw, as if washed-up debris on a beach. It was he who had groaned.

"Kishiro?" Domi whispered, the words making her sore throat burn all the more.

The Tigers of Heaven warrior turned, his head swaying unsteadily as if it was a tethered balloon in the breeze.

"Kishiro, it's me," Domi continued as she scrabbled across the tiles toward him. "It's Domi."

Kishiro groaned again, looking at her as if through sleep. "Domi," he spluttered, the single word sounding breathy with the strain.

"You have any idea where we are, cowboy?" Domi asked, glancing behind him, searching for a door.

"I…" Kishiro began. "I…"

"Forget it," Domi instructed gently. "You were as out of it as I was, I guess. Take your time. It's okay."

As Domi spoke, she felt a strange crackling in the air, subtle, like a change in polarity, and then the lights flickered on behind her. She turned and saw to her surprise that the chamber was longer than she had first suspected. She had initially taken the darkness there for a wall, but realized now that the chamber was lit with such precision that its inhabitant could only see the section he or she was required to.

Lying there, head against his outstretched arm, lay the now-familiar figure of Hassood, his eyes closed, dusky face clenched in pain. Domi recognized him from the footage on the radio transmission unit that she had watched with Grant and the others, and she scampered across the chamber to where the man lay, still holding the knife in one hand, nudging him with a light touch. He was breathing, she saw, but slowly. He appeared unconscious, well out of it.

"Hassood?" she hissed. "Hassood, wake up. I'm a friend, from Cerberus. Wake up."

In response, Hassood groaned and rolled away from Domi's light but insistent prodding, swatting at the air while still asleep.

Vexation furrowing her brow, Domi turned back to Kishiro where he sat behind her, propped against the curving bank of the wall. Her eyes searched over him swiftly. "Kishiro? You have any weapons?" she whispered, keeping her voice low.

Moving slowly, almost like a man under water, Kishiro grasped for his *katana,* only to find the scabbard empty. His hand moved around under the low skirt of his shirt, reaching behind and to the other side, and a smile crossed his features. He nodded to Domi. "My *katana* is missing but I still have my *wakizashi*."

The *wakizashi* was a shorter blade traditionally carried by samurai alongside the *katana*. Not all of the Tigers of Heaven carried them, for they were often considered to be ornamental rather than practical, their short length making them more akin to a knife than a sword. Still, they could be turned to combat if necessary, their blades kept as sharp as the *katana*.

"Maybe whoever put us in here didn't disarm us," Domi told him, keeping her voice low, "but we need to get out of here quickly."

"Where are we?" Kishiro asked.

"That's a good question," Domi told him with a tight smile. She sniffed at the air; it was filtered, but there was a dampness to it, too. "Feels like we're under ground maybe. I can't tell for sure."

As the two mismatched figures spoke, Domi became aware of a change in the lighting out of the corner of her eye. She turned in that direction, scanning the ceiling, the walls. As she watched, the dark wall opposite Hassood began to lighten, its ash color draining away to be replaced by what appeared to be a glowing square, roughly three feet up from the floor and becoming larger as it filled the wall. Light glowed from the square, becoming stronger as the opacity of the wall disappeared entirely, leaving the three-foot-square block clear like a window.

Domi padded toward the square on silent tread, determined to get a better look. As the dull color of the wall drained away, Domi saw that the square seemed to look into another room, with coral-like arches and steps disappearing off into the distance, seating all around. She realized in a moment what the square was—a video screen, or perhaps a window into the next room. The definition was so clear, it could almost be a hole in the wall itself.

Domi examined the room she could see within the square, feeling the coolness radiating from its glassy surface. It appeared empty, and her view remained fixed, which meant it was either a single camera or, as she had suspected, a window that had previously been covered by some unknowable technological trick, perhaps something as simple as a two-way mirror. There were seats there, arranged to face the jutting walls that ran across the farthest reach of her view. The chairs were shaped like champagne glasses, with thin stems beneath the narrow seats, swirling down to the tiled floor in subtle twisting plaits. The walls contained what appeared to be display units, something like the computer terminals used by Cerberus, and there were small glowing pods scattered throughout the ash-colored walls. The pods glowed a putrid yellow like a lizard's eyes, keeping the room in a dusklike luminance. Beyond that, Domi saw darkness, something twinkling subtly within it.

Past the chairs, Domi saw a stairwell reaching upward beyond the level granted by the video feed. Carved in some kind of gray-black, bonelike substance, the grand stairwell looked wide enough to accommodate a SandCat, and it turned in on itself in a languid spiral like the dizzy path of a leaf in fall. There were icy columns there, thin as the bars on a prison window, shimmering in the darkness, just out of sight.

Domi stepped closer, bringing herself to within three inches of the faintly glowing square, her eyes narrowing as she peered into the room in the square. A clattering noise seemed to come from beyond, the sound soft and regular, *clickety-clack, clickety-clack, clickety-clack*. Close up, she could see that the panel seemed to be made of glass, her own pale reflection visible there like a ghost standing in the darkness of the room beyond.

Warily, Domi reached for the glass, touching it first with the hilt of her combat knife, a savage-looking nine-inch weapon with a serrated edge, her sole memento from the six months she had spent as a sex slave in the Tartarus Pits of Cobaltville. As a rule, Domi had little patience for keepsakes. Her Outlands life had been a daily struggle, and one she preferred to forget. However, the knife itself had come to represent something of her triumph over adversity, and as such she invested in it more value than it truly deserved, telling herself, perhaps, that a good knife was hard to find. She had very nearly lost this blade during a tree-top battle less than a week ago, out in the vicinity of Luilekkerville, but it had been recovered by Kane's team when they had come to her assistance.

The knife's scarred hilt tapped against the glass with a dull thud, eliciting a curtailed sound with no discernible reverberation. Solid then, not hollow as she had hoped. That meant the glass of the screen was likely several inches thick, or two panes had been overlaid in the manner of insulated glazing. She peered again into the glass, searching for the telltale double image that generally flared in the reflections, but there was no indication of it.

Without really noticing it, Domi realized that the noise from the screen had become louder, that regular *clickety-clack* sound like an approaching locomotive or the chatter of an insect's scraping legs. What was it?

She tentatively touched her fingers to the glass, feeling the coldness against their tips before they were even pressed against it. The transparent pane was freezing, and it felt damp. As she held her hand there, water trickled across the ridges of her fingers, cool droplets filling in the hollows at the base of her fingernails. More water, she mentally cursed.

Behind her, the dripping became more insistent, and Domi turned irritably, searching for its source. Something glistened on the far wall, twinkling beneath the overhead strip lights. It was a tiny stream of trickling water, fracturing as it ran down the wall in thin, crooked streams like bent fingers.

Domi turned back to the glass pane, and almost jumped with shock. Standing there, his face seemingly a mere foot away from hers, was Overlord Enlil of the Annunaki, his lizard's eyes staring at her.

Chapter 15

Enlil watched Domi through the glass that divided them, a cruel sneer on his reptilian lips, his crocodile's eyes sinister, a single vertical slit down the center of each mustard-yellow iris.

"Let us out of here!" Domi shouted at the glass.

Utterly inhuman, Enlil was a truly beautiful creature, imposing but with such an economy and grace to his movements that he seemed almost like something from a dream, something impossible to behold. At his full height, Enlil stood seven feet tall, a crest of spines curving back from the crown of his skull with a metallic glint, like wires of burnished steel. He wore simple clothing—loose, darkly colored breeches that flared at the hips and ended just past his knees, and a bloodred cloak that was cinched at his shoulders with a golden clasp, glowing like sunset despite the lack of light in the room where he stood. Beneath the golden clasp, Enlil remained bare-chested, his lizardlike hide a coppery-rust, the color of bronze washed with blood. The tiny scales there looked like a pattern of metal that had been sewn into his flesh. He stared directly into Domi's crimson eyes, meeting her gaze with his own. "Cerberus," he stated, the word coming like a curse in his eerie, duotonal voice.

"Let us out of here, you sick, sick bastard," Domi snarled, the knife flashing in her hand.

Domi had met Enlil before now, on several occasions, in fact. Oft considered the cruelest of *Tiamat*'s brood, Enlil had been a near-constant thorn in the side of the Cerberus exiles. Initially, Enlil had plagued Kane, Grant, Domi, Lakesh and Brigid Baptiste in his guise as Baron Cobalt, the hybrid ruler of Cobaltville. In subsequent years, Cobalt had assumed other forms, C. W. Thrush and Sam the Imperator among them. Indeed, under the latter form, Enlil had gifted Domi's aging lover, Lakesh, with a new flush of youth, only to cruelly snatch it away with some genetic succubus that ebbed the life out of Lakesh and almost killed him. However, it was in his current and supposed final form that Enlil had proved his most dangerous. Like the other eight members of the Annunaki royal family, Enlil had emerged from a hybrid body when the starship *Tiamat* had reappeared in Earth's orbit, triggering a genetic download that granted the Annunaki yet another incarnation. When they had first walked the Earth, the Annunaki had been revered as gods by the primitive humans who inhabited the planet; in fact, that godly reverence had also been granted to their slave caste, the Igigi, such was the splendor attached to all things Annunaki—a race whose very slaves were gods.

Enlil and his siblings had reemerged with the *Tiamat* download to take control of the Earth in the twenty-third century. However, they had soon reverted to type, their petty jealousies turning them against one another. So it was that in squabbles with his family, the royal bloodline of the Annunaki, Enlil and his brethren had laid waste to several of the nine baronies of America, causing massive upheaval to the continent and the world beyond.

It had been a while since Domi had last encountered

Enlil, however, and there had been some hope that the would-be world tyrant was finally dead. However, Domi knew all too well the Annunaki's penchant for sidestepping their seeming inevitable demise; seeing him now was a shock, but Domi tamped down her surprise as she faced Enlil.

The overlord stared at her, those eerie lizard-slit eyes seeming to both pierce her and stare through her, as if she was as insignificant to him as a gnat buzzing around his head. And then he spoke once more, the words chiming like the tolling of brass bells, a king's voice in a world ill prepared for such brilliance. "You will be out of there soon enough, apekin," Enlil said, "and more yet, you will be eternally grateful to me for your release. For that release shall be a thing of beauty, child, the release of the butterfly from its cocoon."

"Never!" Domi screamed. Angrily, she lunged at the screen with her knife, driving its point at the glass. The point hit the screen and bounced back with such force that Domi staggered back, too, dropping the blade.

At the glass panel, Enlil began to laugh. It was a braying, mocking, ugly sound made all the more disturbing by its duotonal nature. Domi glared at him, breathing heavily as water dripped around her from the tiled ceiling of the cell.

"I'll never show you gratitude," she stormed, spitting a gob of saliva at the surface of the glass. "The tables will turn, you'll see. They always do. You're a dead lizard who just doesn't know it yet."

Enlil continued to laugh as he turned away from the screen—be it a camera relay or a pane of glass, Domi still could not be sure. She watched as he strode away, his bloodred cape flaring around him, its heavy hem brushing at his ankles. He was barefoot, she saw now, the flaring breeches coming down just a little way past his knees, the curling clawlike talons of his toenails scraping on the tile floor to produce that *clickety-clack* sound she had heard before.

"When the Annunaki first came to Earth," Enlil said, his back still to the screen, "the apekin here, your ancestors, believed us to be a gift from the heavens. And in a way, we were, for we were the children of Anu and we had traveled from Nibiru to bring light and beauty and all things Annunaki to this poor, pitiful ball of mud.

"But you rejected that gift," Enlil snarled, turning back to face the screen, something small and glowing in his clawed hand. "The apekin began to foster delusions of competence, that they—that you—could manage without your gods. We let that happen, allowing our gift to be forgotten.

"But this time...this time the gift will be absolute," Enlil breathed, his voice barely a whisper now. "This time, there will be no denying its value, and there will be no turning back once it is bestowed upon you."

"You're insane," Domi spit, glaring at Enlil through the screenlike medium that separated them.

As she spoke, Domi felt the chill rise in the air, and Kishiro gasped from off to her side. Domi spun and saw Kishiro being pulled to his feet like a rag doll, water pouring around his form in thin streams like a leaking hose. He was being dragged upward against his will, his teeth clenched as he struggled against whatever power it was that had hold of him.

"What is it?" Domi asked, padding toward him. As she got closer she felt the hair on her head part, blown backward by a powerful wind. She realized then what was happening—Kishiro was being sucked up in a

powerful column of air, pulled up toward the ceiling.
Domi looked up there as Kishiro fought against the
incredible force, and she saw the dark tiles there had
drawn silently back, and water was pouring from the
edges of the gap.

Icy water streamed down Kishiro's body, pouring
like a second skin over him, amassing on the floor in
a pool beneath his feet. The proud warrior seemed to
stand on tiptoe for a moment, his whole body stretched
arrow-straight as he was tugged higher and higher
toward the ceiling. Domi grabbed him but was pushed
back, the coolness of the water icy against her own
flesh, the temperature striking through her like a knife.
She staggered back, feeling the bone-numbing coldness running through her, gritting her teeth against
the sudden shock of pain. Then she looked up and saw
Kishiro disappear through the dark mouth in the ceiling, his athletic form whipping up like a rocket.

"Kishiro!" Domi cried as she lunged for him again.
But already she was too late and she knew it. The
Tigers of Heaven warrior's feet shot past her reaching
hands, water pouring off them like a flowing river, and
Domi instead grabbed for nothing but empty air. The
water sluiced across her hands and forearms, so cold
it felt boiling hot against her numb flesh. She jerked
her hands back, crying out in agony.

Kishiro was gone. Above, the hole in the ceiling
oozed closed, coming together like pursing lips before
disappearing entirely, leaving just a bulbous ridge
where it had been.

Domi spun on her heel, her crimson eyes twinkling
like rubies as they searched the strange cell-like room.
Hassood still lay there against the wall, muttering to
himself in delirium. And over by the window screen,

Enlil was watching the room with casual disinterest, the vertical splits of his irises fixed on the middle distance as if in thought.

An eerie shudder ran up Domi's spine as, finally, she recognized that look in Enlil's face. She had seen it time and again in the hallowed halls of the Cerberus redoubt, where the science-brains worked hard on their many and varied projects, learning new applications for the interphaser, testing new theories for the viral drugs that kept their people alive in the radioactive wastes between the villes. It was the look they gave to lab animals as they watched the results of their experiments, considered how next to toy with them to increase their learning.

Domi knew then, without doubt, that she and Hassood and Kishiro—and who knew how many others— were nothing more than laboratory animals to Enlil, there to be experimented on and discarded as necessary, there to die for his knowledge and his whim.

GRANT, KUDO AND ROSALIA hurried along the empty streets of the dragon-shaped city, their movements echoing down the chasmlike labyrinthine alleyways that made up the eerie settlement. Grant remained in touch with Brewster Philboyd and Donald Bry at the temporary Cerberus ops center, taking directions whenever they got turned around in the nightmarish streets. Brewster Philboyd could not achieve any kind of floor plan; indeed the phenomenal city seemed impervious to satellite scan, the details ever changing on screen. All he could do was guide Grant toward the blip of Domi's transponder and advise him if he saw that his team was heading off course.

It was a laborious process, trying to find their way

through those snakelike streets between the white towers glistening in the moonlight. Grant set a brisk pace, guided by the internal beacon in his ear, and the others kept up with him without complaint. But eventually, Rosalia suggested they stop. They had covered two and a half miles eastward, probably closer to twice that with the way the streets kept doubling back on themselves like coiled springs. And the nature of the streets, with their hard surfaces and lack of the signs of human habitation, were disconcerting, encouraging a rising sense of unease in all three members of the field team. There were buildings but no doors. Doorways that opened only onto recessed walls. It was like something from a nightmare, with all the logic of dreams.

"Let's stop for five minutes," Rosalia said as they reached another of the oppressive little courtyards that appeared frequently among the streets. "Catch our breaths and let the dog do his business."

Beside her, Rosalia's scruffy mutt whimpered hopefully as it stared at her with pale eyes before scurrying off to relieve itself by one of the pillars, encouraged there with a simple flick of Rosalia's wrist.

Automatically, Kudo took up a guard position at one of the multitude of narrow entries to the courtyard. Leaning against what looked to be a series of rough stone steps, made from some pale stone like chalk, Kudo took the time to attend to his sword. The *katana* had taken a few knocks during the fight with the water creatures, and Kudo used a portable cleaning kit to oil and cleanse the blade.

"Hell of a place," Grant grumbled, peering around at the towering buildings that clawed their way toward the silver crescent mirror of the moon. The red laser light had stopped firing into the sky, or at least they hadn't seen it fire for almost an hour, and nocturnal birds, owls and sand-colored nighthawks swooped around up in the higher echelons of the abandoned city.

Rosalia nodded her agreement as she perched on the edge of what appeared to be a water trough, the kind used for horses, a horizontal stone bar running at a little above waist height. As she rested against it, her hand scratched across its white surface and caught in a ridge there. Idly, she ran her slender hand along the ridge, working at it with slim fingers.

"According to Brewster," Grant related to his companions, "we're still about two miles out. The location of Domi's tracker hasn't moved since Bry last checked it, so she's definitely settled somewhere. Still can't raise her, though. Something's blocking the signal."

"Technology, huh?" Rosalia said with an resigned shrug. "What would that be, that can block your communications devices like that?"

Grant shook his head. "There's a lot of mineral deposits around here. Could be a localized pocket blocking the signal. Might be radiation off that laser cannon. Could be about a hundred other things. She might just be too far belowground for the signal to penetrate."

Rosalia sat watching Grant without comment, but she was thinking about how these ex-Magistrates—both Grant and his partner Kane—had come to rely so heavily on technology to assist them, with their Commtacts and their mat-trans and their shadow suits. There was nothing wrong with technology in its place, Rosalia considered, but it could be conversely limiting if you became reliant on it. Both Mags had been ignorant of the ways the gangs communicated in the Outlands, utterly unaware of the network of secret signals and hidden signposts that gang members like herself used to pass on information and to mark out their territories. Such information had been crucial to her the first time she had met with Grant, when he had chased after her across the desert of the West Coast of America. Still, despite being outnumbered and in the lair of the enemy, Grant had conducted himself with aplomb, triumphing over greater odds to cage a primal beast whose only expression was violence. For that, at least, Rosalia admired the man.

As she thought these things, Rosalia's fingers idly stroked the ridges in the stonework of the water trough, her nails running along the cracks without conscious thought. Suddenly, her dark eyes widened, and she looked down to where her hand was running across the creamy white stonework. She peered at it intensely, running her slender fingers more carefully across the bumps and ridges as the moonlight painted itself across it with delicate brushstrokes.

Then Rosalia turned back to Grant where the man stood a few feet away discussing strategy with Brewster Philboyd via the Commtact link.

"Bone," Rosalia said as Grant caught her eye. "It's bone. I'm sitting on bone."

Grant's brows furrowed as he heard her, and he swiftly cut the communication with Philboyd, assuring the man he'd contact him the second he needed his help.

"What's that you said?" Grant asked, taking a step toward Rosalia as her dog trotted over from the shadows.

Rosalia flicked her dark ponytail back over her shoulder as she indicated the troughlike structure she had perched on. "I think it's bone," she said.

Grant peered at her warily, still unsure whether he

could really trust this mercenary whom Kane had absorbed into their group. Then he sank down on his haunches and looked more closely at the trough, running his hand along its side. "How can you tell?" he asked.

"It's cold out here," Rosalia said. "No real cloud cover, desert night. If this was stone, it would be colder. And look—look how the ridges work."

Grant ran his hand over the white surface, suppressing the shudder that suddenly ran up his spine. The ridges ran parallel, curving slightly but all of them running lengthwise.

"This is something grown," Rosalia said. "Something organic. We are standing in an ossuary, a bone palace."

She stood then, looking about her at the buildings that towered all around them, at the way the windows and doors seemed to be boarded up with chalky brickwork or wood. Beside her, Grant stood, too, eyeing the buildings with growing concern. "You think…?" he began, and Rosalia nodded.

"We've assumed this whole place was built of stone," she said, "because that's how villes are built. Not one of us looked closely—looked properly—at these structures.

"There are gradations, of course, but the whole settlement is constructed of the same materials, all of it differing shades of cream. The moonlight lies to our eyes. This isn't stone, it's bone. We're in something that's grown. Grown and died."

"A skeleton," Grant said quietly, awe in his voice. "This empty ville covers over seven square miles. If it's a skeleton, we're talking about a heck of a beastie."

"A dragon," Rosalia stated bluntly.

Grant nodded unhappily, like a man who had discovered that the weight of the world was suddenly balanced on his shoulders. "A seven-mile-wide dragon? Someone would have seen it land, surely."

Rosalia looked pensive. "What if it didn't land? What if it…burrowed up from the surface or, I don't know, what if someone placed it here using an interphaser or similar? Possible?"

"Anything's possible," Grant agreed cagily. "If working with Cerberus has taught me one thing, it's that."

Kudo had overheard the conversation from his post, and he looked to Grant with confusion written across his face. "What should we do, Grant? Turn back?"

"No, let's keep moving," Grant decided. "I'm liking this less and less, and I sure don't want to run into whatever killed this thing and left the carcass out here for us to walk through. Let's just find Domi and Kishiro and get the hell out of here."

Rosalia nodded. "Agreed."

IN THE CURVED-WALLED CELL, Domi was still trying to put everything together, even while Enlil continued to tap at whatever tech was hidden just beneath the screen looking in. Far from being sentient creatures, Domi had now concluded that the water figures had been some kind of mat-trans, opening a quantum window through the ether to transport her, Kishiro and Hassood through space so that they could rematerialize within this cell, wherever it was. A walking mat-trans seemed both insane and eminently logical to Domi. Yet less than a week before, she had faced the *bruja,* a Latin American witch who had produced a magic blanket that could be used to anchor an interphaser, plucking an unwary user out of quantum space like a cross-dimensional magnet. And now, these matter-transmitters, be they interphasers or something else, could walk, tracking down and trapping their prey before zapping them to their destination. In some perverse way, it all made sense.

Though Domi could not possibly know it, Enlil had developed this system of transportation as a means to grab humans unawares, plucking them from their locations with pinpoint accuracy. The system used water because of its natural property of attraction. For example, raindrops on a cold windowpane will land separately but be drawn together, and the same is true for the remaining droplets of water in an empty bathtub. Water attracts more water, pulling together. Although limited in reach, the water-based interphaser worked via the same principle, drawn almost magnetically to the water within a person's body to engage in the transfer of matter.

Beyond the cell, out in the room that could be seen within the ice-cold window, Domi watched as Kishiro was dragged to the farthest wall. He was pulled along against his will, almost as if he was a bug trapped in the swirling bathwater as it rushed down the drain. The warrior's lips were pulled back and his teeth grit as he fought against that impossible force dragging him across the low-lit room.

Kishiro was drawn past Enlil where he worked at the console, tapping out a pattern with his clawlike hand, a pattern that held no meaning to Domi. She tried to make sense of it, but it just appeared random and she had the suspicion that the movement of Enlil's fingers was just one part of the programming involved, another no doubt coming from his cerebellum. Domi

watched impotently as Kishiro was pushed up against
the far wall. As she watched, twin bars whipped from
a lip in the wall, firing down from ceiling to floor like
rockets. The bars sparkled, and Domi realized they,
too, were made of some kind of liquid.

Kishiro strained against the bars, and Domi heard
him spit a curse at Enlil. She added her own voice to
the man's, insisting that Enlil let him go.

Enlil turned, and Domi saw the alligator smile that
carved a line across his hideous, reptilian face. "No,"
he said, his eyes meeting with hers. "You shall watch
this, for it is something you need to learn. The Annunaki are your masters. We have always been your masters. You Cerberus fools have had the temerity to stand
against me and my siblings for too long, like termites
trying to change the course of a mighty river. You have
determined to be a part of this, creating conflict where
the Annunaki brought harmony. So now you shall be a
part of it, a part so entrenched within the system that
you shall never be free again.

"Welcome to your future, Domi apekin. Welcome
to the end of humanity."

As he spoke those final words, Enlil gestured with
his clawed hand to something at the control panel
behind him. Domi watched as a bank of amber lights
sprang into life in a sequence of rising, curving, vertical bars, each of them approximately a foot across. The
lit bars illuminated the area by the wide stairwell, and
Domi saw several other people locked there in similar
shimmering bars, one reaching across their chest like
a safety bar on an old fairground ride. These ones were
strangers, but still Domi gasped, unable to stifle her
horror. The strangers were three men and two women,
all of them delirious or sleeping, their heads lolling at

tired angles where they had been held against the wall for so long. They wore simple clothes, and one of the women looked to be well into her sixties, a tangle of gray hair spurting from her head like wire wool. Beside her, three lads in their teens, each thin with hunger, with the similar features of close relatives. They were in fact Mahmett, Yasseft and Panenk. Next to them was a Western-looking woman with long blond hair that fell past her breasts.

Domi felt a deep thrumming beneath her feet then, like a low bass note, too low to be audible, trembling through her body like an earth tremor. She felt it rise through her, rocking her rib cage, vibrating her breastbone. Beside her, a few feet from where Domi stood, Hassood finally woke, yelping in surprise as the tremor took hold of the room.

The Arab blurted something in his own language, and Domi's Commtact automatically translated it so that she could understand, performing the task in real time:

"What is going on? Where am I?"

"Calm down," Domi instructed, her tone brooking no argument.

"Get away from me, demon," Hassood spit in his own tongue, clawing back to the curved wall that was just a few inches behind him, backing away from Domi with his eyes wide in fear.

"I'm not a demon," Domi told him, holding her hands out to show she meant him no harm.

Hassood's eyes fixed on the vicious combat blade in her pale right hand, and he screeched in fear, his body trembling. Seeing this, Domi crouched, slowly and gently, and placed the blade on the floor.

"I'm not going to hurt you," she said in English.

"Ghost girl," Hassood replied, still speaking in his own tongue, the translation sounding ludicrous to Domi's ear.

"My name's Domi," Domi explained. "I'm from Cerberus. You spoke to my partner Grant. I'm not going to hurt you, just calm down."

Hassood eyed her fearfully, his gaze twitching to take in the knife blade she had left on the floor at her feet. "Cerberus," he repeated, emphasizing the word as though it was a question.

Domi nodded once, briefly. "Yeah. We're in a lot of trouble just now, and I need to see what's going on." With that, she turned to look through the scanner or window, she still couldn't tell which.

Hassood leaped forward, making a grab for the discarded knife by Domi's foot. Without turning, she moved her booted heel, placing it flatly but firmly on the handle of the weapon. "The knife stays where it is," she warned.

Things had changed in the room beyond. Domi watched in anguish as Kishiro shook behind the amber bar that held his body upright like a safety barrier. His mouth was open wide, head tilted back in silent scream as some force, some power, drilled through him. Domi could not tell what it was, there wasn't even a hint of what had gripped the brave Tiger of Heaven. But whatever it was, it was clear that the same power was pummeling through the other people locked against the wall between those icy bars.

Domi watched, her hands pressed to that freezing cold screen, water running down her fingers as the people struggled against whatever power had them in its grip. Abruptly, there was a tearing sound from the speaker above the screen and Domi saw that the top on the older woman was ripped at the shoulder seam, tearing away even as she struggled. Then Domi saw the same thing happening to the young man beside her, his breeches ripping apart along the seams, too. Kishiro's top strained across his pectorals, then split down the center as if he had become too big to fit in it.

The light flickered, and Domi was very aware that the thrumming was becoming more powerful, shaking her as she pushed against the screen to get a closer look at the inexplicable horror occurring there. For a long moment, the bars of amber light winked out, and all Domi could feel was the beat running through her, as well as her own heart pounding its frantic tarantella against her chest.

Like a lightning strike, the lights flickered back to life, winking again as more power shook the chamber. And then Domi saw it, saw the first hint of the change in the flickering bars of light. Kishiro's face and body had changed, a hardness to them that Domi had never seen before. It was like staring into the face of a crocodile.

Chapter 16

The once familiar lines of the Cerberus cafeteria glowed with the audacity of the sun itself, shimmering across Kane's vision with a vibrancy he thought reserved only for dreams. He turned his head left and right, feeling how heavy it seemed, how solid. The colors swirled in front of him, the images multiplying and splitting as his point of reference moved, leaving a stuttering trail that took a second or more to catch up to the present. He had gone from near blindness to this, and whatever *this* was, it was so different, so radically advanced from what he had come to know as vision, that it made him vertiginous.

He slumped forward in his seat, feeling the solidity of the table in front of him as he struck it with his chest. The table had a white plastic covering over its wood and, like everything else in the redoubt, it had been assaulted by the creeping rocks, their clawing tendrils spread across it as if to choke the life from its static form. Kane looked at that whiteness now, with its dark streaks of stone, and yet he saw a rainbow of color, a split-prism effect as the whiteness sprouted from the table in a blaze of furious light.

"What have you done to me?" Kane muttered, the words spilling from his mouth and bringing with them the sense that he might vomit. Kane held it back, gritting his teeth and expelling short, sharp breaths through his nostrils. "Balam? What did you do?"

"Keep breathing, Kane," Balam advised, his voice much closer than Kane expected. "The disorientation will pass."

"Dammit all, Balam," Kane spat, "explain this to me, and I mean now." As he spoke, Kane lifted his head and nauseously watched as the world careened around him. Light sparkled across his sight with all the colors of the spectrum, turning the familiar unfamiliar, making Balam in front of him appear to be wreathed in a heavenly glow. Had his world up until now been black and white? Was this color? True color? Kane narrowed his eyes, trying to filter out the brightness, but the effect was much the same. He couldn't tolerate it much longer. The sensation of movement yanked at his innards, pulling at his stomach, pulling the beans and flatbread he had just consumed back up his gullet. Suddenly, Kane tasted the sourness of sick in the back of his throat, then it filled his mouth.

"Balam," he said again as he spit the watery dew between dry lips, muttering the name this time.

"Breathe," Balam said in response.

Unmoving, Kane stared down at the surface of the table, waiting for the numerous afterimages to coalesce and become one image, one straight picture that he could comprehend. He swallowed hard, pushing down the vomit that had threatened to spew from him, feeling his mouth contract at its taste. Finally the world stopped moving, the bright colors settled, poised like neon strips in front of his eyes.

"What did you do?" Kane asked, his words quiet, his eyes still fixed on the cafeteria table as if afraid to look up.

"I have formed a telepathic link," Balam said in his careful, measured tone. "You can 'see,' in a manner, via the bond between us now, thus alleviating you of your blindness."

Kane shook his head, saw the fierce colors in front of him swirl as the lines of the table became an oil-on-water blur once more. Instantly he regretted moving. "I can't live like this," he murmured. "I can't operate, can't function."

Balam reached for Kane once more, clamping the six spindly digits of his hand reassuringly over Kane's own. "Be patient, my friend," he said. "Let it come to you. The link is by no means perfect. It must find its natural level."

Kane felt his eyes widen as he looked around him, saw the rainbow swirl coalesce into the fixed image of the cafeteria once more, its stone-veined arches and dirty walls emerging again amid the racing lights. "Is this…?" he began, and stopped.

"What?" Balam asked, encouragingly.

"Is this how you see?"

The tiny trace of a smile crossed Balam's features for a moment, indulging Kane like a doting grandparent will a child. "You have never questioned how it is that you see," he said, "in relation to how other creatures see. The honey bee, for instance, sees far into the infrared scale, perceiving flowers far differently to the way a human's eyes would."

"And so this…?" Kane began, tamping down the sense of nausea swilling in his gut.

"This is a mental link," Balam explained. "I'll fine-tune it as best as I am able, but you cannot expect it to be the same as the sight you would receive from your own eyes. Think of it as literally a different perspective on your world."

Kane smiled irritably. "That's cute, but I can't function like this, Balam. I can't go into a combat situation if this is what I'm seeing. And you're in no state to defend us."

"You came here," Balam countered, "and you were blind."

"Partially sighted," Kane corrected defensively.

"The Annunaki have played tricks on you from the very beginning," Balam said, ignoring Kane's response. "They are multidimensional beings, their wars, their grievances, fought across many levels, in many ways. And yet you saw them, these aliens to your world, like you, like actors on a stage dressed in fright masks and monster suits. Humans in everything but appearance. And yet you never questioned this."

"What are you saying?" Kane asked.

"This is the Godwar, Kane," Balam told him. "This is how it is fought, not with heat rays and bullets, but with the mind, with perception. Ullikummis wounded you in a way that he hadn't intended, burying a chunk of his own self in your ocular nerve. That chunk is feeding your senses now, obliterating your vision but putting other things in its place. Special things."

Listening to the words, Kane nodded, recalling the weird, dreamlike visions he had been having each time he accessed the interphase jump. This fleck of Ullikummis had been playing the stone god's memories across his ocular nerve like a strip of film, firing those memories directly into the part of his brain that dealt with vision, coloring them with sounds and sensations to make them feel real. The interphaser opened a quantum window, deconstructing and reconstruct-

ing a person in a fraction of a second as it sent them
blasting between two distant geographic points. Each
reconstruction, Kane realized, meant the stone fleck
rebonded with him, reengaged and belched its aliens
memories into his mind.

"The Annunaki are beautiful beings," Balam continued, "multifaceted, crossing dimensions you cannot
hope to comprehend. Their wars are fought on many
planes at once, the nature of their games intersect only
tangentially with Earth and its holding pen of stars.
What you have seen is only a sliver of what the battle
is."

Kane listened, thinking back to a mythical time
in the distant past, a time he had visited with Brigid
Baptiste via a memory trap created by the Igigi, the
Annunaki's slaves. While in that functional memory,
Kane had seen the Annunaki the way the Igigi perceived them. They had seemed beautiful, just as
Balam was telling him, vibrant shining things that
appeared so much more real than the world around
them, color things amid a landscape of gray. They
had seemed every bit as vibrant there as this room
was now, seen through Balam's telepathic link. But
when Kane had faced Overlords Enlil, Marduk and
the others in his role as Cerberus rebel, the Annunaki
had been curiously ordinary. Yes, they were stronger,
faster, supremely devious, but they were—what?—
the thing that Balam called them. Actors on a stage?
People dressed in masks and costumes in some hokey
performance designed for children? Had Kane and his
companions been taken in by a performance, a show
designed to entertain the feeble-minded? Was that all
humans were to them—children?

Kane looked around him, studying Balam through

the unnerving medium of the mental eye, watching the way the light shone around him as if emanating from his flesh. His scabbed chest wound looked vibrant, bright, the stuff of life. The walls behind him blurred and settled as Kane shifted his vision, doubling and tripling for an instant before the accordion image closed like the shutters at the Cerberus armory. Kane's stomach lurched again, threatening to upset, for its contents to spill from his mouth. Kane breathed through his nostrils, working past the nausea. Gradually the swirling blast of lights settled, as if his eyes were becoming used to it, as if his brain was adjusting.

"I can track Ninlil," Balam said, using the child Quav's formal name for the first time since their meeting here. "She is my daughter now and we are linked—she cannot be hidden from me. But I cannot retrieve her alone. I shall require help.

"Your help, Kane?" he added, this last as a question.

Kane looked at the gray-skinned ambassador of the First Folk and, to his relief, the image held rigid, became something he could comprehend without wanting to vomit. "Find the girl and we'll find Baptiste," Kane said. "I feel sure of it."

Balam nodded, his great bulb of a head inclining heavily atop his scrawny neck. "Are you feeling better? Yourself again?"

Swaying a little in place, Kane pushed himself up from his seat to stand. "This'll take some getting used to," he admitted, "but it's starting to make sense. This is what it's like, huh? To be you?"

Balam inclined his head delicately to the side in a noncommittal gesture of supplication. "It is what your brain translates," he observed. "What we see depends

The Reader Service—Here's how it works: Accepting your 2 free books and free gift (gift valued at approximately $5.00) places you under no obligation to buy anything. You may keep the books and gift and return the shipping statement marked "cancel". If you do not cancel, about a month later we'll send you 6 additional books and bill you just $31.94* – that's a savings of 24% off the cover price of all 6 books! And there's no extra charge for shipping and handling! You may cancel at any time, but if you choose to continue, every other month we'll send you 6 more books, which you may either purchase at the discount price or return to us and cancel your subscription.

*Terms and prices subject to change without notice. Prices do not include applicable taxes. Sales tax applicable in N.Y. Canadian residents will be charged applicable taxes. Offer not valid in Quebec. Credit or debit balances in a customer's account(s) may be offset by any other outstanding balance owed by or to the customer. Please allow 4 to 6 weeks for delivery. Offer available while quantities last. All orders subject to credit approval. Books received may not be as shown.

▼ If offer card is missing write to: The Reader Service, P.O. Box 1867, Buffalo, NY 14240-1867 or visit www.ReaderService.com ▼

I accept your offer!

Please send me two free
novels and a mystery gift (gift
worth about $5). I understand
that these books are completely
free—even the shipping and
handling will be paid—and
I am under no obligation
to purchase anything, ever, as
explained on the back of this card.

366 ADL FMQG   166 ADL FMQG

Please Print

FIRST NAME

LAST NAME

ADDRESS

APT.#   CITY

STATE/PROV.   ZIP/POSTAL CODE

Visit us online at
www.ReaderService.com

largely on that, far more so than any physical ocular organ. Do you understand now?"

Kane nodded. "I'm beginning to," he said.

As they spoke, Kane became aware of something else moving in the room. His damaged eyes hadn't picked up the things before, but now, when he looked into the shadows, he could see buds of stone skittering across the walls. Balam was talking about how they could best track Little Quav when Kane pushed himself away from the table, the Sin Eater automatically materializing in his hand.

"What is it, friend Kane?" Balam asked.

"Over there," Kane said, keeping his voice low as he indicated the wall surround over the cafeteria door.

Balam looked at the thick skin of rock that now covered the plaster. Orange light glowed dimly in thin traceries within that rock, illuminating its surface like a web of veins. And there was something moving across it, three somethings, in fact—each one perfectly camouflaged with the rock, each round and about the size of a baseball. "What are they?" Balam whispered.

"Not seen 'em before," Kane confirmed, prowling across the room toward the wall in question. "Definitely more of this Ullikummis shit, though, can't be any doubt about that."

As he spoke, there came a sound like pressurized air bursting from a canister, and one of the ball-like rock things sprung from the wall. Automatically, Kane took a shot at the rock as it rushed through the air toward him, twin bullets hammering into its foremost point with unerring accuracy. They did nothing to slow or alter its trajectory, and in a second Kane felt the thing strike his left shoulder with the force of a hammer, throwing him backward in a spastic twirl of limbs.

Kane palm-slapped the floor with his open left hand, stumbled back to his feet as the spherical rock rolled away across the canteen floor. A growing sense of trepidation rose in his chest as he watched the rock turn, following a definite path as if alive.

"Kane," Balam called, "behind you!"

Kane spun, the sense of disorientation with his new-found vision still palpable, catching a confused glimpse of movement as the next rock detached from the wall and surged toward him like something hurled. Kane was ready for it this time, bringing the barrel of his Sin Eater up and using it like a club to bat the thing away. The metal barrel clanged hollowly as it struck the rock, and Kane felt his whole arm shudder with the blow. Knocked aside, the rock flew at the nearest wall, sticking there as if glued.

Kane's head whipped left and right, checking the floor for the rolling rock and keeping one eye on the wall where the things were emerging like bubbles on a pan of boiling water. With his sight so altered, it was hard to keep track of everything, but Kane dismissed the whirl of color, concentrating on any movements within it. The third rock pulled away from the wall like the others, and Kane watched the way it seemed to elongate like liquid before its strutlike leg kicked off from the wall and tossed the body of the rock toward him.

Kane ducked, letting the launched stone whiz past overhead before turning and blasting it with a burst from his pistol. The bullets carved burrows in the rock's surface as it streaked across the room and disappeared in the shadows beneath a table.

Then the room fell silent, just the eerie sound of

rock scraping against rock emanating distantly from all around.

"Balam?" Kane asked, scanning the walls for movement. "You okay? Anything hit you?"

"Nothing came close," Balam said from behind him. "Whatever they are, they seem to be attracted to you, not me."

Kane was tempted to joke that they must be female rocks, but he bit back the words. Grant or Baptiste might have appreciated his gallows humor, but he was pretty sure Balam would deem him unstable to joke at a time like this.

"They're a trap," Kane said instead. "Like land mines, left here to prey on the unwary. Ullikummis doesn't like us, he made a special effort to target Cerberus once he realized the threat we posed."

"I was here for six days," Balam reminded him, "and I saw nothing of this sort."

Kane glared at him. "They're hot-wired for human DNA, I guess. Wouldn't be the first time I've seen this Ullikummis guy employ something so specific. Rosalia has a stone under her skin that can open stone doors."

"Rosalia?" Balam asked, not recognizing the name.

"Long story," Kane told him. "For now, maybe we'd be best off making a tactical retreat. Can you walk okay?"

Balam nodded, shuffling across the room toward the doors while Kane scanned the area for more of the vicious little rock bursters.

MAKING THEIR WAY FROM the canteen, Kane and Balam headed through the dismal corridors of the Cerberus redoubt, lit as it was by the streaks of magma buried in the walls. Several more of the strange little rock-mines budded from the walls like boils on flesh, throwing themselves at Kane as he and Balam hurried past. There was no question about it—they were very definitely targeting Kane and not his companion, and Kane reasoned that the things had some genetic element in their makeup, working as predators with the specific prey of humans.

"There has long been a truce between my people and the Annunaki," Balam reminded Kane as they trudged down a corridor toward a stairwell. The two-hundred-year-old fire door was webbed with strands of rock. "Perhaps your Ullikummis respects that."

"Yeah?" Kane growled with an edge to his voice. "Well, he doesn't respect much else. I saw this guy mind-wipe a load of Canadian farmers and get half of them to commit ritual suicide without so much as a thought."

"Then he doesn't respect humans," Balam observed pointedly. "Don't forget that your own history is one of segregation based on arbitrary rules, skin color, gender and age all being used to excuse man's inhumanity to his fellow man."

Kane grunted as he pushed at the fire door, making his way into the stairwell without comment. It was darker in here, and it took a few seconds for Kane to adjust. Like a camera, his eyes seemed overpowered with color and brightness until they compensated for the slight illumination of the claustrophobic staircase. Kane had to stop while this change occurred, placing one hand against the nearest wall and taking deep breaths, his head bowed.

"Are you coping, friend Kane?" Balam asked.

"Whatever you did to my eyes, the transitions aren't

so good," Kane explained. "Takes a moment to get working right."

Looking around the almost square walls of the shaft, Balam saw the familiar movements as rock spheres began to bud. "I don't think we have a moment," he whispered.

His head still bowed, Kane listened as a dozen stony protrusions peeled from the walls and launched themselves at him.

Chapter 17

She could still see his face looming in front of her when she closed her eyes.

It was late afternoon in the temporary Cerberus headquarters. Exhausted, Reba DeFore had withdrawn to her room for a couple of hours with Lakesh's encouragement, taking a little time to just rest and gather her thoughts. Kane's last report had suggested he was fine, so she wasn't needed there, at least. She had been the Cerberus on-site physician for several years now, and even though she wasn't a fully certified doctor, she had the training, knowledge and determination to put any twentieth-century general practitioner to shame. One thing that DeFore had been praised for on more than one occasion was her steady hand, her nerve under pressure.

And yet she could still see his face, chiseled from rock, those hideous eyes burning like lava, the smell his inhuman body gave off.

Right now, DeFore lay above the covers of her bed, her eyes wide-open and the drapes pulled closed, with cold sweat clinging to her white one-piece suit. She had been suffering from panic attacks for almost two months now, ever since Ullikummis's people had attacked the once safe haven of the Cerberus redoubt.

And dear Heaven, she could still see him as he cast a shadow over her, the sound of his breath like a pres-

sure cooker, the way he had looked at her with those
burning pits of eyes.

His people had come, proclaiming their allegiance
to stone, their fearlessness engendering an apparent
lack of any instinct for self-preservation, making them
seem almost robotic in their nature. They had swept
aside the first wave of opposition, the security detail of
Mills, Wagner and Ezquerra knocked aside in a heartbeat, limbs broken, one man's face ruined by a volley
of tossed stone, their sharp edges as deadly as shrapnel
from a fragmentation grenade.

A fierce running battle had erupted through the
corridors of the redoubt, DeFore remembered, as the
resident Cerberus crew had fought to defend their home
base. It was too late, of course, and with hindsight they
should have realized that the very moment the cultists had entered the redoubt itself; the only way they
could enter was to be invited by one of Cerberus's own
number, one whose mind had been twisted into a dark
place. That member had been Edwards, who had suffered at the hands of Ullikummis months before, back
when the great stone monstrosity had set up his initial
training camp in the wilds of Saskatchewan, Canada.
Ullikummis had planted the obedience stone inside
Edwards then, left it hibernating inside his skull until
the order was given and his traitorous agent was activated. No one had noticed that Edwards was acting odd
in the meantime, despite the numerous signs. He had
been strangely drawn to a group of cultists out in the
fishing ville of Hope, just a little way along the coast
from where Cerberus had relocated now, and he had
frequently complained of headaches. Furthermore, his
Commtact had failed to operate, picking up signals but

unable to transmit where the tendrils of the living stone had blocked its connections.

DeFore cursed herself for that, for not noticing the little peculiarities in Edwards's behavior. She was the redoubt's physician, dammit all, so she should have realized something was wrong. He had mentioned the headaches only in passing one time when they had lined up together in the Cerberus canteen.

"My door is always open," she had said.

Well, it wasn't open now. Now she cowered behind it, wishing it could hide her from the outside world, the ravages and cruelties that continually threatened. Just as she had hidden behind that other door, back in the Cerberus redoubt, rocking herself back and forth as her sanity had threatened to detach and float away like ashes on flame.

She had been in the ops room when Edwards had returned with the strangers. There had been a problem out in Louisiana, where someone had accessed a long-buried redoubt, triggering an alarm at the Cerberus operations center. CAT Alpha, consisting of Kane, Grant and Brigid Baptiste, had been scrambled to investigate, and Reba DeFore had been kept on hand to monitor their transponders remotely. There was always a risk in sending agents out in the field, and Kane's group seemed predestined to run into the worst trouble whatever the given situation. This time, DeFore recalled, it had been something about the dead getting up and walking again under the auspices of a perverted Annunaki goddess.

The ops center itself was a vast, high-ceilinged room that featured twin rows of computer terminals, a huge Mercator map across one wall and a mat-trans unit in an antechamber off to the far corner. It was the same room where Kane had met with Balam today. Brewster Philboyd had switched the Commtact link to the overhead speakers, and DeFore and the other personnel there listened tensely as Kane relayed the situation, making their way through the undead hordes to reach the disturbed redoubt and shut down the insane dark goddess who had unleashed such abominations upon the Earth. So, like everyone else in the ops room, DeFore had been distracted, worried about the field team and not really thinking that they might be attacked right here in their own home.

Approaching the hidden redoubt without alerting the staff should have been impossible, as there were sensors scattered all around the nearby territory. But Ullikummis had abilities that the Cerberus staff were even now still trying to comprehend—the ability to step through space, to somehow be both there and not there. Afterward, Lakesh had speculated that Ullikummis could somehow use hidden interphase pathways, stepping both in and out of reality, utilizing an extra dimension in his movements. It was impossible to know for sure.

No one had given it a second thought when Edwards had disappeared from the ops center to get some air maybe twenty minutes earlier. When he'd returned, he'd brought a handful of strangers in hooded robes, the troops for Ullikummis. Each of them was armed with a slingshot and a pouch of stones, but they hadn't even needed them at first. They had begun by simply using their fists, channeling the power of stone and hitting people and objects with such force it was like being hit by a sack of bricks.

DeFore didn't even know when she had been hit. It was so sudden she had just crashed to her knees, her head reeling and blood streaming from her lip. There was movement, shouting, and she just lay there on the floor between computer terminals, watched helplessly as the world swam in and out of focus.

Something shattered beside her, and debris pattered across her back, an overturned chair hurtling across the room. She pushed herself from the floor, feeling the movement around her as something distant, her head was still so out of it. Domi, the albino girl, was running past, shouting something that DeFore could not make sense of over the sounds of conflict. DeFore ignored it, reaching up and grabbing the edge of her desk. Something fell from the desk, a pad of notes, slapping against the floor. Strangely—stupidly—DeFore herself reaching for them amid the chaos, then stopped herself.

Then she was standing, her head low as a man in a hooded robe leaped past her, vaulting the desk to land a savage kick in the gut of Donald Bry. The copper-haired supervisor staggered back, falling against a desk so that its computer screen wobbled in place. The hooded man had his back to DeFore, clenching his fists as he approached Bry.

"I am stone," he said, the words coming with the deliberation of a mantra.

DeFore turned and ran, scarpering across the room to the nearby doors. A robed figure made a grab for her as she passed, but was met with something hard and heavy—a computer terminal that Domi had tossed across the aisle at his head. Reba winced as it hit but she didn't slow. She pulled open the door and ran out into the corridor.

And that's where she saw him. Ullikummis.

He was immense, towering over her like some great statue. He stood eight feet tall, his body and face roughly carved out of dark, earthy stone like charcoal, veins of volcanic lava visible across the cracked plates of his chest, arms and legs. He was wide, his broad shoulders dominating the width of the central tunnel that ran the length of the redoubt. A series of thorny protrusions poked from atop each shoulder, like the horns of a stag arching upward toward his head. His face itself was a nightmare vision. It was roughly hewn from rock as if it had been weathered or eroded into shape. It had features—a slit of mouth, two deep-set eyes beneath its brow—but they were misshapen, as if in mockery of a face. The eyes and the mouth glowed like fire, red magma throbbing there in a ceaseless swirl.

DeFore stopped, the soles of her shoes slipping on the dark tiles of the floor where something had spilled, something red. Ullikummis had started out as an Annunaki, reptilian in his appearance like an upright crocodile, but he had been genetically altered while still in the womb, physically manipulated ever since. Now he looked like nothing that had ever lived, like the old Jewish legend of the Golem, the stone giant who brought righteous vengeance on all who defied his masters. Behind him, more of the robed troops were marching down the long corridor that dominated the redoubt's design, their feet in step, echoing from the vast steel girders holding the rock roof up high above. Her body trembling, Reba stared up into those glowing red eyes, feeling them draw her like magnets, north to south, south to north.

Ullikummis looked at her for a moment, the way a man might look at an insect, and then he reached out one of his massive hands, the digits, like the rest of him, roughly carved from metamorphic rock.

"Take heart," he said in a voice that sounded like two millstones grinding slowly together, "the future has arrived."

DeFore turned and ran, ducking beneath one of those great arms and scampering up toward the far-away exit of the redoubt located a long way up the corridor. The corridor had been carved directly into the mountain itself. It looked like a tunnel cavern, with the dark rock walls and ceiling. The ceiling had been left in a natural arch that towered high into the mountain, its apex lost in shadow well above the lighting rigs that ran across it on their steel support girders. Despite the heating of the redoubt, the corridor always felt cold, and DeFore had heard people equate it more to spelunking than walking when they had had to walk the length of the corridor more than twice in one day. Now DeFore ran, her ash-blond hair—carefully plaited that morning in a long rope that curled over her head and went halfway down her back—slapping against her spine as she moved.

There were infiltrators all over. DeFore guessed there must have been more than a dozen of the hooded figures in the corridor alone. Twenty feet away, two of the robed figures were laying into a Cerberus defender named Ezquerra, shoving him against the hard rock wall like so much discarded newspaper. DeFore heard the crack and knew what it was—Ezquerra's neck had broken on impact, and beside him Mills was reeling from a volley of stones that had struck him across the face, ribbons of blood welling into existence even as she turned away. As a doctor—hell, as a human being—DeFore wanted to step in and help her colleagues, see to their wounds. But that thing was just a few feet behind her, looming in the rock corridor like a statue brought to life. So she ran, each breath coming in a loud whimpering sigh.

She dodged, weaving out of the path of the tossed body of a Cerberus operative called Chang. Chang, a slender woman in her mid-forties, slammed into the wall beside DeFore, and blood began to pool almost immediately from her crumpled body.

DeFore turned, feeling nauseous. Behind her was another Cerberus staffer called Wagner. Wagner was a round-looking man better known for his map-reading skills than his combat prowess, and he stood beside security expert Sela Sinclair. Sela had an M-16 assault rifle in her hands that featured an underbarrel grenade launcher for added effect, but she couldn't seem to get a clear shot at the stone monster who stalked toward the three of them down the corridor. Her eyes were fixed on Ullikummis again, DeFore realized, drawn in by those sulfurous pits that burned in his face where his eyes should be. The stone monster moved then with an incredible speed that belied his lumbering appearance.

"Reba, get down!" Sela Sinclair called, trying desperately to fire from the underbarrel grenade launcher against the monster.

Before she could react, DeFore saw Ullikummis reach out and snag Wagner by the head, his huge, bear-like hand wrapping over Wagner's skull in a merciless strike. DeFore backed away, hot tears streaming down her cheeks. Sinclair was shouting something but it no longer registered. She needed to be away from here, away from that moving horror that had come to destroy everything. Her heel cracked back against something hard, and she realized she was pressed up against the wall. DeFore watched as Wagner was snapped apart by the sheer force of Ullikummis's hands, gore coloring his white tunic as he was tossed limply to the floor, a dead sack of bones.

DeFore felt her stomach rebel, tasted vomit in her mouth and turned away. In front of her was the door to a store cupboard where cleaning liquids, mops and brooms were kept. Without even considering it she pushed at the handle and shoved her way inside, closing the door behind her. Inside, the storeroom had a single strip light that blinked on automatically, the tube plink-plinking as it came to life care of the motion sensor. Outside, just beyond the thin barricade of the wooden door, DeFore could hear the cacophonous sounds of violence as battle was waged throughout Cerberus. The noise reminded her of the Fourth of July. The store cupboard itself seemed quiet by comparison, everything muffled now as if she was under water. She sank to the floor as blood swished under the door, a spreading puddle of crimson coloring the room. DeFore sat on the floor, surrounded by the blood, and her shoulders shook as she began to cry.

The words came from her mouth like a child waking from a nightmare. "Go away," she whispered. "Go away and leave us alone."

There came a knocking at the door and Reba screamed, a little sound like a bleat. She was in her bedroom in the temporary Cerberus headquarters on the coast, lying on the bed with the drapes drawn.

The knocking came again, firm and insistent, the hollow sound of knuckles on wood.

"Reba?" a man's voice. "Are you in there?"

The Cerberus medic turned her head and looked at the door. It was just a door, wider than the one in the Cerberus redoubt, the wood pale and unpainted. The floor in front of it was plain, not bloody like the store cupboard she had hidden in listening to the sounds of death and pain just inches away.

"Reba?"

"I'm here," she replied, raising her voice a little to ensure she would be heard. She recognized the voice now; it was Dr. Kazuko, the on-site physician supplied by the Tigers of Heaven.

The door opened just a little, and Kazuko asked, "Are you respectable?" before he proceeded inside. He smiled when he saw DeFore on the bed, a friendly and very human response that she appreciated as her thoughts threatened to consume her.

"I'm fine," DeFore told him, sitting up on the bed. "Must have drifted off for a minute."

Kazuko nodded. "There's been a lot to keep up with just lately," he said, but he was staring at DeFore with puzzled interest.

"What is it?" she asked.

"You're wet," Kazuko said.

DeFore looked down at the one-piece jumpsuit she wore. It was damp, dark patches of sweat showing at the armpits and around the neck. When she placed her hand against her forehead she found that was wet, too, and so was her hair, cold with sweat. "Must have..." she began, correcting herself as she went. "Hot in here, I guess."

Kazuko nodded. "Maybe it is a little at that."

DeFore put a hand through her wet hair, tucking it back behind her ears as she followed Kazuko from the room and off to where Edwards was incarcerated. Ullikummis had never touched her but he had given her something of the future he had promised, she knew. He had given her the fear.

Chapter 18

Shizuka stood outside the low building that had become the temporary headquarters for the Cerberus operation. She wore simple clothes now, a loose cotton shirt and slacks in white that billowed around her and allowed skin to breathe. She had been tempted to accompany Grant on his exploratory mission, but her place was to remain here with the Cerberus op itself. She and her Tigers of Heaven had to protect it against any possible attack.

While things seemed quiet, Shizuka had made her way past the little sunken garden with its hypnotically clacking water feature and out onto the lawn in the lee of the house. She sat there now, cross-legged on the grass, stilling her thoughts. In front of her, she had laid out a plain blanket upon which were two items—her *katana,* a twenty-five-inch blade of sharpened steel held within a dark scabbard decorated with gold filigree, and a small wooden casket, six inches by three, that looked a little like a music box.

Her breathing slow and regular, Shizuka opened her eyes and opened the lid, reaching inside the box. The contents of the box had been placed carefully inside specific compartments, a masterpiece of simple design and economic use of space. There were sheets of thin rice paper, a soft square of cotton, a lightly chalked powder ball and a small bottle of oil. In the front of the compartmentalized box, a tiny brass hammer rested across the longest length, held separate from the other items in the cleaning kit. This was her *katana* cleaning kit, as much ritual as necessity, and its use dated back to the days of feudal Japan when samurai had employed it to ensure that their *katana*—often referred to as the soul of the samurai—remained strong and clean, free from defects that might hinder a warrior in battle. But it was also a ritual, however, one that served to fill and calm Shizuka's mind as she awaited her lover's return.

Overhead, a gull cawed on its way to the sea. Beneath, Shizuka oiled the steel blade and gently tilted it, letting the oil run along its length.

REBA DEFORE didn't want to be performing surgery. She felt tired and irritable and that sense of fearful panic was still nagging at her after she had lain semiawake and found her mind drifting to all that had happened with Ullikummis. Still there was urgency here, a sense that time was of the essence. No one quite understood what was wrong with Edwards, but when she had brought him back to the new Cerberus headquarters, it had taken four men—including an ex-Magistrate called Decard, who functioned as both prince and sheriff for the hidden city of Aten where Reba DeFore and Edwards had hidden—to subdue him. Edwards was like a wild, ravening beast, a constant well of fury and contempt bubbling just beneath the surface. While they had been in Aten, Decard had kept the man incarcerated in a solitary cell, well away from any human interaction. To do otherwise had proved impossible.

Now Edwards lay sedated in front of her on the operating table, looking the most peaceful he had been in almost two months. With Dr. Kazuko standing ready beside her, DeFore held the scalpel poised, staring at the marked spot on Edwards's shaved skull. This was exploratory surgery; no one quite knew what the mass was that was showing up on the CAT scan. The only way to be sure was to cut into Edwards, and as the redoubt's physician, that task fell to DeFore, whether she felt up to it or not.

Normally she would have suggested just a local anesthetic for this type of minor surgery. After all, it wasn't brain surgery but was more akin to removing a cyst. But with the way that Edwards fought everything, the decision was made that it was better if he remained sedated for the whole procedure. They could awaken him when he was back in his bed, strapped down and no threat to anyone.

A few feet behind her, in the room beyond the closed door, DeFore sensed that Mariah Falk and Lakesh himself were waiting anxiously for her report.

Edwards lay on his back, head tilted to his side and rested on a paper-wrapped pillow.

"Shall we begin, Dr. DeFore?" Dr. Kazuko gently urged.

She nodded.

Steadying her hand, she leaned in and made a small incision to the side of Edwards's right ear, putting just a minimal amount of pressure on the sharp blade to cut through the skin. Blood blossomed immediately around the open wound, and Kazuko gently staunched the flow with gauze. Once he was done, DeFore renewed her work, bringing the scalpel down once more and drawing a deeper line into Edwards's head, cutting down behind the ear in an inch-and-a-half gash. She waited, holding her breath as the scarlet flow filled the wound once again.

Kazuko blotted away the blood, letting it turn the white of the gauze red before pulling the block of muslin away and using another to wipe away any excess flow. He was patient, his movements unhurried.

As Kazuko cleared the blood away, DeFore saw the growth for the first time. There, inside Edwards's head, was a dark line. It was a brown-black color, a matte substance that didn't reflect the bright overhead lights, and it sure as heck didn't belong inside a human's head.

Gently, DeFore pushed the tip of her index finger into the wound, touching the dark substance to see what it felt like. It was solid—rock solid—and it stretched off past the open ends of the one-inch wound she had cut in Edwards's head. Blood began to rise around the edges of the wound again, and she pulled her finger gently away.

Stemming the flow of blood, Dr. Kazuko looked at DeFore, one perfectly shaped eyebrow raised on his golden face. "Stone?" he asked.

She nodded. "I think so." There was nothing else it should be. They already knew how Ullikummis operated, how he implanted living rocks inside of people, rocks with different properties depending on the position of the person in his grand operation.

Leaning close once more, DeFore drew another scalpel down, this one with a slightly larger blade, and instructed Kazuko to pinch the wound to hold it open. While Kazuko did as she had requested, DeFore pulled the sharp edge of the scalpel blade over the dark surface in front of her, pushing it with a little effort now to try to carve into its surface. It was hard going, and blood began to ooze over her field of vision as she carved two parallel lines along the surface of the rock. Kazuko cleared the blood away, professionally and silently, so that DeFore could bring the blade in again and finish the exploratory surgery. Fifteen minutes after they had begun the operation, DeFore had removed six thin strips of rock from the solid surface inside Edwards's skull, each one looking a little like a toenail clipping that had been varnished brown-black. DeFore placed the strips in a sterilized metal dish to avoid contamination.

Then, with infinite patience, DeFore took the threaded needle from her operating kit and began to suture the wound. The needle dug into Edwards's skin and DeFore pushed it through, beginning the first stitch to close the black rock back inside her colleague's head. She stopped midstitch, a wave of fear gripping her as she stared at that solid wall of stone that was infiltrating Edwards's skull. It was like looking at him, at Ullikummis. She swallowed, felt the tremor take her hands, her heart palpitating against the cavity wall of her chest.

"Doctor...?" Kazuko coaxed, his restrained voice bringing DeFore back to the present.

The needle was still poking through Edwards's flesh, waiting to find its mark on the other side as Kazuko did his best to wipe away the forming blood. DeFore breathed, not daring to look away from the wound, even though it meant looking at the stone wall inside Edwards. She was steadier then, the infinitesimal trembling in her hands abating. She could do this; there was nothing to fear.

It was right at that moment that Edwards moved, his arm snapping outward and whacking DeFore just below her rib cage with a solid punch.

"What the hell are you doing to me?" Edwards snapped, sitting up on the operating table. He was wide-eyed and looked mad as hell.

DeFore staggered backward, her hands going to her gut where she had been hit, feeling the breath splutter back up her windpipe in a coughing fit.

On the table, Edwards rolled back and over, kicking his feet up to snag Dr. Kazuko on either side of his neck before pulling him back. With a yelp, Kazuko went flying the length of Edwards's body and off the far end of the operating table, landing in a heap by the wall.

Edwards leaped from the table then, a trickle of blood running down behind his right ear, the needle still dangling there by its thread. Struggling to keep her feet, DeFore looked at him under the bright lamps of surgery. He couldn't be awake; that was impossible. He should still be sedated right now. No man could wake up from that dose this soon.

Before she could voice her objection, however, Edwards stomped across the room in her direction and swept an arm out, knocking her aside in a rush of flailing limbs. DeFore fell back against the far wall, crying out in pain.

Edwards ignored her. A trained ex-Magistrate like Kane and Grant, he was already familiarizing himself with his surroundings as he searched for the exit. He dismissed the door to the room, assuming that would hold the best chance to bumping into opposition. Instead he turned to a window at the far side of the pale-walled room. A heavy cotton blind had been pulled down over the glass there to block the sun's rays where they might cast awkward shadows during the surgical procedure. Edwards yanked at the blind's drawstring, ripping the blind from its rail and tossing it aside.

The window itself was roughly twenty inches wide and twice that in height, a single pane of glass with a hinge at the top and a metal handle at the bottom. They were on the first story. Outside through the glass, Edwards saw a vast expanse of neatly trimmed grass, the huge lawn of Shizuka's winter retreat. Edwards grasped the handle and shoved, cranking the window open as wide as he could in a second. The gap was too small for his muscular form to fit through, and his nostrils flared as he glared at it.

"Stone," he muttered.

Behind him, Dr. Kazuko was pulling himself drunkenly up from the floor, a dark red trickle of blood running down his face from the cut on his forehead.

Edwards turned, jabbing his elbow into Kazuko's throat, and the physician fell to his knees, hacking in agony. "Back to sleep, Doc," Edwards instructed.

Then, turning back to the window, Edwards grabbed it by its lowest edge and twisted, turning it against its frame. "I am stone," he said, fearsome determination in every word.

There was a shearing noise of metal scraping against metal, and suddenly the whole window was wrenched free.

It was impossible, DeFore thought as she saw Edwards perform that remarkable feat of strength. First he had recovered from the anesthetic far too quickly, and then this. He was more than human. She had heard of cases of drug users displaying incredible bursts of strength, oblivious to pain, and Edwards's actions reminded her of that.

DeFore watched helplessly as Edwards climbed

through the window and out onto the lawn. But she wasn't helpless, was she? She pushed herself up off the floor, glancing at Kazuko with concern to make sure he was all right. The man had his eyes closed in pain, and his throat looked dark red where a bruise would doubtless form, but he was alive and breathing.

In an instant Reba had grabbed a spare syringe of sedative and she followed Edwards through the window and out onto the neatly manicured lawn. She saw immediately that he had run into an unexpected problem. Shizuka, the beautiful leader of the Tigers of Heaven, had been training out there with her *katana*, as she was wont to do during her quieter moments. She must have come to investigate when she had heard the window being wrenched from its frame. Now she stood in front of him with her sword—still sheathed—held loosely in her hand. Edwards stared at her, tilting his head as if not quite sure what to make of the female warrior.

"You're joking," he muttered.

"What's going on, Edwards?" Shizuka asked warily, well aware that he had been incarcerated here after turning traitor. As she spoke, Shizuka's attention was drawn past him, peering at the ruined window and the second figure clambering through it.

"Be careful, Shizuka," DeFore shouted as she lowered herself onto the lawn, the hypodermic syringe clutched in her hand. "He got loose, beat up Kazuko." And me, she added mentally.

Shizuka nodded once in acknowledgment of the warning, her right hand grasping the hilt of her sword. "Edwards," she said in a cold, emotionless voice, "I'm going to ask you once and only once to stand down.

What happens after that, you bring on yourself. Do you understand?"

Edwards looked at the petite samurai, and a cruel sneer cut across his bloodied face. Then, without a word of warning, he strode purposefully at Shizuka, his legs moving into a jog as he pulled back his fist.

With a crystal-clear note of reverberating steel, Shizuka drew the *katana* from its ornate scabbard, dancing a single step aside as Edwards's clenched fist powered through the air toward her face. The punch whizzed past the side of her head, missing her by just an inch.

Shizuka was already dropping, bending her knees to lower her center of gravity as she jabbed out with the hilt of the sword. The sword's pommel struck Edwards between the ribs, and he yelped in pain as he spun away. Then he was leaping back at the female samurai, his fists cutting the air as he drove punch after punch at her face. Light-footed, Shizuka scampered backward, watching as each blur of fist missed her head by just a couple of inches. She had to keep in mind that this man was a trained Mag, just like Grant, that he was skilled in the arts of combat and would not hesitate to kill anyone he perceived to be an enemy.

In just a few seconds Shizuka had been backed up against the edge of the house, where there was a raised balcony, its wooden decoration painted a vibrant red. She struck out with her left hand, batting at Edwards with the empty sheath of her sword, its hard wood echoing hollowly as it flashed across the man's forearm. Edwards just smiled, the trickle of blood pouring from his ear where the needle and thread were still attached. Then he came at Shizuka again, this time driving his knee at her groin, then kicking higher in an

effort to strike her face. Shizuka sidestepped the first
attack and just barely ducked the second. Edwards had
planned this well; she was too hemmed in here and
needed to get back out in the open.

As Edwards stamped his foot back down on the
ground and prepared his next attack, Shizuka twisted
and leaped backward, kicking out against the topmost
bar of the ornate balcony and launching herself up over
his head. She flipped in the air, her body an upside-
down pendulum over Edwards's shaved head, and she
clapped down with both arms, using the flat of the
sword and its sheath to strike Edwards on either side
of his skull.

Edwards cried out in annoyance as much as pain,
turning away as he reached for the throbbing cut beside
his right ear. Behind him, Shizuka made a perfect two-
point landing, both foot touching the ground just a fraction of a second apart, before spinning and turning to
face her opponent once again.

"I cannot let you leave here, Edwards," she explained, the afternoon sunlight painting her sword like
a bright slash in the air. "Please do not put yourself
through any further pain."

Edwards narrowed his eyes as he glared at her. "I
am stone," he muttered once more.

Then he was upon her again, a furious maelstrom of
punches and kicks directed at Shizuka in a relentless
attempt to knock her down. Shizuka jumped, ducked
and weaved, timing each move with immaculate precision.

Suddenly, Shizuka saw a gap in Edwards's furious
attack, and she struck out once more with the flat edge
of the *katana,* twisting the blade just slightly as she
slashed across his chest. The twisted blade caught the

material of the simple surgery gown Edwards wore, cutting a four-inch horizontal line across it but not meeting the skin beneath.

"The next time," Shizuka warned, "I'll cut you down."

Edwards's eyes met hers, and a thin-lipped smile crossed his slash of mouth. "I am stone," he said.

Then Edwards was on her again, redoubling his effort to knock her down as she darted around like some crazy kangaroo. Shizuka pivoted on one leg, spinning in place and kicking Edwards in the side, but the blow felt like kicking a wall, the man was so solidly built. Edwards retaliated in a split second, driving punch after kick after punch at Shizuka, each one getting closer to striking its mark as she struggled to keep out of his path.

The spectacle was attracting other people from the lodge and its surroundings now. Two Tigers of Heaven rushed from different directions across the vast lawn, and a third man appeared on the higher balcony that ran around the building before charging down the steps and into the sunken garden.

Shizuka aimed her *katana* for Edwards's legs, cutting through the air with a one-handed slash a little above knee height. Edwards stepped out of the sword's arc, then back in as it passed, aiming a ram's-head punch at Shizuka's nose in an attempt to break it and drive the cartilage into her brain, instantly killing her. Shizuka brought her other hand up, using the hard casing of the sword's empty sheath to block Edwards's brutal attack.

Standing close by in the shadow of the building, Reba DeFore watched these two warriors battle mercilessly. Again Edwards was lunging toward Shizuka, reaching for the front of her tunic in a blur of material.

Shizuka pulled away, arching her back as Edwards's hand snatched at empty air, then she kicked out, bringing her toe up to connect with the base of the man's jaw. Edwards's teeth clacked together and he stumbled backward, reeling from the blow.

Shizuka pressed her attack, stepping swiftly forward and sweeping the twenty-five-inch *katana* blade low to Edwards's feet. Edwards stepped aside, but as he did so he slipped on a patch of slick grass, and suddenly he was toppling toward Shizuka.

Shizuka hadn't expected the move—indeed, nor had Edwards—and she found herself falling back under Edwards's weight, her elbows crashing hard against the ground and the breath blurting out of her in a rush. As Edwards floundered atop her, Shizuka shook off the impact and brought her sword up to his throat, balancing the blade there, poised to cut his jugular. As Edwards struggled, Shizuka warned him not to move unless he wanted his throat cut.

"Live or die, it's your choice now," Shizuka whispered close to his ear. "But trust me when I tell you, my blade is true. If you move, it will take you, have no doubt on that."

From behind them, Shizuka saw Reba DeFore dart across the grass toward them.

"Hold him still," DeFore said.

Edwards hissed something at DeFore, pulling against Shizuka as he tried to get free. But as the skin of his flesh touched the cool blade, he must have realized his mistake, and he stopped himself pulling any further. A thin line of blood appeared almost immediately across his throat; had the razor-sharp blade cut any deeper Edwards would have garroted himself.

DeFore leaned close, the hypodermic needle glinting in the sunlight as she brought it down into the vein in the man's arm. Edwards glared daggers at the physician as she pushed the plunger down, shooting the tranquilizer into his bloodstream. If he could have moved, if he had dared, she knew he would have strangled her or tossed her aside. But with any movement he threatened himself with the keen edge of Shizuka's sword, the slightest misstep and he would slit his own throat wide-open.

DeFore stood back as a trio of Tigers of Heaven guards came to join them, ready and waiting to support their mistress as she lay beneath the ex-Magistrate, holding that wicked blade to his throat. DeFore could see it in Edwards's eyes; she had no doubt that right now he would kill her if he could but reach her. It sent a shiver down her spine and, for just a moment, she recalled those other eyes that were seared into her memory, the burning eyes of Ullikummis, the source of all of their current misfortunes.

It took over a minute, ninety seconds or so in fact, before Edwards's eyelids finally became heavy and his muscles ceased tensing. Toward the end of it, DeFore actually began to doubt that the sedative would take effect, worried that perhaps whatever alien thing was driving Edwards inside it had made him superhuman and somehow invincible. Was this the future of mankind? Was this the next step in evolution, a parasitic stone with the ability to guide men's minds and change their physical properties? It hardly bore thinking about.

Eventually Edwards slumped against Shizuka beneath him, his weight heavy against her body. Warily, Shizuka pulled her *katana* blade away from the man's throat, watching for any signs of movement, any hint that this was a feint.

After that, the Tigers of Heaven helped lift Edwards's slumbering form from their mistress, and Shizuka stood and stretched, resheathing the *katana* in its exquisitely tooled scabbard.

"Thank you for your help," she told DeFore.

The clinician shook her head. "No, thank you for yours. He would have got away otherwise. Quite how his system shook off the effects of the first sedative, I can't guess."

"There are many things going on here that still need answers," Shizuka agreed, tucking the sheathed *katana* into her belt, its hilt sticking out so that it might be drawn at an instant's notice.

With surprising gentleness, the Tigers of Heaven carted Edwards back toward the lodge via the sunken garden, and DeFore and Shizuka followed.

"I should finish patching up his ear," the physician said, feeling a little embarrassed by all that had happened. "And after that, we can take a look at whatever it was I scraped out of his skull."

Chapter 19

It was the birth of a god. That's what Domi was watching through the ice-cool plate, she realized, as she watched the thing that had been Kishiro vibrate and shift within Enlil's alien apparatus. Kishiro wasn't simply rocking; he was actually shifting dimensionally, his constitution changing to accommodate the download of an Annunaki genetic template. What started as a man, an ordinary human being, was purposefully evolved through all the stages that had led to the Annunaki rebirth, his muscular form becoming the familiar frail, birdlike shape of the hybrids before taking on a greater shape and size, great flaps of skin sluicing away to reveal the armorlike musculature that was forming from within.

Enlil watched the process proceed, betraying no emotion other than the faintest hint of a smile on his reptilian face.

"Stop it, you monster," Domi demanded, banging her fists against the glass. "Stop it. You're killing him."

Enlil looked at her dispassionately for a moment. "Your whole race should have died out years ago," he declared as if stating a well-known fact. "You are a plague on this planet, nothing more than that."

"And yet you still speak to us," Domi shouted triumphantly. "You still acknowledge us, acknowledge me. For all your talk of superiority, you'll never be better than us and you know it. You'll always just be a lousy, back-biting, fucking scale-face."

Enlil stared at her. "And soon you shall be, too," he said as behind him Kishiro's body trembled, finishing its ghastly cycle from man to monster.

Where once Kishiro had stood, framed within the network of glowing piping that held his struggling body in place, now stood the dormant shell of an Annunaki, a newborn god awaiting activation. Beside him, the five other humans had suffered a similar metamorphosis, turning from man to creature in just a few minutes. Though the procedure appeared to be complete, each of those terrible alien faces held its jaws wide as though in pain, the pain of the gods.

Enlil touched something on his control pad near the screen through which Domi watched, and the amber bars faded, their lines of light winking out in front of the thing that had been Kishiro and the other individuals in the cylinders. Domi saw now that all six had been altered, changed beyond recognition into sinister lizardlike creatures, each one standing nearly seven feet tall with sweeping crests of spines running along their heads. They were hideous yet beautiful, and Domi felt sick just thinking that thought, repelled by her attraction to them.

After a moment it became clear that these new Annunaki were dead, stillborn gods. Enlil strode across the hard floor toward them and ran his clawed hand along the cheek of the one who had been the blond-haired woman. The reptilian thing gave no reaction. Its eyes remained closed and Domi fancied that she could detect no rise and fall of the naked breasts that would indicate breathing.

While Enlil continued to examine the transformed

human, Domi turned back to Hassood, her voice an urgent whisper.

"We need to get out of here," Domi urged, "or we'll be next. You got here before us, Hassood—did you find anything resembling a door?"

Hassood looked bemused. "I...I was asleep," he said helplessly. "I didn't see..."

"Okay, cowboy, calm down," Domi said. "We'll look together. You go check up there—" she pointed "—and I'll see how far this cell goes."

With that, the albino girl padded off into the darkness, her hands outstretched to touch the nearest wall.

GRANT, ROSALIA AND KUDO hurried through the dragon city, their pace never slowing to less than a jog. Rosalia's dog scampered ahead now and again in the restless way dogs will. Nothing had changed and yet it seemed, on some level, that everything had. Now they suspected they were treading on the bones of some colossal creature, that the things they had taken to be buildings were in fact ribs or a spine or an incredible tailbone whose size dwarfed anything they had ever seen before. Grant recalled the gargantuan undersea creatures he had observed a few months ago while investigating the deep-sea Ontic Library off the West Coast of America, but he couldn't make the math work, could not imagine how the bones around him compared to those things.

They scrambled along the cobbled stone, hurrying up a street—or bone, or vein—that was on a steep incline. Rosalia's scruffy dog waited at the apex, tongue hanging out as it panted for breath, peering behind now and then to check that its mistress and her friends were following.

When they reached the top of the incline, two curving, white structures rising to either side of them like the great ribs of some mythical giant, they saw the head of the dragon looming in front of them. Previously concealed by the incline, the head was just a hundred yards ahead of them now, its wedge shape poking up at the sky on a slender, serpentine neck. Grant estimated that the head was at least twenty feet across, probably closer to thirty. Twin red eyes glowed like jewels, set far back along its tapering snout, and its mouth was locked open, wisps of steam winding between its stylized teeth. The creature seemed almost like a work of art, its sleek lines like an art deco interpretation of a dragon of myth, and it made Grant wonder whether the thing was truly alive or simply an elaborate mechanism. In actuality, it was a little of both, Annunaki organic technology wrought large.

It was clear now that the "city" that the Cerberus rebels had been making their way across was made up of the wide-spread wings of the dragon, each jutting building a part of a latticework of bone across which the skin of its wing should have been spread. It stood like a skeleton awaiting life.

Dark-feathered nocturnal birds swooped through the sky, blurting their ugly caws as they fluttered past the vast skull. Without warning, the dragon's head shifted on the neck with a whirring, grating sound, and the mouth wrenched wide-open, blasting two laser bolts into the sky in quick succession, their pulses like colossal red tablets shooting into the air. Insects were lit in that terrible scarlet glow, and Grant shielded his eyes as one of the nocturnal birds was flash-fried in less than a second, feather and flesh instantly turned to ash. Rosalia's dog whined at the blast, which though it couldn't be heard could be felt deep in the eardrums of the humans. What it was doing to the hound's more sensitive hearing was anyone's guess.

"What the hell is that?" Rosalia asked, eyeing the sleek lines of the dragon form in the center of the city.

Grant felt sick as he looked at those familiar lines. *"Tiamat,"* he confirmed. "The mother of the Annunaki."

"You mean *mothership,* right?" Rosalia asked, her eyes fixed on the massive beastlike thing in front of them.

"It's…complicated," Grant told her. "She's a spaceship but she's also kind of alive—at least that's how I understood it. In the last great reappearance of the Annunaki she seemed to have become fed up with the internal squabbles of her children. The part of her that was alive—which is to say, sentient—seemed to rebel, causing her to blow up."

"And this was when? Last year?" Rosalia asked. She had not been a member of the Cerberus team then, and on occasions like this she felt a little as if she was endlessly having to play catch-up.

"Yeah." Grant nodded his agreement. "She looks different now, down here. Last time I saw her she was in space. But she looks broken up, spread out like this. Like you said—she's bones."

Rosalia placed her hand on the dog's head, settling it as it yearned to pull ahead. "You said this ship blew up, though."

"Yeah. Kane, Brigid and me watched as she exploded," Grant confirmed. "We were getting out of there as fast as we could, and the explosion rocked the ship we'd commandeered and lit up the sky. I saw that much with my own eyes."

Kudo spoke up then, his hand nervously resting on the grip of his sheathed sword. "These Annunaki, they're tricky."

"Their tech is like nothing you've ever experienced," Grant grumbled. "The fact that *Tiamat* is here, assuming that really is *Tiamat,* comes as an unpleasant surprise, but not an altogether unexpected one. We thought as much when the satellite feed picked this place up. I just didn't want to believe it, not until I'd seen it with my own eyes."

"And now that you've seen it?" Rosalia prompted.

The dragon's head turned on its gracefully arching neck, and the mouth opened once again, blasting another fiery burst of laser fire high into the sky above the Euphrates River. The sound of the blast was so high-pitched it rumbled the inner ear of the group who watched it, and Rosalia's dog whimpered again, looking plaintively at her.

"Brewster's saying that Domi's in there," Grant confirmed sourly, "and most likely Kishiro is with her. We're going inside, team."

If anyone objected, they didn't say.

BLEARY-EYED, HASSOOD checked the walls of the strange cell close to where Kishiro had disappeared in the eerie reversed waterfall. The walls were plain enough, the lines where they met ceiling and floor lightly curving as if with coving, smoothing away the hard corners.

Domi paced swiftly down the other end of the chamber, her eyes penetrating the growing darkness there. Like Hassood, she could find no suggestion of a door, and she found herself walking further into the darkness with a growing sense of unease. "Just how large is this place?" she muttered, running her hand along the ridges of one of the walls.

But no matter how far she walked there seemed to be no end, and without any light source penetrating this far, it was impossible to gauge how much farther she might have to walk before she found the far wall. It was more like a tunnel, Domi realized, or an artery, and she had the distinct impression those curved walls somehow played tricks on the senses.

Domi peered behind her, checking that Hassood was still there in the light. She was uncomfortable with getting too far from him or leaving him on his own for too long, given what had happened to Kishiro. Cerberus was here to help people, not leave them to the enemy.

She carried on, using her sense of touch to check the walls in the darkness where her eyesight could no longer adequately penetrate.

GRANT'S TEAM HAD MADE their way swiftly down to a bulging wall along the main body of the dragon following the revelation that they had been walking through the vast swoop of its skeletal wings all this time. As they neared, the body seemed to swell on the horizon like a mountain, its scaled skin ragged and broken in blotches, the bones clear through the flesh. It was like a thing half grown, a thing undone somehow before it could truly be born. If this really was *Tiamat,* then she was sick, the ravage of her disease leaving her malformed.

Grant eyed the ruined skin as they came closer, unable to avoid the smell of it now. It smelled rancid like rotting flesh, and there were swarms of nighttime insects feasting on the open wounds along its flank, nocturnal birds picking at its flesh.

Keeping pace alongside them, Rosalia's pale-eyed dog whimpered in dissatisfaction.

"Yeah," she told it sympathetically, "it sure is stinky. Even you wouldn't eat that."

The dog barked sharply in reply before falling back to silence.

Walking beside Grant, Kudo's eyes widened. "I can't see any obvious entrance," he said. "How do you propose we get in, Grant?"

Grant's brows were furrowed. "I'm working on it," he returned, his eyes searching the rotted flesh where engorged grubs blindly wormed.

They were almost upon it now, and Rosalia's nameless dog stood on the spot, not wanting to get any closer to the half-dead creature. She leaned down, holding its head between her hands and staring into its white eyes as she chided, "You're a dog, not a chicken, stupid mutt."

The dog whimpered in response but finally assented to its mistress's wishes. When they joined the others, Grant and Kudo were at the towering wall of flesh, testing it with their hands.

"It's still quite solid despite the damage," Grant explained.

"Feels like metal," Kudo said with surprise when he touched the skin.

"It's Annunaki," Grant announced. "Kind of bridges a halfway house between something born and something constructed."

"That's impossible," Kudo spit. "You cannot grow metal plate. It cannot be done."

"These people—" Grant gave a sour expression as he used the term "—have mastered genetic sequencing. Enlil turned his own son into living rock to overpower his enemies. Whatever preconceptions you have about what's possible and what ain't, let them go before we step inside."

"And how do you plan on doing that?" Rosalia asked as she eyed the great hulk of the dragon's flank.

"Whatever it may look like," Grant stated, "this is ultimately a spaceship, and that means it's hollow inside to allow for living quarters, life support, a star-drive and so on. We burrow deep enough and we'll get past the flesh and into the ship itself."

"At the risk of repeating myself, Magistrate," Rosalia said, "may I ask how?"

Grant reached into one of the small utility pouches that ran along his belt, each one less than three inches across and about as deep as his thumb. After a moment's fiddling, he brought out three tiny spherical globes. They were perfectly round and just an inch across with a dull metallic sheen, and they looked like ball bearings. "We'll make us a little hole," he explained with a grim smile. "Everybody get back behind some cover. Rosie, keep a hold on the dog."

Stepping back behind a riblike strut twenty feet away, Rosalia and Kudo watched as Grant ran his fingers along the rough ridges of the dragon's flesh until he found a gap wide enough to place one of the globes. Forcefully the ex-Magistrate pushed the sphere into the gap, then placed a second across and a little lower down and then a third beneath it. Then his fingers brushed across all three, and there came the very faintest click as something within them was activated.

Grant hurried back from the wall, ducking his head and covering his skull with his hands as he ran for the nearest cover. A moment later there was a mighty triple explosion as the globes blasted a crater into the dragon's scaled flesh.

Rosalia had seen the Cerberus people use something like this before, when she had first met them in the squalid surroundings of Hope. Then, their distaff member Brigid Baptiste had used a spherical explosive called a flash-bang to blind her opponents without wounding them. It appeared that Cerberus had more than one type of explosive device that utilized the same basic design. As the smoke cleared, Rosalia saw a gaping hole in the dragon's massive flank, three feet high and shaped like a long oval. Whatever Grant had used, it certainly had more kick than the flash-bangs.

DOMI WAS STILL CHECKING the cell when the lights behind her abruptly shut down without warning. Hassood yelped with surprise as the whole cell went pitch-black.

"Miss Domi?" he asked, voice echoing along the darkened chamber. "Miss Domi, are you still there?"

"I'm here, Hassood," Domi confirmed, searching all around her in the sudden darkness, letting her well-honed natural senses reach out and feed her information while her eyes adjusted. She confirmed to herself that nothing appeared to have entered the chamber; there was no noise and she could sense no new presence.

Domi waited, listening to the sounds of silence, the only noises the chuntering nervous breathing of Hassood thirty feet away from her. After a few moments of adjustment, she noticed the patch of light high on one wall. It was the square screen via which she had viewed Enlil and that terrible transformation he had triggered in Kishiro and the others. The square of the screen was faint in the dark, almost like something imagined, and Domi realized that the lights had failed wherever Enlil was, as well.

Slowly, warily, Domi padded back toward the screen, stopping in front of it and staring at its picture. Enlil was nowhere to be seen, and the area beyond the room was lit only poorly by what appeared to be emergency lighting. The altered figures of Kishiro and the others had been plunged into darkness, their silhouettes just about visible if Domi looked for their edges. She doubted she would have noticed them had she not known just where to look.

Hassood was beside her now, finding his way in the darkness with all the deliberation of a man walking across a frozen stream. "What has happened?" he whispered.

Domi stepped back from the screen, conscious that they were likely standing right next to any microphone pickup. "Some kind of power failure, by the looks of it," she told Hassood. "Might be our chance."

"Chance for what?" Hassood urged, the strain in even his whispered voice obvious. "There are no doors, just the crazy whirlpool that washed your ally away."

Domi bit her lip in thought. Hassood was right. But there had to be some other way out of here, a locked room was never what it seemed, was it?

ROLLING THREE MORE OF the phosphorous explosive pellets in his hand, Grant examined the hole and decided where to place his second wave of charges.

"Animal, vegetable, mineral?" he muttered under his breath as he worked another explosive charge into the gap.

The first explosion had cut a three-foot-wide hole in the metal-plate skin of the dragon, exposing a clutch of thick cables that reminded Grant more of creepers surrounding a tree trunk than of something animal. The bark itself seemed scraped away from that trunk, leaving a creamy yellow that could just as easily have been wood as bone. Grant tried to put the thought to the back of his mind as he primed the charges and backed swiftly away.

Grant and the others covered their ears and, after a slow five-count, the explosives went off, sending a cacophonous burst of flame through the skin of the grounded dragon. Despite the power of the miniature explosives, the body of the dragon itself did not move; it remained stoically in place as the explosion cut into it like a scalpel.

"It'll take one more at least," Grant stated as he looked at the newly deepened trench in the dragon's unliving flesh.

While Rosalia hushed her dog, Grant went through his utility pouches for his last remaining charges and hoped they would be enough. After that, all he had was acid—and while that might eat away at the hull eventually, it would take a lot more time than he felt they had.

DOMI NARROWED HER EYES as she brought the serrated edge of her combat blade up against the screen. Either it was a window, in which case it would grant them access to the next room if she could break it, or it hid the monitoring equipment that was used to spy on them, in which case disabling it would be a step in getting them their freedom, albeit less directly.

Domi told Hassood to step well back, then with

a grunt of expelled breath, she pushed the tip of the blade into the very edge of the screen, holding it at arm's length in case the screen itself exploded. For a moment nothing happened, and Domi stood there with the blade pressed into the lowermost edge of the square, not daring to take a breath. Then the blade slipped and Domi's hand was drawn with it off to the side, away from the screen.

There had been no reaction. No explosion, no change in the picture projected on the screen's surface, no alteration even at the edge where Domi's blade had pressed as would be the way with an LCD screen.

Domi held her empty hand out protectively, instructing Hassood to stay where he was. "Keep back," she said.

Domi stepped closer to the dully lit screen, examining the place where her knife point had struck. There was a scrape there, a thin white line along the surface with a trace of white dust along its edge. It took Domi a moment to recognize it, racking her brain to recall where she knew that familiar sight from.

Ice, she realized. The whole screen was made of ice, a great, clear block of it inserted in the wall like a window.

Domi turned the knife in her hand and aimed it, point first, at the very center of the square screen. In a few seconds she had hacked out a small cross there, barely an inch across. Then, pressing a little more firmly on the blade's handle, Domi deepened each groove and added a box that connected the lines of the cross, placing the X in an inch-wide square. Swiftly she worked the knife over and over those lines, creating a deeper gash while keeping one eye on the room beyond in case Enlil should return. If she was right about this, she could split the ice and thus break the window, granting her and Hassood access into the room beyond. Of course, that all depended on Enlil not returning anytime soon.

ENLIL WAS MARCHING THROUGH the winding, arterial corridors of the reborn *Tiamat* wombship, his clawed feet clacking against the metal-plate floor with a sound like a sword being sharpened. His scarlet cloak billowed around him as he walked, and he checked a palm-size terminal link that he carried with him, the unit resting in his hand and granting diagnostic access to *Tiamat* herself.

Something had breached the ship's surface, causing a power drop that demanded his attention. *Tiamat* was still in a delicate state, her growth cycle not yet completed, the hardened flesh of her skin not yet ready for space travel. For someone to damage that skin now, after the months he had waited for the ship to regrow, was insufferable. People had mistaken the ship's strange growth cycle for a rogue ville springing up. As such, most had been curious but had ultimately steered clear of the rapidly expanding settlement that seemed to be appearing on the river's bank. Later, those who did venture in became fodder for Enlil's latest experiment, the creation of new bodies that could house the memory downloads of the extended family of the Annunaki. Utilizing water as a means to interphase people from point to point was a glorious inversion of his long-favored weapon, and it held a certain exquisite irony given the physical makeup of the human body itself. The water-based units were limited in scope, however, unable to teleport people more than a few miles and unconnected to the network of parallax points that dotted the globe, but they could be used to shunt matériel short distances, and that was all he needed if the apekin kept approaching. Humans were naturally curious, so let their own curiosity draw them to him. Let that be the end of them.

But of course that had been before the arrival of the Cerberus team. Accursed Cerberus exiles, jumped-up apekin that they were, with not even the basic decency to know their place and to stay in it. If he had tired of them once, it had been so long ago that he could scarcely remember now. He merely knew that no matter what form he had taken, and no matter how their paths had intersected, the Cerberus exiles had always proved a nuisance he underestimated at his peril.

Well, then, Enlil told himself, let them come. For this time, they came to meet evolution, an evolution that would spell their doom and the doom of humankind.

With that, he touched the palm link, willing a command through thought alone. Somewhere deep in the storage banks of *Tiamat,* the waters began to whirl and flow, building to a crescendo of humanoid-shaped waves. The transporters were alive.

Chapter 20

With a decidedly unfeminine grunt, Domi carved another slice of ice from the windowlike screen. There
was a deep rent in the panel now, almost an inch into
the body of the ice yet showing no sign of penetrating
through to the other side. Domi glared at it.

"Just how thick is this thing?" she murmured, shaking her head.

Hassood looked concerned as he saw Domi working harder and harder with little to show for it other
than a smattering of ice chippings powdering the floor.
The surface of the window he had taken for a screen
was marred with a gash of scored ice that resembled
a sunburst, but that mark was still only a matter of a
couple of inches across. "Is there perhaps some way I
can help?" Hassood pleaded.

Domi sneered, eyeing the marred screen the way
she would an enemy. Without answering Hassood, she
took her blade to the ice once more, scoring lines right
across the surface of the viewport, going over them
again and again and bringing each line right out to the
screen's edge. "If we had a heat source we could probably melt this," she grumbled. But they didn't have one,
so that was that.

Domi's blade had been with her a long time, dating
back to her days as a sex slave for Guana Teague. She
trusted it the way one might trust an old friend, treated

it with the same respect she would a person. Right then, she placed the point of the knife into the middle of the cross she had carved, the square of cut ice becoming a frame around it, the score marks running from it like light from a star. Domi held the blade rigid, assuring herself it was straight on, bringing the cup of her other hand against its pommel. Then she pulled her free hand back and drove it forward again in a hard shunt, shoving the knife point deeper into the ice.

It took five attempts, and each time Domi's hand met the pommel of the knife with a loud clap. The last two times she shrieked with the effort, the coldness of the ice conducting through the knife and making it cold from tip to handle. With the fifth shunt, one of the lines she had scored in the icy pane split with a loud cracking sound like splintering wood.

Domi huffed a breath through her nostrils, staring at the icy window. The line leading from the center to the top had split, the two halves of the clear pane rent by a half-inch gap.

As Domi watched, a trickle of dark liquid ebbed down from the top of the frame, drawing a dark line down the crack. Domi touched a finger against it, wondering what it was. A sealant perhaps?

It felt viscous and slightly tacky on her fingertips. Domi pulled her hand away and sniffed the liquid. Though faint, it had that rusty metal tang that she associated with blood.

Domi wiped her finger against her pant leg and got back to widening the hole with the edge of her knife, using the blade as a lever to wedge the two halves farther apart.

Domi worked at it swiftly, driving her blade deeper between the two halves, twisting it in place until finally there came a sudden crack like a gunshot, this one even louder than the first. Domi leaped back as the right-hand side of the split ice tumbled into the room, crashing into the floor in a solid hunk like a dropped brick, its edges skittering off in sharp shards of ice that slid across the cell.

Domi turned to Hassood who looked stunned at this turn of events. "Come on," she told him.

Hassood followed Domi as she went back to the window and pushed out the remaining parts of ice, rocking it several times until it toppled out of the frame and into the next room. Then she lifted herself up by both hands, the knife clenched between her teeth as she squirmed through the now-open window.

"Watch your step," she told Hassood.

Hassood followed Domi through the gap in the wall.

They found themselves in a vast chamber with minimal lighting. It was the chamber that Domi had seen Enlil in, confirming if there had been any doubt that the ice screen had been a window rather than a remote viewer. The thickness of the ice had created the optical illusion of magnification, Domi realized as she looked around her, bringing everything much closer than it really was. Quite probably that was intentional, not for the benefit of the cell's occupants but for Enlil's, so that he could watch the cell's inhabitants the way a scientist might use a microscope to scrutinize the transient creatures that swarm and multiply in a drop of water. That thought reminded Domi of how alien Enlil truly was, and also how human.

The console arrangement that Domi had seen Enlil working at, where he had seemed to stand directly in front of her on the ice screen, was actually set six feet from the portal and formed just one part of a semicircular desk that enveloped its user. Beyond that, Domi saw the organ-pipe-like arrangement of cylinders that held Kishiro and the others she had seen, each of them now transformed into something from a nightmare.

Domi moved farther into the darkened chamber, carefully stepping over the broken ice that had spilled from the windowlike frame. Hassood was just lowering himself down to follow her, grumbling under his breath about how cold the frame was to the touch.

As Domi walked toward the lifeless form that had once been Kishiro, something whirred beneath her feet, and the amber bands that held him and the others in place flashed on in a streak across their chests. Domi stopped in place, her knife clenched and ready as a sloshing sound rushed through the room and the cylinders began to vibrate. Then, as she watched, each of the six tubular mechanisms began to move, twirling in place as if on a child's merry-go-round before lining up like a conveyor belt. Domi watched as all six tubes shuddered across the floor of the room and moved behind the staircase and into the deeper darkness, their amber bands flashing occasionally like orange lightning.

Looking down, Domi saw that the floor was irregular. Where the cylinders had stood, she saw water glistening, some kind of internal stream just a little wider than she was—wide enough to contain the floating, man-size tubes. The six cylinders were being floated upright along the stream, the movement so smooth that Domi could scarcely believe they were traveling upon water. It was a marvel of engineering.

"Stay close," Domi instructed Hassood as she paced forward, keeping her own body low in a half crouch.

Reaching down, Domi ran the fingers of her empty hand through the water, felt its coolness run over her alabaster skin. "This just gets weirder," she muttered to herself as she paced forward, ducking low beneath the delicate arch of the staircase.

It was very dark in the area beyond, and it took Domi a few seconds to adjust to the semidarkness. As such, she felt the immense room's dimensions even before she saw them, subconsciously noticing the stillness of the air, the faint echo of her footsteps on the hard floor. The six cylinder-like frames moved onward into the room, their strips of amber lighting flashing across their slender forms, illuminating the area in front of them in brief, epileptic snatches. Within those snatches of artificial light, Domi and Hassood began to make sense of the room.

It was huge, far bigger than either of them had expected. Shrouded in darkness, the room appeared as big as a sports ground or an ancient gladiatorial amphitheater, and the ceiling stretched to an incredible height, so much so that Domi wondered momentarily if they were still indoors. Channels of water washed across the room, running like tiny rivers throughout the length of the vast chamber. Domi watched the reflections of the amber lights firing across the surface of these canals, guessed from their straight and intricate design that they were all used as some form of transport, somewhat like the way oxygen is ferried around the body in the channels of the bloodstream. In fact, despite the lack of noise and the way the only movement came from the bobbing cylinders, the whole place seemed somehow alive. If a room could be said to be breathing, this one was.

Domi looked up and saw catwalks that crisscrossed

the room, fanning out like barbs from six identical staircases. The walkways themselves were milky pale with no safety rails along their narrow lines, jutting out skeletally like branches over the expanse of the room.

The racing amber lights retreated into the distance as the cylinders trundled on their prearranged paths, and Domi slowed her pace, making sure to keep Hassood behind her. They watched as the cylinders split up, four going to the right while the others— presumably the women's—veered off toward the left wall of the colossal room. As they illuminated more of the room, Domi finally saw the back wall and what was waiting there. Behind her, she heard Hassood say a prayer under his breath.

Hundreds of cylinders were waiting there, each one holding the unmoving body of an Annunaki. They were filed and stacked into groups, males and females, each of them with mouth open in silent scream. Not one of the reptilian figures reacted to the flashing amber lights that lit them; they just remained upright within their coffins as if asleep. They were waiting for something, Domi realized, genetic material waiting for the spark of life.

Domi stepped farther into the chamber, peering all around her as she tried to estimate how many Annunaki figures were waiting there. At least two hundred, she guessed, perhaps a hundred more than that, it was difficult to tell in the inadequate, flickering lights. As she tried to take it all in, she saw there were numerous empty cylinders lining the edges of the chamber, too, waiting ominously to be filled by more bodies for the coming Annunaki, presumably more transformed humans.

"We're surrounded," Hassood said, his voice trembling with awe. "But what are they?"

"Gods," Domi said. "Space gods, and evil as hell itself."

Hassood began muttering another prayer as he stared wide-eyed at the sleeping figures arrayed all around them.

OUTSIDE THE GROUNDED BODY of the starship *Tiamat,* Grant primed the last of his explosive charges and scampered back to where Kudo and Rosalia hid along with the woman's dog. Five seconds later, the charge ignited, blasting a deeper rip within the already damaged flesh of the living ship.

Grant stepped out from cover. "This had better do the trick," he warned as he stalked back to the ship's wounded hull with the others following. "After this, I'm all out of charges."

"But not all out of tricks, Magistrate Man," Rosalia teased.

The explosive had done substantial damage, but it had still failed to cut through to the insides of the ship. The hole was almost square now, five feet high and four across, and it went back into the ship well past the length of Grant's outstretched arm. The wound glistened with seeping liquid across jagged bonelike struts, whole chunks of them disintegrated by Grant's miniature explosives. Electricity arced across the gaps in crackling whips, fizzing through the air and making the whiskers of Grant's beard tingle as he stepped closer. There, in the center of the messy indentation, a sliver of darkness stared like an eye, its lack of color giving it prominence. It was a hole, a tunneled hole no larger than Grant's forearm that went all the way through into the interior of the ship.

Wary of the arcing electricity, Grant commanded his Sin Eater pistol into his hand with a simple flinching of his wrist tendons. The compact mechanism of the pistol unfolded as it slapped into his palm, and Grant was careful not to tense his finger and set off the weapon prematurely. A white slash of lightning hurtled past in front of Grant's eyes as he pushed the nose of the blaster through the hole, assuring himself that it really was a hole into the interior. Once he had confirmed that, Grant hastily withdrew both hand and weapon from the hole, stepping back and assessing it again.

Looking at it, Grant shook his head in irritation. "Damn thing's designed for interstellar travel," he said. "There's a lot of wall to get through yet."

Kudo pulled his *katana* from its sheath with a zing of metal. "The blade is sharp as a razor," he said. "Not ideal, but it will cut it—at least until it blunts."

Grant looked at the blade, then back at the hole. "No," he concluded, sending his Sin Eater back to its holster. "The *katana* is a weapon of finesse, and we don't need finesse here. We need brute strength."

With that, Grant stepped back into the widened rent in the ship's hull, pulled one of his powerful legs back and kicked with all his might. Grant angled the blow as a side kick, ensuring that the whole of his foot drove into the gap, heel first. The material at the edge of the hole splintered just a little, and without pause Grant kicked it a second time, then a third. On and on, Grant lashed out, driving his heel into the gap, chipping away at the weak part of the hole to make it larger as electricity sparked all around him.

"Keep going, Magistrate." Rosalia encouraged him. "You're almost through."

Grant stepped back, breathing heavily as he swapped feet before kicking out again with his other foot. It was hard work, like trying to kick through a rotten tree. The shell of the ship crumbled into splinters under the assault, but it was slow going, and Grant was working up a sweat.

Then suddenly another streak of electricity arced across the gap in a brilliant flash, slashing across Grant's body as he struck out again with his booted heel. Grant clenched his teeth as the electricity raced across the surface of his shadow suit, its incredible weave taking the brunt of the voltage.

Then, with one final kick, Grant booted through a whole great chunk of the inner hull, and a thick line the width of a floorboard fell away with a splintering snap.

Grant leaned down, peering through the gap as the dust settled. It was three feet across at its widest point and came up to his breastbone, a little lower than he would have liked but sufficient to clamber through.

Briefly Grant engaged his Commtact. "Cerberus, this is Grant. Have gained access to the center of the city, am heading inside. Is Domi still showing there?"

Brewster Philboyd's familiar voice came back via the pickup beneath Grant's ear, though it buzzed with static here, standing this close to the living ship. "She's still there, Grant. I have her framed at about a quarter mile directly ahead of you. A little less maybe—the reading's jumping about on screen here."

Grant nodded to himself. "Getting a lot of interference on the comm, too," he said. "There's a localized field screwing with our signals, I guess."

"You be careful, Grant," Philboyd warned. "Don't take any unnecessary risks."

"You're mistaking me for Kane, man," Grant joked. "I never take unnecessaries."

Then he cut the communication. It was time to literally enter the belly of the beast. With a nod to his colleagues, Grant recalled the Sin Eater to his hand and pushed through into the interior of the great dragon-form ship. As he stepped through the ruined wall, the stench of rotting fish struck Grant, some quirk of the makeup of the incredible living starship itself. And then he was through, brushing the dripping glop from his face as he stepped into the ship's interior. Kudo and Rosalia followed, the dog scampering along at their side.

Within, the Cerberus warriors found themselves in what appeared to be a corridor. It was ill lit and its walls were ribbed and rounded so that its cross section had a spherical shape. The floor was rounded, too, and Grant found he had to place his feet apart to feel balanced. Grant peered right then left as his companions made their way through the breach in the wall behind him. The ribs continued along the walls of the corridor, meeting above their heads in arches and running below their feet, making moving along the corridor itself a little like walking through a tunnel made of mismatched tires. Neither end looked especially different in the low lighting, and the corridor curved away from sight on both sides without any hint of a doorway. Grant concluded that they were in the middle of an access corridor, which meant that they would need to go one way or the other to discover anything.

"Where are we?" Kudo asked, recalling that Grant had been inside *Tiamat* before.

"Not sure," Grant said, his voice low. "We're going to have to do a little exploring to figure that out. Left or right—you got a preference?"

Kudo shrugged. "Right."

The muzzle of the Sin Eater pointing ahead of him, Grant led the way warily down the tunnel to the right, with his companions spreading themselves out behind him. They kept just a few paces between them, enough to aid one another without—hopefully—being caught by the same surprise trap.

There were no windows along the corridor and the overhead lighting, though constant, was dimmed to a point that left everything gloomy. Grant wondered whether this was preferable to the Annunaki with their reptile genetics. In pondering that point, he realized something else—they had yet to see any signs of the Annunaki themselves. There was no reason to assume that the ship was occupied. It could be that Domi and Kishiro had been brought here via some automated system.

Engaging his Commtact, Grant tried to raise his missing companion. "Domi, do you read me? Domi?"

There was no reply, and after a moment Grant tried again, keeping his voice low as he stalked through the gloomy corridor. Again no response came and when he tried raising Philboyd at Cerberus headquarters he met a similar silence.

"Comms won't work in this area," he informed Rosalia and Kudo. "We're on our own."

As they continued down the curving, tunnel-like corridor, Rosalia's dog stopped in place, its head cocked.

"What is it?" Rosalia asked, peering where the dog was looking. She called to Grant and Kudo, telling them to halt. "The mutt senses something. Might be we're not alone."

Grant peered down the gloomy tunnel, his eyes searching for movement while Kudo stepped back, checking the way they had just come with his *katana* held ready in his hands.

"You hear that?" Rosalia asked as she came to Grant's side, the dog trotting along beside her. "Like a shushing sound."

Grant nodded. "Sounds like…water."

Even as he spoke, a rush of water came hurrying toward them across the bowled floor of the corridor, two feet deep, its ever-changing surface twinkling in the dim illumination. Grant brought his gun up as the water hurtled at them, watery figures emerging from its surface like burrowing creatures seeking the light.

Chapter 21

The Sin Eater bucked in Grant's hand as he blasted a volley of bullets into the emerging figures who stepped from the water. Once again, the bullets whizzed straight through the watery bodies as they formed and continued on down the corridor, cutting little paths like raindrops from the impossible creatures' backs.

"Dammit!" Grant grunted.

Then the wave hit him and Rosalia, crashing into their knees and lashing past them as it continued down the spherical corridor, causing Rosalia's dog to yelp with an animal's appreciation.

From out of the water three figures stepped, each one humanoid in form but made entirely of the water itself. Grant ducked as the first lunged at him, its ill-defined hands rushing at his face with a swish of spray. With swift assuredness, Grant brought the Sin Eater up and through the torso of the water thing, feeling the water sluice around him as he clenched his finger on the trigger while the gun was still inside the creature's body. There was a strange kind of explosion inside the transparent figure where the gun blasted, cutting a foaming gash inside it like a depth charge going off.

Behind Grant, Rosalia stepped back as the second of the creatures leaped past her, scrambling through the spindrift toward Kudo. Then the third leaped at her, lunging out of the water like the sentient crest of a wave. Rosalia raised the sword in her hands, holding it in the vertical position in front of her as the attacker came at her with the fury of the ocean. She blinked her eyes as the blade split the creature, turning it into a shower of hurtling water as it divided into two.

Rosalia spun as the component parts of the water creature hurtled past her, and she watched as it rained back into the surface of the water around her and the dog's feet, the droplets of water sounding like a furious drum solo as they spattered downward. Already it was re-forming, an arm and head emerging once more from the water as Rosalia pulled her sword back, ready to strike.

Farther along the corridor, Kudo leaped up out of the water as the shimmering humanoid form approached. Water drained from his armor in thick streams as the modern-day samurai grabbed for the ceiling, his hand snagging one of the ribs beside the strip lighting there. Beneath Kudo, the water thing splashed past, swirling over and over as it tried to halt its forward motion.

His grip tight on the ceiling rib, Kudo swung his *katana* one-handed, slicing the two-foot-long blade through the creature's neck and decapitating it after a fashion. The decapitation was effective for a single heartbeat, and Kudo watched in frustration as the watery parts rejoined and the figure turned to face him.

The trio steadied themselves as the next wave of attackers came at them.

BENEATH DOMI'S FEET, the waters stilled as the trio of cylinders that contained Kishiro and the others sailed to their final destinations and locked into position with a quiet hum. All around them, the static figures of other Annunaki, naked but for the containment strips that held them in place, glistened as the lines of amber light illuminated their leathery scales. A moment after, the strips of amber lighting that had blurred across the newcomers' chests faded, and the area beneath the catwalks was plunged into near total darkness accompanied by an eerie silence.

Domi peered ahead of her, her eyes struggling to pierce the darkness that had settled across the room. Then she padded silently toward the nearest of the chambered figures, her combat blade gripped tensely in her hand. The Annunaki were so still that they looked like waxworks, their rigid posture akin to an anatomical diagram or a height chart.

Domi was just a few feet away from them now, a row of Annunaki bodies standing in front of her like statues in the dark. Hassood padded along behind her, flinching this way and that as he noticed more of the creepy figures waiting in the shadows.

Each figure towered to almost seven feet in height and while they were genetically identical, each was subtly different from his brethren. Some had single spiny crests running along the top of their skulls like a Mohawk hairstyle, others had bony protrusions arrayed around them like crowns and still others had smooth heads showing no protrusions at all. All the figures were powerfully built, however, their defined musculature evident across their broad chests and strong limbs. Domi moved across the room, gazing at the females, their rounded breasts and slender waists defining their gender far more than their faces or hidden genitalia.

As she stood there, surrounded by the sleeping forms of more than two hundred Annunaki, Domi felt intense rage welling inside her, twinned with fear of all that the Annunaki had done. Here was the enemy, waiting to be reborn and to wreak havoc upon the planet Earth. And while their bodies slept, waiting for the genetic download that would trigger them to life, here was the perfect opportunity to destroy them, to wipe out their race before it could get a foothold on the Earth again.

Domi glared at the nearest Annunaki, a broad-shouldered female with pendulous breasts and a brown sheen to her scales, and she placed her knife to the figure's throat. It would be the work of a single second to cut the thing's throat, a move she could repeat two hundred or more times until every last one of the ghastly things was dead, stillborn before the personality download process could begin. Her hand trembled as she pressed her knife against the sleeping Annunaki's cool flesh. But she had to be smart, do what Kane or Brigid or Lakesh would do. Killing the bodies would only postpone the birthing process. Whatever Enlil had done, he had found a way to fast track the growth of the Annunaki bodies by tampering with human DNA; killing these bodies was not enough, would merely cause Enlil to seek more victims for his twisted plan.

Domi bit her lip, feeling a coolness come over her as the rage began to subside. She pulled the knife away from the still figure, letting it rest limply at her side. She had to be smart.

In a moment, she engaged her Commtact. "Cerberus, this is Domi. Do you read me? Over."

She waited in the darkness for a response.

GRANT WAS KNEELING ON the floor of the corridor, batting aside the water as it came at his face where the liquid human form tried to drown him. The Sin Eater in his hand jerked as he drilled another burst of 9 mm

slugs into the thing's body, driving the pistol downward
to force the shots to cut through the length of the creature. As he fired again, Grant heard a voice over the
rush of water echoing through the corridor.

"Cerber—is Domi. Do—ou read me? Over."

It was his Commtact, Grant realized, springing to
life at Domi's broadcast. The voice was broken up but
distinct, and Grant engaged his Commtact without hesitation. "Domi? This is Grant. I can hear you. Do you
read me?"

The water creature in front of him slapped its
mittenlike hand over Grant's mouth, and he felt the
wash of water running up his nose, making him see
stars. Intentionally, Grant toppled backward, falling to
the floor and away from the thing's liquid hand.

"Got some of th—Grant. Where are you?"

"Close by," Grant told Domi as her fractured message piped into his ear. "But kinda busy." Even as he
spoke, he was rolling through the shallow water away
from the thrusting arms of the water thing. "Brewster's been tracking your transponder, but the Commtact signals are being disrupted somehow." He drew
his blaster up, shoving the tip into the water thing's
face and pumping the trigger. Slick runnels of water
charged from the back of the thing's head along with
the bullets, carving a path toward the far end of the
corridor. "Looks like you're inside *Tiamat*."

"*Tiamat?*" Domi was unable to disguise her surprise when she responded. "But—ought she exploded.
—ver mind, we have bigger worries right n—"

Grant spun backward as the water creature swished
its leg up for a vicious head kick. The kick connected
with his cheek, splattering it and again searching for

his nostrils and mouth in a determined effort to drown him. "What worries?" Grant demanded. "What's going on?"

Static came back over the Commtact as Domi's reply failed to come through clearly.

Grant whipped his pistol up with little hope, blasting another clutch of 9 mm slugs deep into and through his attacker's torso. Behind him, Rosalia and Kudo were engaged with their own foes, struggling to find some way to gain an advantage.

"Please repeat, Domi," Grant urged. "I didn't catch that."

DOMI'S DESPERATE WORDS echoed through the vast chamber of sleeping Annunaki shells. "Enlil's using the ship to create a new pantheon of gods," she shouted, willing the message to reach Grant. "He's grafting Annunaki DNA to human bodies.

"Do you hear me?"

There was no response, and Domi cursed vehemently, wishing there was some way to communicate with Grant. As she searched the room, wondering what to do, an ugly voice echoed from behind her.

"You're smarter than most credit you, Domi."

Domi turned as Enlil stepped from the shadows of the staircase, batting Hassood aside with one powerful flick of his arm as he lunged toward her. He stopped in front of her, a cruel reptilian sneer appearing on his features. "For an apekin, that is."

Before the last word had left Enlil's mouth, Domi pounced at him, leaping into the air. Enlil brought his arm up to bat her away as the albino girl slashed the knife at his face. Her blow missed his face, instead striking his upheld forearm with such force that it cut through his natural armor with a gush of blood.

Then she was spinning away, landing on the floor and rolling over and over to slow her momentum. She was up again in a heartbeat, feet pounding against the hard floor as she leaped into the air once again. Enlil was ready for her this time, his right arm shooting forward and snatching Domi by her outstretched arm, swinging her out and away from him.

Domi sailed across the chamber before slamming into a wall of cylinder frames, several of them containing the lifeless bodies of the adult Annunaki. She shook her head, trying to clear it as Enlil came charging toward her, leaping the little streams of water as he powered across the chamber, his scarlet cape billowing out behind him like a bloody mist.

"Grant, listen to me," Domi shouted, hoping their Commtacts were still linked. "Enlil's regrown the Annunaki pantheon. Two hundred space gods, and he's about to bring them to life."

Enlil kicked out as Domi tried to roll away, and his multiclawed foot clipped her across the chest, driving the air out of her in a strained gasp. Domi brought her knife down between the alien's toes, ripping through the scales and driving it point-first into Enlil's soft flesh.

Enlil bellowed in reply, stepping away from Domi with the blade still wedged between his claws. Coughing as she took another breath, Domi pushed herself back, using the struts of one of the empty cylinders to drag herself to her feet. Before she could do more than that, she felt Enlil strike her on the back of the head. She fell forward, crashing face-first into the back wall of the empty cylinder. A trace of tiny lights sprang to

life on the wall in front of her, and Domi saw the illumination from behind her as the cylinder's amber bars
came to life, locking her within its tubelike form.

"And now," Enlil railed, "you will finally become
useful."

Domi turned in the cramped space, her mind
screaming at her to get free. She was a child of the
Outlands and as such she detested being caged in any
manner, far more so than the folks who had grown up
within the rooms and high walls of the villes. "Let me
out," she snapped, twisting her body to see what was
occurring on the front side of the narrow container.

Enlil ignored her pleas as he pulled the knife from
his foot and tossed it aside, a spit of blood bubbling
there. Then he picked up the fallen form of Hassood
and placed the man's unconscious body in another of
the empty cylinders. With a flick of his palm control-
ler, Enlil strode out of the main chamber and past the
stairs, and Domi and Hassood followed within the cylinders, bobbing along the narrow canals of water that
crisscrossed the room.

Domi hammered against the edges of the cylinder as
it journeyed along the stream toward the stairs. Though
she couldn't feel it directly, some kind of invisible field
held her in place, solid like hardened air. "Let me out,
you lousy snake-face," Domi snarled.

Now standing in front of his control console, Enlil
turned to Domi and smiled. "Rejoice. Evolution has
arrived," he thundered.

Domi watched helplessly as he depressed a lighted
switch on the control board.

Chapter 22

The grimly illuminated shaft of the stairwell resounded with blasts as Kane depressed the Sin Eater's trigger again and again, rapidly loosing bursts of bullets at the oncoming torrent of rocks. Behind him, Balam watched in amazement as the baseball-size stones seemed to peel from the face of the walls and tumble into the air, throwing themselves at the Cerberus warrior with no sense of order or reason.

"This was a mistake," Kane scoffed. "We've triggered some kind of death trap, and it's building its attack."

"Stoned to death," Balam responded as another of the spherical rocks hurled itself at Kane's head. "I imagine it's a nasty way to die."

"Let's not find out," Kane said as he knocked the rock aside with a jab of his fist.

In a moment they had turned back, stepping out into the corridor once more and slamming the stairwell door behind them. "That'll contain them," Kane said.

"But it traps us here," Balam observed.

To Kane's ears, Balam sounded maddeningly calm about the whole situation. He could afford to be, Kane realized—the rocks didn't seem to be interested in attacking Balam of the First Folk.

Kane scanned the corridor, his vision popping as it tried to adjust to the change in lighting. He clenched his teeth, feeling strangely disconnected from what he was seeing now, the process of sight no longer truly connected to his body.

The corridor, like the rest of the old redoubt, had jagged struts of stone depending from the ceiling like stalactites now. The walls were rough, blisters of stone running unevenly along them with veins of magma churning through them to act as lamps. Kane led the way back toward the canteen, turning down another corridor, the floor plan of the ancient redoubt still familiar despite the cosmetic changes. As he walked, he heard something moving off to his right, that fabled point-man sense alerting him even before he became consciously aware of the danger. He turned, his free arm going up to protect Balam where the shorter creature walked behind him, his Sin Eater aiming at the noise even though he hadn't identified it.

There was another of the ball-like rocks there, charcoal dark and rolling across the wall in an uncanny way as if magnetically attached to the vertical surface. Without warning, the rock popped, leaping from the wall and hurling itself at Kane's head.

Kane snapped off a blast from his Sin Eater as he shouted the command to Balam. "Run!"

Missing Kane by just two inches, the flying rock continued along its arc, smashing into the far wall with such force that it kicked up shards of broken stone from the surface.

Kane was already moving, urging Balam to keep going as more of the strange rocks formed across the surface of the walls and began launching themselves at the intruders.

The two of them ran back to the canteen, Balam waiting just inside the double doors, holding them open for Kane to enter. Ducking from another volley of the palm-size rocks, Kane slid through the doorway on his knees, instructing Balam to close the door as he entered.

"The whole redoubt's primed to kill us…me," Kane said, correcting himself without thinking.

"Then we need to get out of here," Balam concluded, his reedy voice ringing in Kane's ears as the ex-Magistrate's eyes struggled to adjust once more, much to his frustration.

"We'll use the interphaser," Kane said after a moment's consideration.

Balam bowed in supplication. "I know—it is how I came to be here. But how do you propose we access the chamber itself?"

Kane scanned the walls, searching for more of the rock balls. They seemed to take time to generate, drawing from the surface of the walls, he had noticed. But it would not be long before they reappeared in this room, tossing themselves at him with savage purpose. He and Balam had to move quickly.

Kane marched across the canteen until he was at the table where they had eaten, sending his Sin Eater back into its hidden housing beneath his right sleeve. With a swift flick of his arm, he cleared the remaining crockery and snatched the plastic tray up in his hands. "Come on," he told Balam, pacing swiftly back to the double doors.

A moment later they were out in the corridor, hurrying along at a jog, with Kane taking the lead. The curious, spherical stones rolled across the walls as Kane ran by, disengaging and tossing themselves at him with no warning. Kane sidestepped the first and ducked the second, paying no attention as the stones slapped against the floor.

When the third budded from the ceiling and dropped at Kane's head, the ex-Magistrate responded with lightning-fast reactions, bringing the fourteen-by-eight-inch rectangular tray up and using it like a shield, batting the rock aside. A fourth stone fired out of the wall to Kane's right, slamming against the ex-Magistrate's flank before he could move his makeshift shield into position. Kane grunted with the impact, grateful for the shadow suit he wore with its armored weave. Even so, he still felt that blow, and had to move swiftly to sidestep a fifth stone missile.

"Keep going," Kane said, indicating the door to the stairs.

"What about you? Are you hurt?" Balam asked.

"I'll be fine," Kane assured him. "You go on ahead of me. These rocks won't attack you, so just make your way to the mat-trans chamber and I'll follow as soon as I can."

Balam pushed against the heavy fire door leading to the stairwell, turning back once to give Kane a further piece of information. "You must stay close or our bond will lose coherence," he explained. "You'll lose your vision again."

Kane nodded. "How close?"

"Perhaps fifteen feet," Balam advised. "There will be no mistaking it," he added ominously.

Kane leaped back as another of the stones bulged from the wall and hurled itself at him. "Just go as fast as you can," he instructed Balam. "I won't be far behind."

As Balam pushed into the stairwell he wondered whether Kane was brave or merely crazy. He was re-

minded of that ancient human saying, of how fools
rushed in where angels feared to tread. Kane had lost
Brigid and his home, and was beginning to lose his
eyesight. Could his grip on sanity be slipping, too?
Balam dismissed the thought as he hurried down the
staircase, lifting the skirts of his indigo robe just a little
to allow his feet free movement. From above, he heard
Kane battling with the bizarre rock guardians, knocking them away or stepping out of their line of fire as
he made his own way down the internal stairs.

One turn of the stairwell above, Kane eyed the walls
warily, his vision popping with specks of light. Even
through the controlled environment of the shadow suit,
Kane could tell that the stairwell was icy cold; the temperature of the whole redoubt had dropped since it had
been abandoned, its air control broken. The glowing
veins in the walls, however, remained burning hot, and
when Kane neared them it was like waving one's fingers through the steam of a boiling kettle: a sudden,
palpable heat that seemed to snatch at the skin.

Kane continued down the staircase, his booted feet
clattering against the uneven steps that, like the rest of
the redoubt, had been overcome by rocky growths.

As he turned the bend in the stairs at the midstory
landing, another of the hard, round balls of rock dis-
engaged from the wall and threw itself at him. Kane
whipped the plastic meal tray up to block it, brac-
ing himself for the impact as the hard chunk of stone
slammed against his makeshift shield with a clatter.
The rock dropped away, leaving a hairline crack in
the surface of the tray. Kane sidestepped as another
rock burst from the stone-clad wall, firing across
the cramped stairwell toward him with the force of a
cannonball. The ball-shaped rock whipped past Kane,

missing his broad chest by an inch as it hurtled onward and into the floor.

Kane watched for a moment as the rock rolled unevenly on the rough surface of the step, before it turned in place and careened back into the wall there. A moment later, like so much dough, it had been absorbed by the rocky surface of the wall itself, the bulge smoothing over as quickly as it had appeared.

Kane moved onward, scurrying down the steps and making his way past the next story. Abruptly his vision seemed to lose color, the bright veins of magma turning to a white-streaked gray in an instant.

I'm too far from Balam, he realized, redoubling his pace and taking the stairs two at a time. Up ahead, Kane heard the heavy fire door crash open as Balam made his exit. Beside his head, another of the budlike stones was forming into existence.

ON THE DISTANT PACIFIC COAST, Lakesh stood on the balcony outside the makeshift ops room, reading the results of the spectrographic study of Edwards's skull. The man's head was full of rock, running around the inside of his skull casing in thin, weblike strands. The rock had completely blocked his Commtact, which explained why Edwards had seemed out of touch during field missions in the weeks prior to the successful attack on Cerberus.

"Dr. Singh?" A man's voice came from behind him, firm but gentle, respectful of his solitude.

Lakesh turned, saw one of the Tigers of Heaven standing there in his techno armor. The man stood with head slightly bowed, his hands clenched loosely together in front of him.

"Yes…Ryochi?" Lakesh said, recalling the man's

name after a moment's hesitation. Lakesh believed in good personnel relations and he had made an effort to learn the names of every one of Shizuka's men who had come to support them.

"There is something that you should see," Ryochi said, "out by the East Gate."

Lakesh nodded, following the warrior without question as he made his way around the raised wooden balcony that surrounded the winter retreat.

"He was spotted by my partner," Ryochi explained, "and we brought it to Mistress Shizuka's attention straight away."

Indeed, Shizuka was standing at the balcony on the other side of the house, a set of field glasses raised to her eyes as she scanned the easternmost edge of the vast property. At her name, she lowered the binoculars and turned to greet Lakesh.

"It seems we have jackals at the door," Shizuka stated ominously, handing the binoculars to Lakesh.

Placing the lenses to his eyes, Lakesh located the east gate in a moment. Constructed of steel and painted red, the gate was made up of two dozen eight-foot-high metal struts, standing vertically like spears carried by an invisible army. The gate was more than a dozen feet wide and a sentry box stood beside it. Typically one of Shizuka's warriors would man the gate, granting access only to those he deemed acceptable. The road beyond was largely unused, an out-of-the-way track off the beaten path. Only those seeking the mansion itself would come up it intentionally.

Steadying the binoculars with both hands, Lakesh scanned the area past the gate until he spotted a figure poised by the long-hanging foliage. The figure was dressed in a dark robe, the hood cinched up to hide its face, a small leather pouch tied to its waist. Loose-fitting and shapeless, the robe left Lakesh uncertain as to whether the figure was male or female. Even so, he knew what the person was and—by association—what he or she wanted.

"Firewalker." Lakesh cursed, recalling the term Brigid had applied to the devoted warriors of Ulli-kummis before her recent disappearance.

"He's been there twenty minutes, perhaps more," Shizuka informed Lakesh. "He doesn't seem to be moving, just waiting."

"He senses we're here," Lakesh conceded. He pulled the binoculars from his eyes then, and she saw the weariness cloud his face for a moment.

"Lakesh?"

"We still understand so little about our foe, this Ullikummis," Lakesh said. "How he communicates with his people, how he spreads his message. It's part religion but there's more to it. This…monster seems able to see things beyond what's there. It's like facing a grand chess master, knowing you are utterly outclassed yet unable to see the killing move until he strikes."

Handing the binoculars back to Shizuka, Lakesh turned away from the balcony. "There is a pawn on the fifth rank," he said. "Tell your men to watch him, but do nothing to attract any further attention. For now, all we can do is wait."

"As the vultures circle," Shizuka added as Lakesh departed.

IT HAD TAKEN EIGHTEEN minutes to reach the operations room, a journey that normally would have taken perhaps three or four. Balam arrived first, standing at the open doors beneath the Mercator map. The map was

vandalized, rocky spines stretching across it and turning it into something nightmarish—like an alien, stony
hand crushing the globe.

Balam watched the corridor beyond, its arching roof
a spiny plethora of stalactites. It was silent, showing no
signs of movement. Balam waited, watching the heavy
fire door he had exited not thirty seconds earlier, waiting for Kane to appear. Their bond was breaking apart,
he realized, and Kane's vision would be in flux until
he came close enough to reestablish it.

Suddenly the fire door crashed open and Kane came
hurtling through, batting at something with the plastic
tray he held. He looked to where Balam stood in the
open doorway. "Keep moving," he ordered through
gritted teeth.

Balam turned, hurrying farther into the ops room.

Alone now in the corridor, Kane stumbled forward,
feeling the ache in his muscles where he'd been batting the flying rocks aside. Once again, his vision was
sailing in and out of reality, the rocky corridor walls
swimming in front of his eyes. "Come on, Kane," he
told himself. "Keep it together."

In the ops room, Balam waddled past the twin rows
of rock to the chamber that contained the mat-trans.
Like Kane, he had traveled here by interphaser, and
he had hidden the device in a rocky nook close to the
chamber. The device itself was priceless, and it would
not do for it to fall into the wrong hands.

As Balam set up the interphaser within the mat-
trans chamber, he wondered whether his wounded body
would be able to cope with the journey through quantum space. Such travel could be hard on an injury, he
understood, but for now they seemed to have run out
of other options.

Balam looked up as the twin doors to the operations room shoved open and Kane came staggering in, the tray still clutched in his hands. He looked tired, his unshaved face streaked with dirt and sweat. Even as Balam called to him, something began to form on the rock surface of the wall that housed the Mercator map. Small, circular rocks budded there, taking shape in front of Balam's weary eyes. A second later, as Kane strode toward him across the vast room, one of those rocks fired from the wall as if shot from a cannon, throwing itself at the Cerberus warrior. Kane reacted before Balam could even shout a warning, spinning on his heel and hoisting the tray high, deflecting the hurtling rock.

Then another rock—and another and another—popped from the wall, blasting across the room at Kane as he stood in place like a batter on the mound.

"Get the interphaser fired up," Kane called to Balam, sidestepping one of the rocks even as he shielded himself from the impact of the next.

Balam turned back to the interphaser, his spindly fingers playing across its command pad, setting the coordinates in a swift flurry. The silver-sided pyramid waited patiently, accepting Balam's instructions in silence. Then the unit began to hum, a low note that seemed to vibrate through Balam's body. He stepped back as it appeared to open up, a stream of swirling light emanating from top and bottom as the gateway began to form.

"It's opening," Balam stated, his eyes fixed on the magical rush of colors that formed a cone over the little metal pyramid. A mirror image of that cone appeared beneath, penetrating impossibly into the floor.

Balam turned, watching for a moment as the powerfully built ex-Mag pulled the tray across his shoulder, using both hands to hold it at one end. Then, as the next rock launched across the operations room, Kane swung the battered tray in a swift arc, knocking the stone aside with a clatter of cracking plastic.

More stones were attacking Kane, dropping from the ceiling and budding in the twin aisles where the Cerberus desks had once stood, launching themselves at the intruder in their midst. Kane leaped over one that fired low, gasped as it clipped his foot, knocking him to one side. Then another rock was falling from the high ceiling, rushing at his face with a whistle of wind. Rolling onto his back, Kane held the tray out once again, letting its plastic surface take the brunt of the blow. The tray snapped as the rock was pushed aside, and Kane tossed the two pieces away as he leaped to his feet.

Up ahead of him, Kane could see the flickering lights of the interphaser window through the open door to the mat-trans chamber, Balam's bulbous-headed silhouette waiting amid the crackling cone of swirling lightning. Kane kicked off the floor, running across the room and dodging as more of the spherical rocks formed and dropped at him in a barrage, like some nightmarish parody of a snowball fight. Two of the hard rocks struck him, slamming into his chest and abdomen, the force of the blows unmistakable even through the protective weave of the shadow suit. Kane grunted with the pain, never slowing, hurrying on to the open door.

Then, in the blink of an eye, he and Balam were gone, the swirl of colored light imploding into nothingness.

Chapter 23

The water creature swung both hands at Grant in a double fist as he listened to Domi's frantic message playing through his Commtact receiver. "Grant, listen—" Domi began, static interrupting her urgent words. "Enlil's—nunaki pantheon. Two hundr—gods, and they're abou—brought to life."

Grant shoved his Sin Eater into the water creature's jaw and blasted off another burst of lethal fire. "Domi's in trouble," he shouted as the thing splashed over him like a cloudburst. "We need to figure a way to her right now."

A few feet away, Rosalia's mangy-looking mutt was up to its belly in the rushing water as it barked at the vicious beings that attacked them. Rosalia's wet hair whipped heavily around her as she peered left and right down the curving corridor. "Doors," she shouted to Grant. "Find some doors."

"What good's that going to do us?" Grant snapped as he sidestepped another lightning-swift attack from his liquid-bodied opponent.

Rosalia kicked up the water as she ran past him. "Better than nothing," she told him.

Grant could hardly argue with that logic. If nothing else, at least they would be moving in the right direction to meet with Domi. He engaged his Commtact once again, blurted a message to Domi hoping that she would hear. "Domi, we're coming. Just try to keep Enlil busy until we get there." Of course, he couldn't possibly know if she would hear the message or not.

At the rear of the group, Kudo dropped down from his perch on the low ceiling, splashing into the water wielding the *katana*. His own foe was behind him now, and Kudo dropped, swinging an upward kick at the thing's eerily half-formed face. The creature's head burst into a cascade of water, splattering the walls, and for a moment it swayed there, headless.

Kudo ran, arms pumping at his sides as, behind him, the creature re-formed, its head reappearing atop its stub of neck. There were two more of the water creatures still standing in the tunnel-like corridor, but Kudo didn't slow his pace. Instead he merely ran close to the left wall, using one of the riblike struts to kick off and dart around the first creature before ducking the attack of the second. In a moment he was in the clear, but all three water creatures were charging after him with the relentlessness of a tsunami.

The corridor continued its shallow curve inward, leading the three Cerberus warriors deeper into the guts of the grounded spacecraft. Water continued to splash around their feet, and Rosalia's dog took to swimming through the deluge, its paws just barely reaching the floor otherwise. Thigh deep in water, Rosalia was leading the way, the *katana* flashing in her hand beneath the subtle illumination of the organic-feeling corridor. Immediately behind her, Grant peered over his shoulder, assessing how far away the water figures were. To his surprise they were gone; it was just Kudo now who was splashing through the water a half-dozen paces behind him.

"Where the fuck did they go?" Grant muttered, a scowl furrowing his dark brow.

Then the water seemed to swell behind Kudo, and a humanoid figure came lunging for him, cut off at the waist and far larger than a man. Kudo increased his pace, desperately trying to outrun those grasping hands.

Automatically, Grant slowed his pace and rattled off a stuttered burst of bullets, aiming them far to Kudo's right where they pinged off the riblike walls in a shower of sparks. The water giant reacted to the sparks, swaying aside as it grabbed for Kudo again.

Up ahead, Rosalia spotted a doorway that led off to the left. She turned back, saw that Grant had slowed as he tried to provide covering fire for their Tigers of Heaven ally.

"Get your head back in the game, Magistrate," Rosalia bellowed.

Grant turned back, saw the swish of her long hair as the woman ducked through the doorway and disappeared. Her dog leaped over the lip of the doorway after her, its fur heavy with water.

Grant trudged through the hip-deep water to the doorway, stepping half in and waiting there with his Sin Eater targeted back down the corridor.

"Come on, Magistrate," Rosalia teased. "Get in."

"No one gets left behind on my watch, sister," Grant told her, rattling off another burst of fire as Kudo struggled to keep ahead of his watery pursuer.

Kudo leaped through the doorway, and Grant pulled it shut behind him.

Rosalia looked at Grant sourly. "Your nobility will get us killed one of these days, Magistrate."

Grant ignored her, looking down at the pooling

water beneath their feet. It was shallower here, just a half-inch layer like a carpet over the floor of the room, running perhaps six feet into the room itself. The room appeared to be another corridor, wider this time with a more traditional, almost square shape to its design. As Grant looked around, a series of brighter lights stuttered automatically to life farther down the length of the walkway.

"So, what's the plan?" Grant asked.

Rosalia smiled. "This is it," she said, and she began marching off down the corridor. Dutifully, the dog trotted along at her side, shaking water from its fur and looking up at her for encouragement.

Behind Grant, Kudo was shaking his head as he checked the door. "This won't hold them," he decided.

"Kudo's right," Grant agreed. "This thing doesn't even have a lock."

Rosalia turned back, giving both men a withering look. "You ever hear of the naiads?" she asked. "They were water spirits in Greek mythology who acted as guardians and deities for the rivers and tributaries across Greece and its islands. When their source dried up, it was said that the naiads died."

"What, so you think we're fighting these naiads?" Grant asked.

"The water was crucial for transport between the islands in ancient times," Rosalia reminded him. "It acted the same way a road system would. It seems that Domi and Kishiro were transported here via some secret network of water, not the same but close enough."

"Secret rivers," Grant muttered, nodding slowly as he began to comprehend.

"The world is full of secret things," Rosalia quipped.

"Sometimes it's down to the way you look at something before you really get to see it for what it is."

"Which doesn't address our problem," Grant urged. "How do we keep them from coming through the door?" As he spoke, the sloshing sounds of the water behind him swelled in volume, crashing against the door.

"Find the source and cut it off," Rosalia said with a superior smile. "Even money says that's in this ship somewhere."

"A spaceship will have water tanks," Grant said slowly, nodding once more in agreement. "If we can shut them down or seal them somehow, then in theory, our watery friends will lose their impetus."

Rosalia nodded. "You catch on quick for a Magistrate."

Grant jogged along the corridor after Rosalia, and a moment later Kudo was following them, checking over his shoulder that the door was still sealed. Water was pooling there, seeping through the bottom of the door.

"We still have to find Domi and Kishiro," Grant told them. "That's priority number one. The water things, we'll deal with when we can."

DOMI SQUIRMED AGAINST the invisible wall that seemed to bind her, feeling the floor and walls of the cylinder vibrate as a low thrum echoed through the room. Over to her left, Hassood was still slumped in his own container, creating the bizarre illusion that he was leaning forward against nothing, like some sinister mime act. Domi saw his body shudder as the vibration struck him.

Enlil was busy now with the organlike control board, his back turned to Domi and her companion.

The board was arrayed in a fan, with large, wedge-shaped keys running across it like slices of a pie, reminding Domi of a musical organ more than a computer. To her, the unit's operation seemed almost mystical, and she concluded it involved not only the dimly glowing keys of the board, but also a small unit that Enlil held in his palm. Enlil would take long blinks between certain manipulations of the keyboard, suggesting to Domi that there was also some kind of mind link involved in its operation. It was unfathomable.

Now, while Enlil was diverted by operating his device, Domi still stood a chance of escape. But that window of opportunity was rapidly narrowing to nothing.

If only she had her knife she might just have a chance to free herself, Domi realized. But the knife was back there, lying discarded on the chamber floor between two channels of water. Still, there had to be a way out of here, didn't there? She had found the weak point in the ice cell; how much more difficult could this trap be?

Domi stopped squirming, felt the pit of her stomach drop as that wicked resonance coursed through her fragile form. Surreptitiously, she ran her hands over the back wall of the cylinder, the solid section that appeared to be carved of blackened bone. There were nicks and gouges there, but she could not feel any seams to suggest a rear door. The front then, or the top.

THE RISING WATER SWIRLED around their feet as Grant, Rosalia and Kudo hurried along the flat-walled corridor. It was still just an inch deep, but the pool was expanding, reaching out from the closed door behind them in a dark stain that swirled across the floor as it grew.

They continued running, desperately trying to outpace it. Ahead of them, the corridor split in two, and there was a ladder cut into the wall. The rungs of the ladder looked like the bones of the spine, curving as they disappeared in a narrow hole in the floor. The hole itself was circular with a raised edge, the lip lit in a semicircular, soft crimson glow. Grant knew he needed to take charge, be the leader that Kane would have been in the same situation.

"We need to split up," he decided. "Someone has to drain the water tanks or these naiads or whatever they are, are going to keep hindering us."

"I'll go," Kudo volunteered. "But you'll need to point me in the right direction."

"Water's heavy," Grant reasoned as he handed Kudo something from one of his belt pouches, "so aircraft tend to carry it low down, close to the undercarriage. I don't know enough about alien spaceships to know if that rule holds, but it's all I've got."

With a single nod, Kudo grasped the rungs of the ladder and began clambering down to a lower level of *Tiamat*. "Good luck, friends."

"And to you," Grant said.

"What about me?" Rosalia asked, the dog scampering on ahead of her down the forked corridor.

Grant pulled a sour face. "I've met Enlil before and I sure as shootin' don't want to tackle him on my own if I can help it. Domi's last message didn't make a whole lot of sense, but whatever's going on I'd appreciate the backup."

Rosalia nodded solemnly. "Then I guess we keep going."

The dark stain of water expanded across the floor behind them as they ran, reaching the hole in the decking where Kudo has disappeared and swirling around the gap like a living thing.

Domi's palms ran across the invisible front plate of the cylinder, the section that had locked in place with some kind of force wall. The strip of amber lights was glowing frenetically there, a crazy pattern playing across her retina in golden hues. Though beyond her range of sight, the wall seemed absolutely solid, and it was utterly smooth to the touch like Jell-O popped from a mold.

At the strange console, Enlil continued to tap at the keys, his clawed fingers darting this way and that as he played some nightmarish, silent orchestration, faster and faster to reach an imagined crescendo. As he did so, Domi heard a voice beside her and turned to see Hassood just waking up.

"Where—? What happened?" he asked, looking barely awake. From inside the cylinder his voice sounded as if it was coming from an old-fashioned diving suit, echoing and tinny, as if spoken down a long iron pipe. Then his body tensed and he arched his back, his breastbone jutting out toward the front of the chamber. "What is—" he began, rising fear in his tone.

"We're in a lot of trouble, Hassood," Domi told him, her hands still testing the walls of the pod. "My friends are on their way."

Hassood looked frantic, his eyes wide and his voice cracked as he spoke. "Look at all the good they did for my cousin!" he shrieked before reverting to a muttered prayer, his lips working through the syllables as he closed his eyes. His body strained upward, as if being drawn there by powerful magnets.

Domi looked away as the man screamed, turning her full attention back to the walls of the cylinder.

THE *KATANA* AT HIS BELT slapped rhythmically at his side as Kudo clambered hand over hand down the bone-like ladder. He found himself plunging into darkness once more, and could not see how deep the ladder went before it might access another deck. It certainly brought home just how huge the spaceship *Tiamat* was.

As he clambered on, water began dripping from above, finding its way through the circular cut in the floor. Kudo looked up, saw the crimson semicircle glowing there, felt a single drip of water splash against his cheek.

He hurried onward, his hands and legs working in unison as he sought the next deck down. The rungs of the ladder became slippery, slick with water as he continued urgently toward the next level. The constant dripping sounded like a dinner bell in his ears, and all he could see was the wall behind the bonelike ladder as he urged himself to greater speed.

In a moment he was there, reaching the floor of a vast, echoing chamber whose next closest wall was so far away that he couldn't even guess at its distance. Kudo extricated himself from the ladder and began searching for the water tanks, even as the ladder itself became slick with water.

The gloom painted shadows across everything, and a low rumbling seemed to echo through the floor plates of the room. As water trickled down the ladder behind him, Kudo unsheathed his sword once more and stalked warily into the room.

HASSOOD WAS SCREAMING, a stream of howled words shrieking from his taut mouth as witchfire ran across his body in the containment field of the pod.

Domi tried her best to ignore the noise. She reached up, trying the ceiling of the little cylinder she had been caught within like a bug in a jar, her chalk-white fingers scrabbling frantically to find some weak spot, a seam in the construction.

Domi's eyes were drawn to her left once more, where Hassood was struggling within his invisible bonds. The man was shaking now, bouncing in place as his body vibrated. Barely four feet from the spectacle, Domi found she could no longer ignore it. Hassood shrieked, a strained, hoarse sound as his body shook itself faster and faster within the containment field. With a sudden rip, his cotton shirt tore, splitting along the arms and across the chest, the buttons springing from it as their threads snapped, firing forward with the speed of bullets until they struck the invisible force wall and abruptly dropped to the floor of the cylinder.

Hassood screwed his eyes up in agony, and Domi wanted to scream in sympathy. When he opened them a few seconds later, they were changing. The coffee-dark irises shrunk to nothing and a yellow wash seemed to bleed into the whites like paint dropped in water.

When Hassood blinked again, Domi saw the eyes were reptilian now, a match for Enlil's. The soft skin around his eyes was changing, too, tautening into a harder substance, flakes appearing and affixing themselves. At some point—though Domi hadn't noticed when—the man had stopped screaming, his agonized shriek curtailed with the abruptness of a guillotine. His jaw was altering shape, too, she saw, its lines becoming harder, more angular, the center of the face jutting outward more like a snout. He was Annunaki now, she realized, his genetics twisted, recoded, immutably changed beyond repair.

As the thing that had been Hassood slumped lifelessly against the walls of the containment cylinder, Domi felt the plate beneath her vibrating, felt her whole body begin to tremble and shudder as if with intense cold. "Stop it," she begged. "Stop it now."

It did not stop.

GRANT AND ROSALIA HEARD Domi's pleas coming from up ahead, and they redoubled their speed as they ran through a narrow room lined with chairs. Each chair stood on a single leg, and their backs were uncomfortably arched in a manner that made them look more like the buds of flowers waiting to be open in bloom. Each chair contained a headset attachment on a swivel arm that stuck out close to the headrest, the unit working via some kind of pivot arrangement.

Rosalia's dog dashed ahead of its mistress, paws padding against the hard deck as it sought the open door that led into the next chamber. Grant almost tripped over the mutt when he caught up, for the animal was standing just inside the doorway, peering into the room beyond.

Her breath coming hard, Rosalia joined them a moment later. "What is it?" she asked, keeping her voice to a whisper.

"Look for yourself," Grant said.

They were on an open catwalk with an uneven, arched floor and no safety rail. Beneath them waited the vast chamber full of the sleeping Annunaki, two hundred or more poised in their slumber, just waiting to be brought to life.

Chapter 24

Domi shrieked again, and Grant pinpointed her position by the noise, spotting the flashing lines of amber light that illuminated her containment pod over at the far end of the room.

"That's Domi," he growled, already in motion, hurrying along the catwalk as swiftly as he could.

Rosalia followed, the dog bounding past her to get ahead. "What do you plan on doing?" she asked as she ran.

Grant assessed the crisscrossed catwalks, searching for a way to the room itself. "I don't know yet," he admitted. "Find a way to stop Enlil."

They ran, taking a turn where two catwalks crossed, tromping toward where a staircase met the high avenues. The room seemed to be vibrating, a low shuddering playing deep in their ears. Below them, Enlil swept a clawed hand over a softly lit semicircular podium and a series of ghostly lights flickered there for a few seconds.

"What is he doing?" Rosalia asked in wonder.

"I can't tell, but Domi said something about more Annunaki," Grant warned.

Then they heard Domi scream in pain and the amber bands that locked her in place grew brighter, coursing with energy. Enlil's hideous, duotonal voice pierced the air as he raised it over the sounds of Domi's agonized screams.

"Welcome, my sister. You shall be Lilitu."

Grant's Commtact burst to life at that moment, as Domi's shrieking voice drilled into his skull. "Grant, where are you? Where—?"

Grant, Rosalia and the dog were at one of the stairwell entrances now, and Grant clattered down it without slowing, taking the curving stairs two at a time.

"I'm coming," Grant snarled over the Commtact link. "Be there in a minute."

Following Grant down the bowed stairs, Rosalia glanced around her and saw the cylinders waiting in the shadows, each one populated with a sleeping Annunaki figure. "Grant, we're outnumbered here," she shouted, advising caution.

Grant ignored her, hurrying down the stairs, the Sin Eater ready in his right hand. As he reached the bottom of the stairwell, still fifty feet from where Enlil was charging Domi's form with new DNA, altering her form beyond recognition, Grant skidded to a halt, his feet stopping just in front of a shimmering line of dark water that was all but hidden in the gloom. Then the blaster in his hand coughed, launching a cluster of 9 mm titanium-shelled bullets on rapid fire at the scarlet-cloaked form of Enlil.

Some sixth sense warned Enlil in time, even over the sound of the energy surging through Domi's cylinder, and he stepped aside as the bullets raced toward him. Missing Enlil, the projectiles drilled into the control podium he had been standing at just a moment before, and there was a burst of sparks from its side. Enlil walked backward, scampering away from the control console as more sparks fizzed from its front panel and an arc of electricity came to life across its keyboardlike surface. Domi began to shriek with pain, the amber bar turning white as a crest of lightning blasted across the front of her cylinder. In the cylinder beside her, Hassood's altered body burst into flame.

"What—?" Enlil demanded as he spied Grant charging toward him. "Do you realize what blasphemy you've committed, apekin?"

"Fucked something up but good," Grant declared as he bounded toward Enlil, the Sin Eater spitting bullets.

Then Grant was upon the Annunaki overlord, his muscular body barging into Enlil's reptilian form and knocking the Annunaki back. Enlil reacted instinctively, his left hand grabbing Grant's wrist below the Sin Eater as his right lunged for the ex-Magistrate's face with sharpened talons.

Grant tried to pull away, and both figures made an uncoordinated dive toward the floor. Enlil recovered with a swiftness that belied his massive form, even as Grant rolled to avoid his next attack. Grant was just too slow, and the sharp claws of Enlil's hand raked across his cheek, leaving three bloody lines as he tried to move out of reach. Grant found himself backed away from Domi's prison, his knee sinking in a shallow stream of fast-flowing water.

"Cerberus apekin," Enlil swore as he rose from the floor. "Will you never learn to accept your place?"

Grant pushed the blood from his cheek in a red smear. "We'll never bow down to you, you psychopathic monster."

Enlil barked a cruel, ugly laugh at that. "'Psychopathic'? How little you comprehend. Your feeble understanding has no place judging the actions of your betters." He took a menacing step toward Grant, his hands unfurling, sharp claws glinting as they reflected the sparkle show that crisscrossed Domi's cylinder. "Now it ends. I shall replace you and all your kind with my brethren—as *Tiamat* wills."

Grant whipped his blaster up as Enlil came stalking toward him across the darkened chamber, his sharp-clawed toes clacking on the bonelike plating there.

A DOZEN FEET AWAY, Rosalia reached the lowest step and stared around the room full of cylinders, the *katana* held loosely at her side. Nearby, the control board sparked and Domi's cylinder was alive with witch-fire while the one beside her was a column of flames. The dog nosed against Rosalia, letting out a plaintive whimper.

"Okay, mutt," Rosalia said without looking at him. "Shut up and let me work this out."

Grant was being overpowered by the lizard man, but she had to do something about the albino girl first. Domi looked as if she was being roasted alive in there, or worse. In a moment, Rosalia dashed away from the stairwell, ignoring Grant and Enlil as she hurried to the sparking pillar of the control board.

The dog yipped as it neared the control column, clearly uncomfortable with the electricity arcing across its surface.

"Yes, I know it looks dangerous," Rosalia reassured the hound, "but we have to do something to earn you dinner, don't we?"

A few feet away, Domi was screaming, a twisted line of electricity playing across her arching form. The front panel of her cylinder sparked and flashed as the amber bar's intensity grew. The two events were linked; Rosalia was sure of that, but there was simply no way to know how the alien console operated. In burying a half-dozen slugs in its side, Grant may have unintentionally sealed his colleague's fate forever.

TWO DECKS BELOW, KUDO had located what he concluded were the water tanks to the mighty starship *Tiamat*. He stood in a vast area at least a mile across as water dripped down from high above him, bulbous mounds with a metallic shine looming over him and reaching to three-fourths the height of the towering ceiling. Curved and fattened to the size of city blocks, it was near impossible to guess what each of the vast units was, but Kudo pressed his ear to the side of each, listening intently for the familiar slosh of water and searching for piping that might lead it through the ship itself. Several of the units were almost silent, giving off a faint hiss as of steam or flowing gas, and Kudo wondered if these might be the mighty drives for the fantastic space-faring craft.

Ultimately, the modern-day samurai had found twin units poised next to one another like a bloated zeppelin, with hard shells and a multitude of pipes coming from several points on their surfaces. When he pressed his ear against them, Kudo had heard the distinctive swish of water, and the pipes he could reach vibrated subtly to his touch as something was pushed through them under pressure. The floor beneath one of the units was sodden where water had dripped onto it over a long period of time—Kudo felt reassured by that thought. He felt certain he had found what he was looking for.

The warrior reached into a pocket of his tunic, pulling loose the items that Grant had handed him before they had split up. These were explosives of a sort, though without the fearsome power of the units Grant had used on the ship's hull. Each was round and about the size of a squash ball with a tabbed seal. Unlike the others these were marked with a chemical symbol for sulfuric acid, one of the strongest known to man. Kudo stared at it for a moment, checking how the seal worked. Then he pulled at the tab on the first, revealing an adhesive strip on the side of the spherical unit which he shoved against the side of the first water tank. In a couple of seconds Kudo had added two more close to the first and was hurrying across the gangway to the other water tank. He had two more of the devices, and wanted to get the process under way as soon as he could.

A tiny charge was contained inside each ball-shaped device, and once they had been primed by removing the tab, a timer fuse ran down for roughly thirty seconds before cracking the shell and flinging acid out in a vicious spray. It was a nasty little weapon, to say the least. As Kudo placed the final two charges on the other water tank, the first explosions set off, three blisters of acid appearing on the surface of the other tank. The skin of the tank fizzed under that deadly onslaught, astringent white mist pouring up toward the ceiling as the shell of the tank was eaten away.

Something appeared at his side as Kudo was finishing at the second tank. He turned as he primed the charge, just in time to see the figure emerge from the trail of dripping water and lunge at him.

Like being mowed down by a tidal wave, the brave Tigers of Heaven warrior was knocked back by a savage, sopping-wet blow.

ENLIL'S FOOT KICKED OUT, striking Grant in the chest as the man squeezed the trigger of the Sin Eater, sending a burst of gunfire into the air. Grant found himself knocked backward as the kick connected, knocking him up off the floor so that he rolled through the air before finally tumbling down again on the decking a dozen feet from where he had started.

Grant recovered quickly, raising the Sin Eater once more and sending another burst of fire at the approaching form of Enlil stalking between the channels of glistening water. The bullets zipped into Enlil's swash of crimson cape, leaving burned holes where they cut through the material and out the other side.

Enlil was unfazed, his lips curling back in a savage grin as he charged toward Grant, bloodlust in his reptilian eyes.

"It's too late, apekin," Enlil boasted. "The hour of your demise has arrived."

Grant heard a crackle behind and above him, and when he looked he saw a great chunk of the overhead catwalk spark with expelled energy from the ruined console, a streak of lightning ripping through the air.

STILL STANDING BY THE sparking control panel, Rosalia bared her teeth in frustration, unconsciously mimicking the scruffy-looking dog at her side as another lethal burst of energy shot from its open panel. Beside her, the cylinder holding Hassood was alive with fire, the freshly made Annunaki body burning to a crisp.

She had to make a decision. Domi was dying in that other cylinder, and it had something to do with this control unit. But it was alien technology; there was just no way of knowing how it worked. Her sword still clenched in her right hand, Rosalia reached forward with her left, finger jabbing out to press a key with a red glow, hoping against all odds that it just might be the off switch. Beside her, the dog growled warily, a deep, throaty noise of warning.

Rosalia looked at it, her hand still poised over the keyboard as sparks like lightning hurtled across its surface. Another blast shot upward, snagging one of the skeletal catwalks in a shower of sparks. The dog looked up at her with its strange eyes—white with just the slightest cerulean highlight—and it whined again.

"Dammit," Rosalia spit, pulling her hand back.

The dog was right; there was no way of knowing which button to press. The odds of alien tech working with the same logic as human were incalculable.

But a cell—now, that was another matter altogether.

Rosalia hurried over to the cylinder where Domi was trapped, staring emotionlessly as the albino warrior cried out in agony, her chalk-white body charged with sparking, twisting tendrils of current. The cylinder wrapped roughly halfway around a circle, with the front panel missing. In its place, Rosalia saw, was a simple bar of amber light, flashing angrily as Domi squirmed against the power source within. Though it didn't appear to have a front, Rosalia watched the way the sparks played in front of her, realized there must be some barrier of force there, visible only beyond the human optical range like something ultraviolet or infrared.

Domi's crimson eyes met Rosalia's for a moment as she writhed in agony, and she spit out three words, each one strained with desperation. "Get...me...out."

"What is it with you Cerberus people?" Rosalia muttered to herself. "Everything in such a rush all the time. 'Less haste, more speed.' That's what Sister Superior used to tell me."

SEVERAL DECKS BELOW, Kudo struggled to regain his senses as the water creature threw him aside. It was similar to the others he had fought, only this one was thinner, as if emaciated. Kudo looked at the floor at the creature's feet, saw the bare trickle of water it was drawing from to generate its body.

"All over for you," Kudo snarled as he dived at the watery figure, arms outstretched. "Your source is about to dry up."

At that moment the second set of charges went off with a pop, and a spray of acid fired in all directions, burning into the body of the liquid thing and striking Kudo across the face. Kudo's lips pulled back as the burning pain hit him.

From somewhere high above him in the belly of the ship, Kudo heard the sound of lightning ripping the air apart. Then the water struck him and he was swept off his feet.

GRANT LAY DISORIENTED on the decking, trying desperately to gather his wits as a great chunk of catwalk crashed down just feet from his face. Enlil was stronger than him—much stronger, in fact, with the natural body armor of an Annunaki's scaled hide. As Grant struggled to get back to his feet, Enlil yanked him from the floor by both hands, his claws digging into the armored weave of Grant's shadow suit.

"Your infantile race is finished, Cerberus man," Enlil raged.

Grant sneered at him. "I've heard that before," he spit, driving the muzzle of the Sin Eater into Enlil's gut. He pulled the trigger, sending a stream of bullets into Enlil's torso from point-blank range.

Enlil howled in agony, tossing Grant aside as he

stumbled back, doubled over. Grant slammed against the deck once more, struggled to hold on to consciousness as dark spots swam in front of his eyes.

Clutching the oozing wounds at his belly, Enlil loomed over Grant, driving one cruelly clawed foot down on the ex-Mag's right hand, locking it—and the Sin Eater it held—onto the deck.

"*Tiamat* waited patiently for the hybrid barons to rise to power," he told Grant, "sufficiently developed shells that we, her children, might have bodies in which we could manifest and grow. That process took centuries, with millennia of planning behind it. The Annunaki are infinite—we believed we had time. Knew so."

Grant sneered at him, struggling to loose himself from where the overlord's foot had him pinned. "We destroyed *Tiamat,* destroyed all of you," Grant taunted. "We didn't realize that, like any cancer, you weren't really dead—you had just gone into remission. But that's fine, 'cause now I get to beat you all over again."

Enlil glared at him, and Grant saw something twinkling in the palm of the monster's left hand—a tiny circular device that appeared to be carved from charred bone. "I have come to realize that a race with infinite time stultifies, their plans never realized. So I have changed the plan, accelerated the schedule."

Grant glared at him as he struggled to free his trapped arm.

"Your race is finished, Cerberus man," Enlil told him, a cruel sneer appearing on his lips. "Replaced forever on the planet you have clung to like an infection."

Grant watched helplessly as the device in the overlord's hand began to glow, a series of lights coursing across its surface. There were colors there that Grant didn't even have names for, fractal colors from other dimensions not meant for human eyes.

"What…?" Grant asked, still struggling to free his hand.

"*Tiamat* is ready," Enlil explained. "The download begins."

Past Enlil's shoulders, Grant could see movement in the cylindrical canisters that dominated the room as more electrical blasts ripped across the ceiling like a thunderstorm. The cylinders were shaking as the things that waited inside shuddered into life.

STILL KEEPING HER DISTANCE, Rosalia studied Domi's cylinder, the dog at her side. There were no seals, no locks that she could see, no handles or keypads that might operate the device. Presumably, Domi had tried to push from the inside, which meant that the force wall could not be simply shoved aside.

"I wonder if it can be cut," Rosalia mused, muttering to herself as she glanced at the dog. "Let's hope so, huh?"

Then, with a determined thrust, she drove the tip of the *katana* into the front of the unit and a web of sparks fired into life across its surface.

GRANT HEARD SOMETHING moving behind him now, too, and he automatically turned his head, seeing a wall full of cylinders shaking where they waited.

"The hybrid barons were formed of human DNA," Enlil explained to Grant, pitching his voice high over the sounds of the rocking cylinders all around them, "and in turn a downloaded viral catalyst allowed them to mutate into their ultimate, glorious form as Annunaki. These past months I have worked with *Tiamat* to bypass that procedure, to turn humans into Annunaki with no need of that wasteful, initial mutation.

"What you see here before you are not resting Annunaki, Grant—they are the bodies of your own kind, altered forever into the glory of the Annunaki. You apekin—you *humans*—are the building blocks of our new pantheon. And thus, you have become obsolete."

With an incredible show of strength, Grant finally pulled his hand free, the claws of Enlil's foot ripping great gouts of skin from his wrist in the process. "Not today, snake-face," he announced as he pulled the Sin Eater up to target Enlil's head.

A SHOWER OF SPARKS BURST forth as Rosalia drove the two-foot-long *katana,* point-first, into the front side of the cylinder that held Domi. Domi's pained shriek turned into a desperate cough as she struggled to take a breath.

"Hang on, chicken," Rosalia urged, talking as much to herself as to the trapped albino warrior. Sparks like lightning played across the steel of the blade, zinging with a resonance like an insect's wings behind glass.

Beside her, the unnamed dog backed away, its pale eyes fixed on the hideous light show that was playing out across the cylinder. To the dog's right, the control panel was blistering as electricity raced across its surface, firing wanton bolts of power around the room as it went into an irreversible meltdown. The dog barked once even as its mistress slashed the blade through the force wall that held Domi pinned in place.

Suddenly the amber strips of light that had raced across the cylinder went out and Rosalia heard Domi cry out. The dark-haired mercenary clung to the handle of the sword as if magnetized, unable to let go as energy coruscated up its silver blade.

Behind her, the dog growled angrily, and then Rosalia tumbled backward as she finally pulled the blade free of the cylinder. And what she saw next would stay with her to the grave.

AS GRANT PULLED THE TRIGGER of the Sin Eater, the whole chamber shook with a low rumble. His blast went wide, even as both combatants looked around them to see what was happening. On every side, the amber-banded cylinders had gone dark. And, emerging from those silent cylinders lining the walls, dozens of Annunaki had awoken, their eyes fixed on Grant and Enlil.

Enlil's laughter echoed through the belly of *Tiamat,* grating on Grant's ears like the sound of a braying hyena.

"Say goodbye, Grant apekin," Enlil boasted as more than two hundred Annunaki came to life around him, stumbling like mannequins across the water-lined floor of the vast chamber as their bodies were charged with life. "Your gods have returned to judge you."

"Oh, shit," Grant growled as two hundred snake-faced gods came hurrying toward him from all sides.

Chapter 25

Kudo was plunged beneath the water, losing his footing as he was dragged away by the current. Caught up in the torrent, his face burning with acid, Kudo was tossed away from the ruined water tanks as their contents spilled out across the deck. The sword he had been holding was wrenched from his hand in an instant by that sudden burst of water, and he found himself spinning so violently that, for a moment, he lost all sense of where he was.

The water was spewing from the twin water tanks with increasing force, ripping at the small holes Kudo's chargers had made and making them larger as the pressure was released and the contents spilled over the floor. Kudo was below the water now, eyes open in the semidarkness as he struggled to find the surface, to find air. His arms whirred as he tried to right himself, slamming into the deck beneath him as he was swept up in the thunderous surge.

Then he surfaced, bobbing up above the water line for a moment before disappearing beneath once more. The whole of the vast works room was filling with water from the ruined tanks, and Kudo estimated there must already be enough water spilled to fill three Olympic-size swimming pools, and the tanks still had more to disgorge.

His armor was dragging him down, the warrior realized, its weight heavy with the wetness. He loosened one of the buckles at his shoulder, clawing at it with desperate hands as he struggled to release it. There was a surge in the current then, and a blurt of air escaped from Kudo's mouth in a series of fat bubbles, scampering to the water's surface in mockery of his own desires. Kudo watched them go as he plucked at the buckle on his armor. The bubbles hurried past his left ear, running diagonal to his vision and showing him that the surface was not where he had imagined it; the water had already thrown him into confusion.

Then the buckle was open, and he yanked at the chest piece of his supple armor, pulling himself out of it as his feet suddenly scuffed the deck's surface. Kudo bent his knees and kicked off, leaving the chest armor behind him as he swam up to the surface.

The water was already eight feet deep and the outpouring from damaged water tanks—now thirty feet behind Kudo—showed no signs of abating. Lights shimmered into luminance on the walls, and Kudo became subconsciously aware of a buzzing tickle behind his ears—some kind of automated alert signal, he guessed, the kind that might be perceived differently by the spaceship's otherworldly owners.

The water continued to hurtle outward from the vast water tanks, spilling across the room like the contents of a tipped bowl. It was all Kudo could do to remain afloat, taking breath after watery breath as he was thrown across the vast room on the spindrift. In front of his eyes, things were trying to form on the surface—figures like the ones he and Kishiro had battled with over the past few hours. He saw their faces and necks trying to take shape on the ruffled surface of the water, malformed like something stillborn, aborted.

There was too much water now, moving so fast that they could not draw enough into themselves to make a shape.

Kudo was hurrying toward one of the ladders that dotted the room now, and he shifted his body, reaching out for it as he bobbed passed, his hand locking around one of the rungs. In a moment, Kudo had pulled himself up, and he began climbing the ladder out of the rapidly filling chamber below, hurrying toward the upper deck.

OVER TWO HUNDRED SETS of clawed feet marched across the bone-tiled deck of *Tiamat*, their talons clacking on the hard tiles.

"Witness the God machine in action," Enlil decreed as the new born Annunaki paced across the deck toward where he loomed over Grant. "Witness the final evolution of humanity, at last become the very thing you worshiped."

Grant raised his Sin Eater, knowing full well that he had zero chance of defeating more than two hundred reborn Annunaki with the tiny weapon. He had been a fighter all his life, once a Magistrate and then a rebel for Cerberus, a warrior for all humankind. Even now, in the face of impossible odds, he would not give up, would never admit defeat. Around him the walls of the chamber resounded with the sparking sound of unleashed energy as chunks of *Tiamat* were ripped away and came crashing to the floor in flaming bursts like comets.

Taking a steadying breath, Grant centered the Sin Eater on the nearest of the Annunaki as he chased across the tiled floor toward him, just behind Enlil. The creature was at least seven feet in height, his naked body defined by taut muscles and spiny ridges across the crest of his skull, the armorlike scales a glistering platinum that shone like the moon. His eyes were a vibrant indigo like the depths of the ocean, and his lips were pulled back in an ugly sneer. Grant knew that look, knew what it meant—it was bloodlust. Reborn, the Annunaki wanted blood, wanted carnage, wanted death.

Grant stroked the trigger of the Sin Eater, calculating where the Annunaki would be when the bullet struck. The Sin Eater bucked in his hand, spitting its deadly cargo at the first of the fearsome lizards. But to Grant's astonishment, the Annunaki stepped away, out of the path of the bullet, and he watched with incredulity as the platinum-hued Annunaki reached out—not for him but for Enlil, grasping the cruel overlord by the back of his head with such force that Enlil was thrown to the decking.

Grant watched confused as more of the reborn Annunaki hurried to assist the first, piling on Enlil as he struggled beneath their weight.

"What the hell—?" Grant asked himself as, one after another, the reborn Annunaki came to join in the massacre of Enlil.

ROSALIA LAY IN A CRUMPLED heap on the floor, watching as her dog stood beside the control console, its scruffy body shuddering with powerful vibrations. Knotted and mangy though it was, the dog's fur stood on end as if brushed with static and its mouth hung open, the jaw slack. Emanating from the dog, dozens of ghost images leaped out, their spirits charging toward the sparking control console as electricity played across it. They looked like the dog, with their long jaws and crouching bodies, but they looked like something else, too. Rosalia didn't know what it was.

Something within the dog was entering the console, she realized. Something that was disrupting everything that Enlil had worked for.

"You brave animal," she chastised the hound, reaching her hand to the dog as it wavered on its four legs, shaking in front of the wildly sparking machinery. "If we both get out of this alive, I'll get you a prize steak, promise."

As her hand neared, Rosalia felt the incredible, breathtaking force throbbing from the animal, playing across her outstretched palm in a wave of heat and power. The dog didn't react, didn't even move other than that terrible trembling. Instead, it continued staring at the control column, and Rosalia noticed something she had never seen in its familiar face before. The dog's eyes were turning dark, a brown tinge swelling within the once-white pupils.

Rosalia watched helplessly as the dog shuddered and dropped, its body sagging as it collapsed to the dark plate of the deck. Whatever they were, the spirits had left it, piling into the console and disseminating through the waiting bodies of the Annunaki.

As Rosalia reached for it, the dog whimpered, its dark eyes looking plaintively at her. "It's okay, boy," she whispered. "It's okay now. You can rest now."

The dog snuffled as it lay on the deck in front of her, not moving as she stroked its head one last time. It felt so hot, as if its flesh had been scalded beneath the fur. "You just rest," Rosalia whispered, her hand running through the dog's matted fur as the life ebbed out of it. "Good boy. Nice little dog."

Behind Rosalia, a woman's voice groaned. The dark-haired mercenary turned and saw Domi lying there in front of the broken cylinder, her white body stained with dirt. The charred *katana* lay beside her, its once-silver surface turned obsidian black.

Rosalia stroked the dog's mangy fur one last time, feeling its belly rise and fall as it struggled to take its last breath. As it did so, Rosalia muttered a prayer under her breath, her eyes never leaving the sorrowful eyes of her loyal friend. Then she turned, taking a deep, steadying breath as she went to help Domi.

"Come on, Cerberus *chica,*" she said as with weary limbs she reached down for the albino. "Probably best if we get out of here before something else blows up."

CAUGHT UTTERLY UNAWARE, Enlil fell to that first blow, crashing to *Tiamat*'s deck before he even realized he had been hit. Disoriented, he lay sprawled on the floor for a moment, reeling as blow after blow struck his body as more Annunaki attacked. Around him, the wombship herself was falling apart, quaking insanely as the unleashed energy rushed across her bow.

They were piling on him now, one after the other, a great angry mob of perfect Annunaki bodies, each one naturally armored with scales as tough as metal plate, each possessing the strength of five men or more. He had wanted them to be perfect, and so they were. Perfect predators. Enlil, too, was strong, a natural survivor and one of the greatest Annunaki who had ever walked the Earth. It took him but a single breath to begin fighting back, striking out at the first attacker even as two more came to assist him, and three more after them.

But he was outnumbered. Every last one of the reborn Annunaki had turned against him, attacking him like a swarm, their uncompromising hatred for him like a single thought shared between a whole community. A uni-thought.

Enlil could not get to his feet, could not even get his arms up properly to protect himself. As he lashed out with one clawed hand, striking a coal-scaled Annunaki female across the jaw with such force that her lips split, another Annunaki had kicked him in the back, the sharp talons of its toes ripping across his scales where his rib cage met with his belly.

He was surrounded now, with nowhere to turn. He could barely even see the light of the gloomy birthing chamber, such was the density of the mob all around him.

Enlil drove a fist upward, striking a figure in the belly, lashing out and ripping something fleshy from another, its genitalia shredding across his sharp claws. But as he moved, another creature set upon him, and another and another. Relentless.

"Get back," Enlil demanded, spitting the words out at the crowd that surrounded him. "I have given life to you. *Tiamat* is your mother, but now I am father to the Annunaki race. Without me, none of you would be standing here. Don't you realize that? Can't you see?"

In response, 213 sets of eyes gazed back at Enlil, staring with absolute hatred at the one who would be their master. And in that moment, Enlil finally saw what he had failed to notice before. They were not truly Annunaki. Somehow the Annunaki bodies were host to the Igigi, the slave caste of the Annunaki, turning now against their betters. Once, millennia ago, Enlil had killed them all, a consequence so trivial he could barely recall it.

They were called the Igigi, and they were known as "those who watch and see." According to Sumerian myth, there were one thousand of them and each one was a god. They never achieved names, however, for they toiled under the Annunaki, a slave caste made up of gods, whose function was to ensure that the day-to-day running of the Earth went smoothly. Bureaucrats cast as gods. The Igigi loved the Annunaki with all their hearts, and in return for that love they were ignored and dismissed, their value diminished by the very fact that they were not Annunaki. Finally, they had been seen as collateral damage when Enlil had unleashed the Great Flood upon the Earth to wipe out humankind.

But some of the Igigi had grown wise to Enlil's scheme for, as their epithet suggested, they would watch and see, their knowledge of the workings of the Annunaki royal family far more intricate than any had given them credit for. When they learned that Enlil planned to wipe them out, a rebellious group of Igigi had acted quickly, copying technology from *Tiamat* to grant them a second life, allowing their minds to be reborn into new and spectacular bodies. They were destined to rule the Earth in splendor, a race of new gods to replace the departing Annunaki.

But there had been an unforeseen flaw in their plan. They had been forced to act surreptitiously, hiding their intentions from the Annunaki and had hidden their bootlegged tech deep beneath a mountain in the San Francisco range. A failure in the so-called shadow box that the Igigi had transferred their bio-prints into left them trapped without bodies for thousands of years, their essences slowly leaking out to affect the consciousnesses of the local Pueblo tribes. Whatever individuality they had once had had become lost in a miasma of muddled thought. Ultimately, an earthquake had reengaged the technology less than a year ago, and the damaged tech had created one body for the whole society of Igigi, locking them in a memory trap while they sought new bodies so they might finally become individuals thousands of years after they had first hidden beneath the earth.

However, when the Igigi souls tried to download into reluctant humans, an added complication arose— the human vessels simply could not take the power of their blazing souls, and the bodies would be burned through within the space of a few hours. It took Cerberus teammates Kane and Brigid Baptiste to finally quell the monster, overpowering the Igigi souls locked inside the trap of memory by turning on themselves, in the mental equivalent of shadow boxing. What neither Kane nor his companions had realized was that an aspect of the Igigi souls had already fled the monstrous shell before they had first tangled with it, and that aspect had gained purchase not in a human but in the body of a dog. The canine had been owned by one of the crofters who lived in the bleak Californian desert and the creature had been driven half mad by the transfer, while its master had been burned alive from the inside by a similar trade of Igigi souls. While the master had died, the dog had survived, its genetic makeup just close enough to that of the Igigi that it could accept the spiritual transfusion. The dog was both one and many, for like a shattered piece of a hologram, every Igigi download attempt had contained all of the personalities that had gone into hiding.

Rosalia had been with the Cerberus rebels when they had first encountered the monster that housed the Igigi souls, and she had returned to the little settlement seeking shelter. While there, she had found the mongrel with its eerily pale eyes and insatiable appetite, or arguably the dog had "found" her. Rosalia had taken the hound under her wing, feeding it and trusting it to act as a guard dog as she traveled alone across the ruined territory known as Cobaltville, little suspecting that the creature housed the rebellious Igigi souls within it. There had been occasions when the beast had seemed somehow more than real, moments when it had appeared to be more than one dog, more than one creature, but neither Rosalia nor her companions had begun to suspect why.

Now, faced with 213 Annunaki shells waiting to be filled, the Igigi within the dog had seen their chance to be free. Their spirits soared through the air, charging out of the dog's body in a joyous burst, hurling themselves via the control console into the dormant shells of the Annunaki gods. And with the Igigi gone, whatever remained of the dog had been used up, a dying husk left in its place.

Thus, 213 pairs of Igigi eyes stared at Enlil, the cause of all their pain and suffering for the past four thousand years. And in unison 213 pairs of Igigi eyes narrowed in fury.

GRANT WAS STANDING TO the side of the altercation, watching in slack-jawed astonishment, the Sin Eater forgotten in his hand.

"Magistrate?" Rosalia called to him. She stood propping up Domi, three channels of glistening water between them. "Are you coming or not?"

"We can't leave it like this," Grant shouted to her, his mind racing. Something dropped from the ceiling then, flaming like a firework as it hurtled into one of the canals before fizzing and dying.

"They won't hurt us," Rosalia said, indicating the swarming Igigi who were beating Enlil to death. "They're—" she shrugged, struggling to explain "—grateful."

Grant looked at the dark-haired woman across the sparkling streams, recalling how she had met the Cerberus team as their enemy. Kane had brought her aboard, and he had vouched for her, said that she could be trusted. Kane would trust her now, Grant knew; Kane would trust the woman's judgment. And while Grant might never really trust her, he knew to trust Kane and all his nutty instincts.

Sin Eater in hand, he hurried across the disintegrating room, skirting past the crowding mob as they overwhelmed Enlil, pulling the overlord apart piece by bloody piece. *Tiamat* was doomed—whatever Grant's bullets had hit in that control console had unleashed energy forces that would tear the whole chamber apart. The living ship rocked and quaked as another blast of energy rang across its innards.

In truth, Grant might never really understand. At most, he and his companions would piece together as much as they could afterward, making their best guess at what had really occurred when the corrupted download began.

For now, however, it was time to leave.

Chapter 26

When Kane emerged from the quantum jump he was met by a wall of rock, close to his face, dark and impenetrable. It was so close he could feel his own breath striking against it, making its presence felt even in the darkness. The rock was shaking and so was he, shaking as if a great engine stood beneath his feet, a great turbine all around him. His heart was pounding in his chest, thumping harder and harder against his rib cage.

And then the vision began, the vision within the vision. A face materialized in front of his eyes, a female Annunaki, her sleek scales beautiful, her eyes piercing and direct.

"My son," she said, an animation floating in darkness, "though we have rarely shown affection for one another, what happens to you today leaves a stain upon my heart. You were born in horror, for your father only knows how to take. Because of that, I have found myself unable to look upon you the way I might a child born in other circumstances. But still, my love for you has always been pure, Ullikummis. Your father is considered one of the greatest planning minds to ever be gifted to an Annunaki, and your own life has been just one part of those convoluted, never-ending schemes. You must understand that, even as you entered this awful prison, Enlil saw to it that you were playing yet another role in his schemes, and that your ultimate failure was simply another tactical move on his immense game board."

Kane felt himself nod as he listened to the female's words, the rock prison shuddering all around him.

"I couldn't stave off your execution nor ensure that you would live, my son," the Annunaki continued, her voice ringing in Kane's head, "for I knew that appealing to your father's mercy was a pointless gesture. And so, I spoke with Ningishzidda as you asked me to, and he came to visit as you waited in the cell beneath the palace.

"Ningishzidda has done something so that you cannot betray him, lest your father learn of your audacious plan. He has altered the direction of the gravity beam by one degree, so slight that Enlil will never know. Thus you shall be launched into space, as expected, but you shall return to this planet   Ki, in the tongue of your forefathers—after you have completed one orbit of the heavens.

"With love."

Abruptly the female's face disappeared, and Kane felt a strange sense of loss as if orphaned. It was Ullikummis who felt these things, he knew, Ullikummis whose memories he was privy to. And the figure in the vision, the face that spoke loving words was his mother—Ninlil, the one reborn as Little Quav.

"Kane?" The voice was nearby and it had no place in the memory.

Disturbed, the vision faded away like a dissipating fog, and in its place Kane found himself sprawled on the smooth-tiled floor of a vast room. A pattern was painted on the floor, concentric circles that lit in oranges and ambers, the colors fading even as Kane acknowledged them. Beyond that, he saw shelves of equipment, most of it unrecognizable in either form or purpose. A bank of vast cylinders like jumbo jet engines waited by one of the shelves, and as Kane became more aware he saw more objects that had been left in the aisles between the shelves, each one sparking his curiosity. Balam stood over him, peering at Kane with his expressive, wide eyes.

"Kane? Are you all right?"

Kane looked at him, feeling the strain within his head. "Where are we?" he asked.

"Agartha. In the museum sector," Balam replied.

"This is a museum?" Kane asked incredulously.

Balam waved his hands through the air as if playing cat's cradle with an invisible thread. "The term is imprecise," he explained. "Some concepts translate better than others."

"Yeah," Kane muttered, pushing himself up from the floor, "and I'm just a dumb ol' human."

Either Balam did not hear the comment or he chose to ignore it. "How are your eyes?" he asked.

"I can see," Kane assured him. "Getting used to it, I guess. How about you? The trip do anything nasty to your injuries?"

Balam touched his chest. "Nothing of note to report," he said, intentionally vague.

"We should have gone to Cerberus," Kane said as he and Balam walked through the storage room of alien artifacts. "New Cerberus," he added. "Reba DeFore could have looked you over, made sure that wound was patched up properly."

"I shall be fine," Balam said a little too curtly.

Kane left it at that, surprised to find Balam give such a display of macho pride. Maybe there was more to it than that; Kane didn't know.

Together, they made their way toward a curve-sided cube that arced up to the high ceiling of the room. The walls of the cube were transparent, creating a shimmering effect in the air. Kane broke the silence as they trudged toward it.

"I had another vision," he explained. "One of Ullikummis's memories."

"There can be no such thing as one memory," Balam corrected. "Memory is memory. Singling one out is like trying to understand a river by watching a single ripple on its surface."

"He hates his father," Kane said. "But there's something about his relationship with his mother, something unresolved there. Stupid as it sounds, I think he wants her love. Like it's something he needs to fix."

Balam halted at the edge of the cube, forcing Kane to come up short. "Seeking a mother's love is not that unusual," he mused.

"I think he wants to turn Little Quav into Ninlil so that he can make things better," Kane said. "The attack on Cerberus—none of that mattered. We're tiny to him, insignificant. He got us out of the way, yes, but what he wanted to create was something so that she would be worshiped when the time came. A new religion for a new world order. At least, that's what I'd guess."

Balam touched his chin, long fingers running along his pointed jawbone in thought. "Then he needs *Tiamat,* and we shall stop him before that can happen," he said.

"But *Tiamat* got destroyed," Kane said.

Balam turned back and gave Kane that maddening half smile of his, as if indulging a child. Then he scooped his hands together and pushed into the wall of the cube, stepping through it as if through a waterfall. Warily, Kane followed.

Within, the cube smelled of plant life, of things living and organic, like mulch. It was twenty feet across, but it contained just one object—a chair. Kane had seen the chair before, or at least one very much like it. It was a navigator's chair used on the Annunaki spacecraft known as *Tiamat*.

"Like calls to like, Kane," Balam said. "You need to call to your *anam-chara*."

To Brigid, Kane realized.

"Okay," Kane said, his eyes fixed on the navigator's chair. "Show me."

Chapter 27

Domi couldn't stay conscious, so Grant had been forced to carry her listless frame as they made their way out of the disintegrating body of *Tiamat*. Rosalia kept pace with him, the charred *katana* cinched in her belt like a trophy. Whatever was going on behind them, nobody had cared to check. They could hear the inhuman screams and shrieks as the Igigi tore their master apart, the cries of agony as Enlil fought with the slave caste he had abandoned all those millennia ago. Hearing the terrible screams was enough—it had to be.

The artery-like passageways had been ankle-deep in water, but nothing further emerged from its swirling depths to attack them. Whatever had powered the watery figures lay with Enlil, it seemed, and once his mind was locked on other matters he lost all ability to generate the naiads that had caused such calamity to anyone who approached the dragon-shaped city.

As they reached the ship's exterior wall, searching for the point where Grant's explosives had damaged her, Kudo appeared, calling to them from along the curving corridor. He looked hurt and, when he came closer Grant saw the man had a nasty streak across the left-hand side of his face—his eye was a grim shade of red and it looked as if the flesh around it had been melted, running to a puckered wound above the warrior's mouth. He was also soaked through, and his black hair clung to his head in tussled curls.

"What happened to you?" Grant asked, hefting the deadweight of Domi over the threshold and through the hole in *Tiamat*'s hull.

"I mistimed the charge," Kudo said wryly, offering nothing further by way of explanation. "Did you find Kishiro?"

Grant looked solemn. "He didn't make it," he said.

Rosalia clambered through the hole last of all, checking back to the water-logged corridor that they had exited to ensure they were not being followed. For a moment, automatically, she looked down for the familiar form of her faithful dog, breathing sharply when she realized it wouldn't be there.

Outside, the sun had risen, painting the streets in the colors of bone.

"We should destroy it," Kudo said, staring angrily at the spaceship that nestled amid its own spreading wings, each of them a series of ordered bones that gave the illusion of streets and buildings.

"We don't have anything that can do that," Grant told him, "but we can come back. Bomb the wicked place out of existence once and for all."

Rosalia stepped from the craft then, brushing the dark hair from her eyes where it had come loose from its ponytail. As always, she looked beautiful and withdrawn, her thoughts ever her own.

Grant looked around and a question occurred to him then. "What happened to your dog?" he asked.

Rosalia glared at Grant, but her fierce mask dropped and a smile twitched at the corner of her mouth. "He saved your life," she said.

If a further explanation was coming, Grant would wait for it. Now was not the time to probe.

Without water tanks, the ship *Tiamat* could no longer snatch people via its bizarre mat-trans. As the Cerberus warriors walked away through the streets of bone, the dragon form behind them was just a husk waiting to be brought back to life, as much of a threat now as an abandoned cannon left rusting in the rain. Let the aliens do what they wanted to one another. For now, humanity was safe.

And so they began the long trek out of the empty city, making their way back to humanity.

IN THE TEMPORARY CERBERUS base on the Pacific shore, Mariah Falk sat watching Reba DeFore as she impatiently paced the study. Lakesh sat in a chair across from her, while Dr. Kazuko had taken up a position by the door. All of them looked concerned, their faces fixed in thought. The results of the CAT scan and the exploratory surgery were laid out across three desks in the small room, and a computer unit hummed to itself in one corner as its hard drive whirred, processing further analysis.

"There's no 'right' way to destroy rocks," Mariah explained to all assembled. She could feel that twinge in her leg where she had taken a bullet a few months back, scratched at it absently as she muddled over their dilemma. "I mean, you can smash them, pulverize them, break them up in numerous ways—you don't need my geology degree to tell you that."

"And obviously we can't use that kind of force inside a human skull," DeFore said. "We're stymied."

Lakesh steepled his fingers in thought. "No, we're

not. We need to consider noninvasive surgical techniques," he said.

"Such as?"

Lakesh considered for a moment. "I recall reading something about focused ultrasound being used to destroy tumors. That was a long time ago, however, and the details escape me."

DeFore nodded. "We'll look into it, Lakesh," she said, and Dr. Kazuko confirmed he would see what equipment they had access to.

As Mariah began speaking enthusiastically about the use of seismic waves in undersea rock study, Lakesh took his cue to leave them to it. A good leader knows when to trust his troops, he reminded himself.

Outside the room, Lakesh allowed himself a little self-satisfied smile, pleased that the Cerberus operation was slowly getting back on its feet. Ullikummis had struck them such a blow that it had seemed, for a while, that they might never recover. If they could crack this secreted stone virus that had attacked Edwards, Kane and several others, there might just be a chance of regathering his full complement of personnel and overturning the living nightmare that they found themselves in.

As he made his way down the wood-walled corridor and into the temporary ops room, Lakesh could hear Brewster Philboyd and Donald Bry talking in excited voices. When he stepped through the doorway, Lakesh saw the two men huddled over the computer terminal that displayed the satellite feed.

"We're on it now," Bry said, speaking into his microphone.

"What has happened?" Lakesh asked as he hurried across the room.

Bry looked up as Philboyd busily tapped out an urgent sequence into the computer, altering the sharpness of the satellite image on his screen.

"It's Kane," Bry explained.

"Put him on speaker," Lakesh instructed, and Bry padded across to his own terminal and flipped a switch. A moment later the hiss of dead air crackled from the speakers.

"Kane?" Lakesh began, speaking into a portable microphone. "This is Lakesh. Donald is just bringing me up to speed now."

"Just tell me when you can see it," Kane replied, his voice reverberating through the computer's speakers.

Lakesh tilted his head quizzically, looking at Donald Bry for explanation.

"He's with Balam," Bry explained, shaking the dangling copper curls of his unruly fringe out of his eyes. "They think they've located it."

The image on the computer terminal whirled and blurred as Brewster Philboyd tweaked the view, and for a moment all they could see was the featureless blue of the ocean's surface. Lakesh looked at the coordinates that were shown in a pane to the bottom left of the screen, wondering where they were.

"Atlantic Ocean," Bry said, as if reading his mentor's mind. "A few miles out from the New England shore."

As Lakesh watched, something came into focus at the edge of the screen, and Philboyd recentered his feed to get a better view of it. There was an island there, formed of slate-gray stone, its jutting spikes like some kind of nightmarish fortress. Narrow channels ran through the island, and Lakesh had no doubt that they would be almost impossible to navigate by boat.

"What is it?" Lakesh breathed, the words barely audible. "What have they found?"

Before Bry could reply, Kane's voice boomed over the Commtact link again.

"Do you see it?" Kane asked.

"Yes, but what is it?" Lakesh responded.

"Ullikummis's home," Kane said.

The words hit Lakesh like a physical blow, and he stared at the satellite feed for a long moment, wondering why the picture feed seemed suddenly so ominous. Slowly, his hand trembling, Lakesh pressed the tiny microphone closer to his mouth and spoke into it, his voice cracking before he finally got the words out:

"Are you there now?"

He waited for Kane to reply.

* * * * *

TAKE 'EM FREE
2 action-packed novels plus a mystery bonus

NO RISK
NO OBLIGATION TO BUY

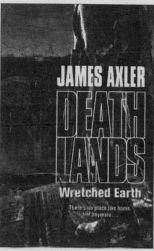

AleX Archer
LIBRARY OF GOLD

History has a way of hiding its secrets.

Ivan the Terrible was one of Russia's most infamous rulers, and he alone held the key to a legendary library filled with rare and priceless tomes. When the opportunity to unravel the mystery presents itself, Annja can't resist. But Annja soon finds herself deep beneath the Russian soil in a dangerous game of cat and mouse…. Will she be the next to mysteriously disappear from history?

Available in July wherever books are sold.

www.readgoldeagle.blogspot.com

GRA37